SINS

1.

'Are you out of your mind? Why wc

walk? It would be bad enough if it hadn't been raining but this is

treacherous.' Bee said, glaring at her friend Sindy.

Devon was a hilly county and a lot of the fields in their surrounding

area, rather than being flat, gentle, grassy areas, were steep and

unforgiving. Sometimes you'd pass farmers' fields with tractors

working on a gradient that you would think a mountain goat would

struggle to negotiate.

They'd dealt with uneven steps, carved into the steep slope, then

walked across the top of a field that felt as if you were trying to

cross a precipitous slippery grassy hill with a mind of its own, just

waiting for you to lose concentration before it threw you off to

tumble down the hillside, then it had the nerve to end with an

unmaintained stile with no step up to enable you to get over it,

especially if you were only 5' 2".

'Lovely views,' Sindy said, with a smirk, from the other side of

the stile, adding, 'You'll have to get over it, else go back.'

Bee looked behind her with horror, there was no way she was going

to retrace her steps, with a monumental effort, she heaved herself

over the stile and fell at Sindy's feet.

Her friend turned away so Bee couldn't see her smiling, then said,

'Well done, that's the furthest you've walked all year and now we can take our time. It's plain sailing from now on.

Bet you didn't know that walk would end here. We don't even have to go back the way we came, the car is on the side road behind this house.' Sindy beamed, very pleased with herself.

Bee gave a long blink intended to show her displeasure and resigned herself to at least another half an hour of walking.

They were now strolling, with their dogs on one of their regular walks, Ashleigh Manor, a disused manor house set in gardens and woodland teeming with wildlife, the dogs loved it. It had rained heavily all week, big puddles covered most of the pathways and the upper green was sodden and boggy. The grey clouds hung over them like huge, waterlogged hammocks about to burst at any moment. The dogs darted around them, as if they were at the start of the walk, rather than at the end.

Chilli, a miniature labradoodle, her coat reddish blonde the colour of the Devon soil, Harley, blond and curly, a typical Cockerpoo always on the go and Mac, a small black dog of indetermined breed but with Cocker, Poodle and Schnauzer traits, not to mention the herding instincts of a collie. They carried on exploring and chasing other dogs and squirrels, not showing any signs of being tired.

Since the pandemic, people were emerging from their isolation changed, some had let themselves go, eaten whatever they wanted, spending time watching endless repeats on the television, others had watched exercise blogs and podcasts and religiously followed an exercise plan. Many had become creative, writing books, composing music, or deciding to learn a new skill, some a bit bizarre.

As a Post Office clerk Bee had worked throughout lockdown but not wanting to be left out, she had abandoned her eating plan and overindulged in takeaways and sweet treats.

'All my clothes have shrunk since lockdown, every single one,' she moaned.

'Funny that,' Sindy said, a glint in her grey eyes 'perhaps it's your washing powder.''

'Do you think?' Bee said, eagerly clutching at the offered straw.

'No, I don't, you numptie. I'll help you get fitter if you like. We'll get back into our old routine, meet up every day, go on longer walks, like we've done today.'

Bee screwed up her face. They were walking past a bench, and she had been about to suggest they sat down. Sindy marched past, oblivious, stomping through the puddles in her green wellies. Bee had the same pair in silver. Sindy thought they made her look like a singer from the 70's and would start singing 'come on, come on, come on, come on...' rather unkindly, every time she looked back at her.

Bee would counter with the Scottish comedians' wellie song, but it didn't have the same insulting tone to it, being catchy and quite sweet (If it wasnae for yer wellies, where would ye be, you'd be in a hospital or Infermeree ...)

A man passed them, staring a moment too long. Bee glanced back 'do you know that man? He gave us a filthy look.'

'He works in our street and acts offended that Gemma and I would open a Bakery within 50 yards of his poxy corner shop that he doesn't even own. He always looks at me as if he's trying to work out what 'an' I am'.

'Anne?'

'My ethnicity. Indian, Malaysian, Tibetan.'

Sindy was part Malaysian and part European, so she was at least two 'ans' mixed together, with a strong cockney accent. She had short silvery hair which currently stood up in bristly spikes that glittered when she turned her head.

Bee, who was not known for her tact, couldn't resist. 'He was probably staring at your hair. You look like a demented hedgehog that fell in a glitter jar. What's with the sparkles?'

Sindy rolled her eyes, 'Gemma waylaid me this morning, she was putting edible glitter on some cupcakes, we tussled, glycerine was involved, and it set like glue. Don't worry, I'm not keeping it.'

Sindy stomped a bit faster, her head sparkling with every step. Bee put a spurt on, 'good job the sun isn't out, you'd look like a firework. Can I call you Sparkle?'

'Have you finished? Good. I can't wait to get home and have a shower. Do you think it will wash out easily?'

'Nope, sorry Sparkle, hot water will probably make it set harder, you'd better have a cold shower.'

'Fuck off... oh morning vicar,' Sindy said, cringing, as they walked past a middle-aged lady walking her little dog.

'You made me swear in front of Susan.' Sindy hissed, glaring at Bee.

'Don't blame me for your potty mouth. Is she really a vicar?'

'There are lady vicars you know. She comes in the shop every Saturday for her weekly treat. Wake up and smell the 21st century.'

'That's coffee. Wake up and smell the coffee,' Bee sniffed as if she could smell the hot beverage, 'some things smell better than they taste. Take bacon sandwiches, they make your mouth water when they're being prepared but never taste as good as they smell.' Sindy gave her friend a quizzical look, 'you know very well that I don't eat meat and stop talking about food, I didn't have time for breakfast.'

Bee had but could easily fit in a second breakfast if it was offered, and call it brunch, with the walk they'd done today, she'd earned it.

'Let's finish the walk and go back to yours. You and Gem make a good coffee, it tastes even better when it's accompanied by one of your croissants.
How is Gemma by the way?'
Six months ago, Sindy s partner Jo had suffered an accident in the home. She had banged her head on a solid oak kitchen cupboard,

then to add insult to injury, a heavy pot had fallen out and hit Jo on the head causing a concussion. Jo had fully recovered with only one side effect, she insisted everyone call her Gemma, even changing her name by deed poll. It had taken some getting used to, but they all called her Gemma now, as Bee had pointed out, it could have been worse, some peoples' personalities changed after a blow to the head, so wanting to be known by another name was nothing. Bee had wondered, out loud, if she could hit her boyfriend, P.R. Ross accidently on purpose, would he forget his name was Poodie and want to be known by his middle name Rohan?

'You call him Rohan most of the time anyway whether he likes it or not.' Sindy pointed out.

'Talking of Rohan,' Bee began and was interrupted by Sindy saying 'Poodie'. Bee shook her head slightly then proceeded to tell her friend about visiting Poodie on the Isles of Scilly and that Poodie s boss had organised the firms' helicopter to pick her up from Cornwall and it had been a magical few days, he was still there but due home soon .' Bee stopped talking just in time to watch Mac follow Harley through a deep muddy puddle.

'No,' she wailed, 'he's just had a bath.' Glaring at Sindy as it was obviously Harley s fault, Mac always copied him.

'Stop whinging, it's going to rain all week anyway, no point giving him a bath. Come on, let's make a move. We've got time for a quick coffee, then I've got things to do, are you working in the morning?'

Bee confirmed that she wasn't, so could do the morning dog walk with Sindy.

They liked to organise their dog walks a few days ahead so that they knew what they were doing. One of their friends called them boring for not being spontaneous but 'spontaneous' was overrated in their opinion.

The next morning Sindy and Gemma pulled up outside the bakery in their royal blue jeep. Bee followed in her old red Honda Civic waiting to pick up Sindy and drive to one of their regular walks. Her friend transferred Harley and Chilli into the back seat of Bee's car and went back to help Gemma.

The boutique cake shop was called Sins and it was in a small row of shops in a quiet part of the seaside town of Torquay. Sindy and Gemma bustled about, unloading cake tins from the car, unlocking the door and carrying everything in. After putting her apron on, Gemma tied a pretty scarf around her curly chestnut hair then she started setting up, telling her partner that the answer phone was flashing. Sindy pressed play.

You have 3 messages, the answerphone stated. Message 1, message received on the 29th of April at 11.15 pm. A gruff masculine voice said 'I want pink frosted icing rubbed on my private parts...'
Sindy jumped to the second message 'I'd like to order 30 of the champagne pop cakes, pick up midday. My name is Maddie Nudge my phone number is 079710554487.

Answerphone clicked to third message; a sexy, throaty voice asks 'have you got a list of your sins? Call me.'

Sindy groaned as she went to help Gemma finish setting up, 'all nuisance calls, haven't they got anything better to do?'

'You wanted to call us Sins. You said it was a clever play on your name and the desire to indulge in a sweet treat. Besides, one message was an order.'

'No way. Maddy Nudge? Really? If she is a genuine customer, I'll do all the housework for a week. Anyway, I didn't think calling us 'Sins' would lead to dirty phone calls every day, what's wrong with people?'

'It's too late to change the name of the shop now, we'll have to put up with it. I'll ring her back to check and see if it's a real order, bit short notice but I'll get hold of Jack and see if he can get them done for us.'

Jack was their part time baker. He usually came in at 4 and was gone by opening time, an amiable giant of a man, he rarely said no to any challenge they sent his way.

The bell above the door dinged as Bee came in with Harley and Chilli, both dogs pulling madly to get to their owners. Harley jerked suddenly and Bee dropped his lead, the cockerpoo jumped up to the counter and managed to snatch a doughnut.

Sindy turned round, glaring at Bee while grabbing Harley and dragging him back to the door. 'Why didn't you leave them in the car? Heaven's sake, Bee, what did you bring them in for, I said I was only going to be 5 minutes, he'll get the squits now.'

Bee gave Gemma an apologetic smile, saying 'they wouldn't settle, they wanted to see you and I wanted to tell you Poodie is home, he just messaged me,' she sniffed, as if her actions were justified then dragged the dogs back to the car leaving Sindy to grab her dog walking stuff, she said a quick goodbye to her partner and a quick hello to the couple waiting to come in, who were old friends of theirs. Mark and Kay, a couple in their 30s, originally from London, they had moved down to Devon after visiting their friends several years ago and had fallen in love with the place. They had taken to the quieter pace of life in Torquay and liked to take a morning walk with no ulterior motive other than to enjoy the scenery but today, they were obviously on a mission as Mark was carrying a large cake tin, Gemma looked at it suspiciously, then nodded at Mark in a way that meant 'go on'.

'You remember Gabriel? He works with me at the college, he's made a vegan traybake and wondered if you'd take it to sell on a regular basis.'

Gemma rolled her eyes, she was too soft hearted, and her friends knew it, she didn't even want to put them to the trouble of carrying the tin home again.

'I suppose I could give them a go but not on a regular basis unless they sell. Gabriel got you to ask me, that was a bit sneaky, presenting me with a fait accompli. Is Gabe vegan? He doesn't look vegan'.

Kay snorted, 'Vegans are not a race from a sci fi film, do me and Sindy look vegetarian?'

'You know what I mean. He's a fit, athletic looking guy, always on the go...'

'No, I don't know what you mean. *I'm* always on the go. You can't tell by looking at people if they eat meat. In theory we should be fitter, we have a healthier diet than you carnivores. What you are really thinking is that he should look weak and wishy washy, are you sure you are living in the 21st century? Healthy eaters are better for the environment, it could almost be the other way round.'

Gemma said indignantly, 'I eat a lot of fish and I look great!'

Kay raised her eyebrows sceptically 'covered in healthy batter and accompanied with healthy chips? I wasn't having a dig at your diet, you eat what you want, I don't care.'

Gemma snatched the cake tin from Mark and looked for a tray to display it on, 'I will eat what I want thanks and actually, I like my fish poached or breaded.'

'Whoa a bit sensitive there Gemma,' Mark said, 'it's okay, we'll pick on Bee instead, did she buy a cake? She loves cake, you can tell!'

'Mark! You shouldn't talk about her behind her back,' Kay reprimanded.

'What? We talk about all our friends behind their backs.'

Gemma frowned, 'I don't, what have you been saying?'

Kay widened her eyes and glared at Mark, 'stop stirring it, of course we don't talk about you, Gem.'

'Only because you never do anything for us to gossip about. Back to Gabe, I think I would know if he was vegan. I work with him. People who don't eat meat make sure everyone knows about it. They all have a slight air of superiority, apart from you of course, hon.' This to his partner who was still glaring at him, her glasses had slipped down her nose, and she looked like a stern schoolteacher, reprimanding the class clown.

Mark continued: 'they like to say they are following a plant-based diet.'

'I've never heard anyone say that'. Kay lied, knowing the phrase was spoken, advertised, on food labels, in supermarkets etc.

'They all do. It's the in thing to say and with climate change I'm surprised we're not in the minority. At least you and Sindy will still cook meat for us carnivores, but I can think of at least 10 celebrities that have made a point of telling the world about their vegan diet, like people used to tell you what their star sign is.'

Gemma chuckled, 'Bee still does. We're all meeting tonight for a walk if you want to come with us, before you ask, yes it will probably end up at a pub or beer garden. I might even treat us to some organic sausage rolls and some veggie sausage rolls of course.'

She carried on chatting to Kay as Mark picked up the phone as soon as it rang, it was obviously another rude phone call as they heard Mark say, 'this is a cake shop. Because the owner is called Sindy …

with an S.' He glanced at the two women, 'the cheek of it he hung up on **me**. I love answering the phone here, can I give up my I.T job and become your P.A?'

Gemma walked over to the door to change the closed sign to 'open'.

'Yes, and you can be my Saturday person as well, as she hasn't turned up.'

Kay tutted in sympathy, 'What again? We'll stay and help for a couple of hours, won't we, love? We've got nothing else on today.'

Mark frowned and said a bit grumpily, 'I was going to polish my guitars.'

Gemma gave him a strange look.

Kay laughed, 'it's not a euphemism, he's got 7 now and they take up a lot of his time, along with his quest to grow the hottest chilli pepper in the world. Nah, they'll keep. We'll stop for a bit, till the morning rush has died down.'

They walked into the back to wash their hands and put aprons and hair nets on. Mark had what might be called a pleasant, homely appearance, laughter lines creasing his blue-grey eyes and a smile which rarely left his face.

He wanted to look more rock and roll so had scraped his short brown hair into a small ponytail therefore, he reckoned, a hair covering, unless it was a bandana was bad for his street cred.

'What street cred?' Kay muttered under her breath to Gemma as Mark continued to moan about wearing a head covering, saying it made him look like he was about to have a shower, but he didn't really mind.

The first customer of the day came in, one of Gemma s regulars. Mark and Kay watched Gemma serve the burly builder type with a delicate cupcake.

The man greeted her: 'Morning, how are you?'

'I'm fine thanks and you?'

The man replied, 'not three bad.'

Mark and Kay exchanged a glance, Kay whispered,

'good job Bee s not here, she hates that expression, she'd explode!'

'It's not an expression, nobody ever said it in London, it must be a Devon thing. Bee has a regular customer who comes into the Post Office, he says it every morning. She doesn't know his name, just refers to him as 'not 3 bad'. Pete the barman says it too, it's simply weird.'

The customer left, oblivious to their discussion. Mark couldn't resist commenting to Gemma that he thought the builder type would have gone for a couple of pasties.

'If you're going to help, don't judge my customers. He's a regular and he loves those dainty little cakes.'

Mark brushed some non-existent crumbs off the counter as he settled himself in for the morning commenting that Gemma was stealing all his fun and he hoped they'd get a lot of dirty phone calls.

On cue it rang, and they looked at Mark as if he were psychic, he picked it up and put his telephone voice on, then quickly changed to himself.

'Oh, hi Gabe, yes she'll give them a go for a couple of weeks,' ducking as Gemma tried to take the phone from him ...'yes they look very tasty, O.K. mate, see you Monday.'

Gemma glared at him 'I didn't say a couple of weeks ... hello Betty,' this to an older lady who had entered the shop, 'you used to work in a Bakery didn't you? and you keep saying retirement isn't all it's cracked up to be, fancy a Saturday job?'

Betty put down her shopping bag and rubbed her hands gleefully, she was short, slightly built and quite hard of hearing. Gemma had been half joking and hadn't really expected Betty to understand her. Betty said 'I do get bored of a weekend, but I may be a bit rusty, never mind, I'll give it a go, see how my old knees hold out. When do you want me to start? I've got nothing planned for today, just came out for something to do. So shall I start now?'

'I thought you might want to take some time to think about it but why not, no time like the present.'

Betty rushed into the back room to get kitted out. The others looked at each other, Gemma shrugged her shoulders.

'You've got more staff than customers now and Betty's a bit deaf, do you think she'll be all right?'

'I'm sure she will, no discrimination in this shop. Customers can always point to what they want. Do you want to go?'

Kay said, before Mark could speak, 'we'll stay for a bit. It'll be fun, it's not like you're paying any of us for today.'

Gemma looked on the back shelf for her list, she loved writing a list, crossing things off and adding things on. She put Mark in charge of the till and Kay, who loved to clean and tidy, took herself off into the back room as Betty made her way out just as a customer came in, he looked at Betty and asked, 'any baklava?'

Betty looked at Mark repeating 'is he a bachelor? No love, he's with someone.'

'Baklava.'

Betty turned to Gemma, 'balaclava? You only sell food, don't you? I could knit 'im one if he wanted, as long as he didn't want it for nefarious reasons.'

Gemma said under her breath to Mark, who was trying to keep a straight face, 'don't say a word.'

Another customer came in, so Gemma asked Betty to serve her.

'I'll deal with this gentleman Betty, while you see to that lady. Actually Sir, I don't usually sell it, but I do have a small tray of baklava.'

The man corrected Gemma s pronunciation as she gritted her teeth and carried on, 'as I said, we don't usually have it. You're in luck.' She put the tray with six slices on, into a bag and Mark took the card payment.

The little shop bustled with customers, and they were kept busy. A man came in and looked around the shelves.

'Can I help you?'

'I'd like a Nuns Puff.'

Mark, Gemma and Betty looked at each other.

The man said, 'I heard it on a quiz show.'

Mark called for Kay to come out, but she hadn't heard of it either.

'It's definitely a cake.'

'Betty, google it.'

Gemma glared at Mark knowing that Betty was a bit of a technophobe, she could barely operate her mobile phone.

Betty had raised her eyebrows as she tried to work out what Mark had said, 'Goo glit?' Oh, I know, you've got some of those cakes with edible glitter on, what will they think of next? Glitter on cakes, wouldn't fancy it myself, eating glitter? No. I don't understand gold leaf either, why do they sometimes put gold leaf on food? They might think it's luxurious but it literally sets my teeth on edge.' Betty shuddered.

Mark, who had commandeered a stool, placed it next to the till and looked settled in for the day, looked at his phone and read out the description 'Nuns Puff, it's French, sometimes called a Nuns Fart ...' he and Kay snorted, the customer didn't, Mark cleared his throat ' it looks like a small doughnut, rolled in cinnamon and sugar.'

'We haven't got any,' Gemma put in, 'what about an actual doughnut,' then took pity at the customer s crestfallen expression

'I'll make some for next Saturday, how many do you want?'

'One.'

'One?'

'I might not like it. I only wanted to try it.'

'Well do you like doughnuts?'

'They're okay. Right, see you next Saturday.'

He left before Gemma could reply. 'Blast, I didn't even get a name.'

'You're too soft Gem, you say yes before you even consider the question.' Mark said, 'Tell you what, put a couple aside for me too.'

'Thanks,' she sighed 'oh well, if I label them people might buy them for the novelty factor. I'll put them in the window and create a talking point. It's good to stretch yourself, I always say. Let's hope I can make them,'

'Well, can you make doughnuts?' Mark teased, echoing Gemma's remark to the customer.

Ha ha, I can but I haven't made them in ages. I'll do a practise run in the week and if they are rubbish, I'll put them on Jack s to do list, bet he's never heard of them either. I'd better add it to my notes in case I forget.'

A short stocky man with mousy coloured thinning hair and a scruffy beard that he had tried to do some creative shaving to, walked in, glowering at them.

'Can I help you?' Gemma asked politely, recognising the man as the manager of the corner shop and trying not to stare at his chin.

'I'm the manager of Tollys, our bin is the one with the blue top, stop filling it with rubbish, we pay for that service.'

Mark said, as he finally recognised him, 'I know you, Carl, isn't it? You used to have the fish and chip shop down at the harbour.'

Gemma informed Carl that their shop had its own bin, and they hadn't been using the corner shops one, suggesting that it might be their own customers or passers-by and by the way, didn't it lock?'

Carl walked out without replying.

Mark shook his head, 'he's a bit of an odd character, think his last place went bust, not very friendly, is he?'

Gemma said 'I've only ever been polite to him; he doesn't like me for whatever reason. He doesn't like Sindy because the dogs growl at him, he doesn't like Bee because Mac barks at him, are you sensing a theme here? maybe the dogs can sense something dodgy about him. He can get on with it, I don't have time for people like that but it's a shame when the traders don't help one another or get on. The last manager of Tollys was okay, pity he left.'

The morning flew past and before they knew it, it was midday. Gemma s mystery lady had collected her champagne cupcakes, done and delivered in the nick of time by Jack, Gemma insisted that all her helpers took a cake or two before they left, Kay picked a couple of slices of Rocky Road. Betty, hearing them, asking what 'floppy road' was. Kay and Mark laughed, said they had enjoyed the morning and agreed to meet in the evening for a dog walk. It was a routine they had got into, at least 6 of them would meet up on most Saturdays, usually for a walk and usually somewhere they could take the dogs. Betty picked a couple of pastries, told Gemma she had had a lovely time and asked if she should come back the following week? Gemma paused, not sure what to say so Betty took control, informing her that she only wanted to be paid in cakes, she would return the next Saturday and they could see if they suited each other. Gemma got as far as saying 'um ...' when the phone rang, Mark picked it up and they could hear Sindy s voice loud and clear, he passed the phone to Gemma, and they heard Sindy ask if Noonie Nudger had turned up. Mark spluttered as Gemma said 'Sindy! You're loud, the whole shop can hear you. Maddy has literally just picked up her order and left, thank God, else she would have heard you calling her Noonie, so she was a real customer and I have proof. Mark and Kay can back me up. I'll look forward to a restful week, putting my feet up when I'm not working. Anyway, all my helpers are going now, remember Betty? She used to work in a bakery, she is coming in to help once a week, this is all because Poppy didn't turn up again. Can you make a sign asking for Saturday staff and bring it with you later just in case Betty doesn't work out or want to do the hours?'

'Ask Mark and Kay if they want the job.'

Mark heard. 'Noooo. Don't work Saturdays.'

Kay said at the same time 'Uh uh.'

'Why do you want me to do a sign if Betty is going to do it? Oh, never mind, we'll talk about it when I see you, just finishing off some computer work. See you later.'

Gemma said, before Sindy could hang up: 'I would do the ironing before you do anything else if I were you.'

They heard a groan from the other end before the phone was put down.

Gemma beamed at her friends puzzled expressions and explained about the bet. 'I love it when I'm right, and I hate ironing,' giving a slightly evil chuckle, ' see you around 6 tonight, thanks again guys.'

The shop cleared and Gemma started clearing up and pottering about behind the counter, two minutes later Bee appeared carrying a box. Gemma narrowed her eyes, glaring at Bee.

'What's that look for? I've just made some salted caramel brownies; will you sell them in the shop?'

Gemma reluctantly took the box, 'Bee, we're not going to make much money if we keep selling the cakes our friends have made, plus we close soon so they're not going to sell now, also, how do I know you've followed the hygiene regulations?'

'Because you know me and how o.c.d I am around food? I got the basic food hygiene certificate last year just in case I wanted to start baking cakes and selling them. Look, just buy me a drink tonight, I don't want cash. Freeze them or take them home and eat them but if they sell like … um … hot cakes we can come to some arrangement. Got to dash, see you later.'

Gemma muttered to herself, as she tried to make space on the counter, annoyed with herself for not being firmer but slightly amused that no-one except perhaps, Gabe, wanted to be paid cash. Paying people in kind, seemed like quite a good idea.

2.

'Holy Mother of God, you need to go faster than that to get to the top, we don't want to be coming down in the dark.' Poodie said, his handsome features screwed up into a mock frown. Looking back at his girlfriend as he waited for her to catch up.

It was a cold, crisp spring day, and for once it wasn't raining. Poodie and Bee had taken the dogs out to one of the more out of the way places that Poodie wanted to explore.

'You've only been back a couple of weeks; how come you've picked up the gang s penchant for exaggeration?'

Poodie raised his eyebrows and watched with hidden amusement as his girlfriend tried to get out of finishing the hike.

Bee sat down on an old log and pretended she had something in her shoe, 'and don't be quoting Genesis lyrics to me, thinking I won't notice, you've never said 'Holy Mother of God' in your life even if you do have an Irish father.'

They both loved music and bands from the 70's and 80's. Poodie was 7 years younger than Bee, but they had the same taste, she was sensitive about the age difference which Poodie took full advantage of when he was in 'teasing mode'.

'I say it all the time, shows how much you listen to me. Come on, old woman, up you get. This was your idea, remember?

All those texts when I was away about how you couldn't wait to go on long walks with the dogs, you walked miles when you came to see me.'

Bee huffed, 'miles, as if. We had a stroll around Tresco. Besides the Isles of Scilly are flatter than here, Devon is so hilly. I haven't recovered from the walk Sindy made me do yet. We walked for hours.'

Poodie had spent half of the previous year working away. He was a tree surgeon and gardener and after a lucrative contract was able to pick and choose his jobs and could spend more time with Bee and Copper, his pretty spaniel and in doing up his run-down cottage. He hadn't been back long, but he had filled every moment catching up with friends, family and spending quality time with Bee.

The dogs appeared, running down the slope, their ears flapping and tongues hanging out. Mac the small, black crossbreed, crossed with several breeds of dogs and what looked like the dragon from an old film called Never Ending Story. When he ran, they laughed and said he looked like a little cartoon dog. Copper was a pretty, cinnamon coloured spaniel with a tail that never stopped wagging and a nose that never stopped sniffing.

The path they were on was overgrown and continued winding up a seemingly endless slope, it was not quite muddy, yet not quite firm either, stubborn tufts of grass pushed through, hinting at a verdant grassy path to come. The trees had yet to come out of their winter dormancy, it had felt like a long cold winter followed by a cold wet spring, but the leaves were starting to break through and some of the birds had decided to start nest building. A crow flew past carrying a large twig, the blackbirds were singing their complicated song and they could hear a woodpecker knocking on a tree.

'Every time I hear that,' Bee said, 'I think of Sindy doing the Woody Woodpecker call ... eh eh eh eh, eh eh eh eh eh... all because I said I wondered what the call of a woodpecker sounded like. Now she does it whenever we hear one, which is every dog walk this time of year.'

Poodie laughed, he'd missed his slightly eccentric girlfriend s stories. He looked at her now, her cheeks red, her blonde hair getting wilder by the minute, she was wearing her not quite warm enough navy coat and her not quite waterproof boots, poo bags and one glove about to fall out of one of her pockets. Bee insisted that even if she were to pay a fortune for an outfit, it would look like something from a charity shop within 20 minutes of her wearing it, so why bother? Bee had said that Poodie found her refreshing after his last girlfriend Dawn who had been obsessed with fashion and appearance both of herself and of Poodie, whom she would always call by his full name Paudric. She hadn't approved of his friends, barely tolerated his family and even though they had split up some time ago she still criticized his choices and the circles he moved in. She did not approve of Bee and looked down her nose at her, any chance she got. Torquay was a small town and they still bumped into her now and again.

'Come on, scruff bag, let's keep moving.'

' that's rude, who dresses up for a dog walk? Last time we bumped into Dawn she implied that I'd dragged you into the gutter with me and hinted that your clothes were not doing you any favours. Admit it, you'd rather be slumming with me, than waiting for Queen Dawn to find the exact shade of lipstick to wear with her designer outfit or landscaping her private parts.'

Poodie snorted and couldn't resist saying, 'I'm a landscape gardener' holding out a hand to pull his girlfriend up.

'Well, you're not trimming my bush.' Bee said with a glint of humour in her eyes and turned to go back down the hill, declaring that the dogs had probably reached the top and that was good enough for her. Her sense of humour was the thing that Poodie loved most about her, a day didn't pass when they didn't laugh, something he'd never had before, and he treasured it.

'Can't believe that Jo...emma and Sindy have opened a cake shop,' Poodie commented, running his hand through his dark, almost black hair, which was getting too long, he just hadn't had time to visit his barber.

'Gemma. Seriously, I told you, she changed her name to Gemma and goes mad if anyone forgets and calls her Jo. It was a very strange side effect after that blow to her head.'

Poodie curled his hand around hers as they walked back, Bee secretly revelled in the fact that Poodie was holding her hand, they'd been together nearly two years, and she'd been single for a while before she met Poodie. She found it hard to get over the age gap and sometimes couldn't quite believe he was serious about her, he attracted women like bees to nectar with his dark good looks and brooding eyes, but he had assured her that he wasn't interested in playing the field and was perfectly happy with her. She tried not to seek assurance, not wanting to come across as needy and lacking in self-confidence but didn't always succeed. Bee always tried to live in the moment and enjoy her relationship which had started out of the blue when she hadn't been looking and had thought she was content to be single. She squeezed his hand, loving the warm feel of his calloused palms. Bee glanced at him out of the corner of her eye, not wanting her boyfriend to catch her ogling him.

Despite the opinion of his ex, Poodie wore good quality casual clothes, jeans, white shirt and his old dark brown leather coat which had softened with age, worn but much loved, even though neither of them would buy leather goods now due to their love of animals, they didn't see the point of discarding items that were years old and still serviceable.

Still discussing Gemma s accident, Poodie commented that he found it hard to believe that she could get concussion from walking into an open cupboard door even if it were a solid oak one. He supposed that the crockpot falling out and hitting her hadn't helped. They walked in silence for a few minutes, soaking up the peace of their surroundings and taking pleasure from watching their dogs running back and forth and sniffing at all the scents along the way, Mac was looking for the right type of grass to have a nibble on, he added various grasses to his diet on most walks and had taken a liking to a sticky one that stuck to his fur. Bee tried not to stop him as she assumed he knew what he was doing.

Bee said, 'It's just as well we're heading back, I need to pick up some bits from the supermarket in case they close and we're meeting the others at 6.'

Poodie s lip quirked slightly, 'what, the 24 hour one?'

'Yep.'

'Nutter.'

'Last time I went they had a sign on the door that said closed for shelf stocking, so I don't believe in 24 hr shops.' Bee said firmly, determined to have the last word, as they reached Poodie s van, put the dogs in and set off. Neither of them enjoyed food shopping and consequently, got round the store in under ten minutes. Poodie paid for the goods, turned down the offer of a bag and began stuffing the groceries under his coat and up his sleeves as Bee watched, shaking her head in disbelief.

'buy a bag.' She snapped.

'Don't like bags, besides I'm eco-friendly.'

Bee, holding the bread and milk, gave him a dark look.

'You're a man. Men don't like carrying bags. Mark does it too, hanging on to as much shopping as he can and refusing to buy a bag, which are biodegradable by the way. You look like you're on steroids with those tins shoved up your sleeves. '

Poodie grinned, 'pass me the baguette, I'll find somewhere to stick it.'

Bee rolled her eyes and led the way out of the shop. The carpark they were in was bordered by shrubland and neglected areas that nobody took responsibility for. They had parked near the verge and Bee noticed a pile of rags next to the wheel that hadn't been there when they had arrived, she was about to comment on the litter when it moved, and a pair of very pale blue eyes glinted up at her.

'Poodie look, I think it's a puppy.'

He bent down and scooped it up. 'It's thin, must be a stray or dumped,' checking the matted bundle of dark grey fur for a collar. 'look at his eyes, they're like chips of blue ice. I'll call him Blue.'

'I'll call him Ice,' Bee said at the same time, 'It's better if I look after him for now,' trying to take hold of the little bundle.

Poodie swerved, swiftly, before realising that he had to get in the van. ' We'll share responsibility. Get in and I'll put him on your lap and don't let him nibble the baguette, he'll need puppy food. Then we'll see if we can find a vet free to check him over.'

'A free vet? No chance.' Bee quipped as she got in the passenger side and the puppy was settled on her lap. She was secretly pleased that Poodie wanted to share him, feeling that it made their relationship more permanent. 'He looks more wolf than dog and look at the size of his paws, he's going to be a big boy.'

They found a vets, who had time to check the puppy for them, dropped the pup off at a friend's house, who bred dogs and had equipment, baskets and food suitable for a young dog and was happy to mind him for a few hours he also kindly offered to give him a bath as he was rather fragrant. They took up the offer of an old basket, two dog bowls, a harness and lead to take home, telling Poodie's friend Joe that they would return them when they'd had a chance to visit the big pet shop.

They then went back to Poodie s cottage for a quick snack and a freshen up before going to meet their friends.

3

It was a pleasant evening for a walk, mild and still dry, which was a bonus. The group of friends had met up, as they did most weekends. The dogs had had a run on the green and now they were all walking along the seafront, a few people were strolling along, enjoying the fresh sea air, the gentle breeze and the noise of the waves as they rhythmically flowed towards the sea wall, gulls rode high above them, gliding and riding on the light breeze. Crows perched on the wall, watching everything, looking for food. Wagtails darted about on the path in front of them, looking for insects. A teenager went past on an e.scooter, setting Chilli off. She had a low tolerance for bikes, skateboarders, teenagers, children, in fact almost anyone who wasn't part of her extended pack, she would bark or growl or grumble, earning her the nickname 'Mismog'.

Sindy apologised to the teenager, saying as she always did, 'sorry, she's just nervous, she won't hurt you.'

Kay said under her breath: 'bet she would.'

A large white Mitsubishi pulled up and parked alongside. A short comfortably plump woman with dark hair swept up into a short ponytail, got out.

'Hi Rosa,' Kay said to their friend, 'just in time for our walk, well the rest of it anyway.'

'What day is it?'

'Saturday.'

'Don't do long walks on a Saturday, I'll sit on this bench and wait for you to come back, we're ending up across the road at the bar anyway.'

Kay groaned and said to the others 'she thinks she's funny and she thinks 'walk' is a rude word.'

They strolled the length of the seafront, enjoying the fresh cool sea breeze. The dogs weren't allowed on the beach from May until the end of September, so they made the most of what would probably be their last walk on the main beach for a few months. They picked up Rosa on their way back and saw Bee and Poodie hurrying to meet them, Mac and Copper trotting beside them. Then all made their way to the beachside bar, Bee recounting the story of the puppy, without pausing to take a breath.

'We've left him with a friend after the vet checked him over and gave him a jab, didn't want to give him too much excitement in one day. He's a big pup, looks like a wolf, we're keeping him, joint custody and joint names. Blue Ice.'

Gemma laughed, 'hope Mac and Copper take to him, he sounds like he'll end up as pack leader. Harley s nose will be put out of joint'. Harley was definitely pack leader. He led, the other dogs followed. Mark said to Poodie, 'so you found a possible wolf cub by the side of the road, immediately decided to keep it with no discussion. That's very strange. I knew what Bee was like, but you're obviously made for each other.'

Poodie raised an eyebrow, 'When you put it like that, I suppose it does seem a bit odd, but it didn't cross my mind not to look after him and for your information, he's not a wolf cub.'

Gemma settled in her chair and raised her arms above her head, stretching, releasing the tension of the day, and sighed, 'I love these dry evenings, and it's quite mild for the time of year, we're so lucky to live here.'

Bee said sarcastically, 'yeah, in sunny Devon, where it rains 6 days out of 7. It's not that mild either, I'm cold.'

   Rosa told her to stop moaning, Sindy asked if she wanted them to sit inside and Gemma offered Bee her scarf.

Bee wrapped the scarf around her neck and decided they were fine where they were. Mark said, 'older people feel the cold more.'

Poodie raised his eyebrows as Bee snapped at Mark, 'where were you when tact was handed out? I'm 35, that's only a bit older than you and by the way, what's that little tuft sticking out round the back of your head?'

   'and the rest.' Mark scoffed.

Bee was 39. Sindy narrowed her eyes and said, 'she's picked her age and she's sticking to it.'

   'I think you both missed out when tact was being distributed,' Poodie said adding, 'what is it though, mate?'

They all laughed, as Mark patted his head, feeling to see if his hair was still in place and told them not to diss his ponytail. Mark was the most laid back of the group, easy-going, never got angry or offended, he enjoyed teasing and winding his friends up. He and Kay were also animal lovers, but both had full time jobs so didn't have any pets themselves, instead often looking after their friends dogs if any pet sitting was required.

Kay got up and started clearing the table, she took their drinks order and went inside with the dirty glasses.

Gemma said, 'she's too kind-hearted, she can't help herself.'

Sindy gave a little shake of her head, 'pot meet kettle? Kay can't help herself; she has to tidy up wherever she goes, and you can't say no to anyone. Not being funny but … you ought to stand in front of the mirror and practise saying the 'n' word.'

   'No, no and hell no. There you go, I did it.'

Sindy didn't react to her partners sarcasm, 'well done, luv, keep saying it.'

Kay returned with a bottle of wine and some glasses, told them she had ordered some food and that the staff were bringing the rest of the drinks. They sat enjoying the view and the company, telling stories and bantering.

After an hour in which Harley had got into trouble for pinching a piece of Marks garlic bread, Mark got into trouble for not being vigilant, as garlic was a member of the onion family, and everyone knows that onion is bad for dogs. Bee had spilt drink down herself (she couldn't eat or drink without spilling something, it was a standing joke). Sindy gave all the dogs a chew calling Harley by his nickname 'Harley Shark' which led to Gemma singing a very annoying silly song about sharks which irritated almost everyone except Sindy who laughed and joined in.

The dogs suddenly erupted from under the table, barking and growling, at a man who was walking past. He glared at them as Poodie apologised.

After he had moved on Mark told Poodie, 'that's Carl, he's manager of Tollys, he's got a grudge against Sins or the girls or the dogs. I think they sense something off about him and always react to him. He came in the bakery and moaned about his bins; reckon he's following us!'

Poodie shook his head, 'takes all sorts, I guess.'

Kay and Bee finished their second glasses of wine at the same time and upended the bottle to get the last dregs into their glasses, both a little tipsy, Bee tended to get louder and Kay, for reasons best known to herself would put on a Welsh accent.

'I love sitting here, I do,' she said, trying to do the accent. As far as they all knew, she had never been to Wales, even though she swore she'd been to Cardiff or somewhere with a similar name, nor did she have any Welsh relations nor even a thing for a well-known Welsh singer.

Having managed a sentence without anyone commenting, she felt

safe to throw in another couple, informing them that she loved pink
Prosecco 'I do' and she loved their pack meets 'I do.'

They stayed for another couple of hours before taking their leave
and arranging to meet in a week, a week in which Blue Ice doubled in
size, Rosa, who struggled with walking but missed having a dog, she
adored them all, especially Mac, who she wanted to cuddle at every
opportunity: started saying she wanted a dog, and the bakery had
another new Saturday person starting.

Sindy and Gemma were getting the shop ready to open and talking
about whether Rosa would be a suitable owner for Blue Ice, and
should they suggest it to Bee and Poodie as a puppy was hard work
and a big responsibility? Then went on to talk about the new lad.

'What's he called, Oliver? What about Betty, is she coming in too?'

'She said she was, she's a bit of a character, quite bossy, doesn't
want set hours, she wants to go home when she's had enough, quite
funny really, I've always had a soft spot for Betty, but we have to
have a regular Saturday person who will do a full shift, hence
Oliver but on the plus side, Betty only wants to be paid in cakes, the
customers love her, they prefer her to me.' Gemma sounded slightly
miffed.

Sindy laughed and told her not to be daft.

'They do. She butters them up, especially the men and calls
everyone 'my lover'.

'Well, that's Devon through and through. Most counties have their quirky regional sayings. Your cockney gran used to call everyone 'duck' and my Scottish gran called everyone 'hen', well, the women anyway. Remember my uncle Barry? He called every man he met 'John. All right John? Cheers John. Come to think of it, he even named his son Jon.'

Gemma chuckled, 'I know. It sounds odd to me though,' she put on a Devon accent and said, 'alright my lover?'

'You can't be jealous of Betty, she's twice your age and she's an asset if the customers like her.'

Gemma picked up her pad from the back shelf to give Sindy her shopping list and checked to make sure nothing else needed to be done. She kissed her partner goodbye and ruffled her hair, earning a comment along the lines of: 'there better not be more glitter on my head' then Sindy took off to walk the dogs with Bee, changing the shop sign to 'open' as she left, brushing shoulders with a regular customer coming in for his fairy cakes.'

Gemma greeted him knowing what was coming and the man didn't disappoint.

'Not 3 bad. I'll have a couple of my usual cakes please.'

Gemma served him, giving a little shake of her head as she did. After he left, she arranged the rest of the cakes and double checked her list, crossing off one or two things. Betty arrived carrying a mug with a sunflower on, holding it up to show Gemma.

'Morning love, I know I'm early. I've brought my own mug so we can start the day with a nice cup of tea, 'adding 'what do you think of my perm'? patting her tight white curls, she told Gemma she'd done it herself with the help of a friend as she didn't think hairdressing salons knew how to do old ladies' hair these days. Betty hooked the door open stating that an open door looked more welcoming, and she didn't want people to walk past thinking they were closed, then went into the back to put her apron on.

Gemma muttered to herself that the door could be closed, the lights off and people would still try to come in. She looked at her watch and noticed that the new lad was late, just as she thought it, a teenager who looked like he had just got out of bed, walked in, holding his mobile and texting.

Betty came out, having decided to leave the tea till later.

'Betty, this is Oliver, he's starting with us today.'

Betty sniffed, 'you're late. What do they call you?'

The lad looked at Betty as if she were mad, 'Oliver. I had to wait for my dad to give me a lift.'

'I thought they might call you Oli. There was a puppet on telly called Oli Beak, wasn't there Gemma?'

'How old do you think I am? No idea Betty but there's a singer called Oli; I like him.'

'Oh, I know who you mean, I love him. I know another singer in a group, called Oli, he acts as well.'

Gemma took control of the conversation before Betty went through all the Oli's she knew. She told Oliver to have a look around and familiarise himself with the cakes and prices, she said Betty would help him.

Oliver didn't seem impressed; he took his eyes off his phone for a second to say, 'I think I can manage, it's only selling cakes,' he paused before adding 'I got an A star in Science.'

Gemma and Betty exchanged a meaningful look. Gemma told him where to go to wash his hands and gave him some basic hygiene instructions, asking him to relinquish his phone to which he said he couldn't as his dad might have to reach him urgently, then, dragging his feet, took himself off into the back room.

Betty shook her head and tutted. An elderly couple walked in and looked at the cakes.

The lady said 'oh I can't decide, they all look so nice, oo do you know what I haven't had for ages? Battenberg.'

Betty frowned, 'Is it right outside the shop?'

'Is what outside?'

'I thought you said you'd flattened a bird. Have you killed a seagull? The baby gulls don't care, they stand in the road just waiting to be flattened and then the parent bird will come down and poo on your windscreen. They never forget your car either, the traffic warden was harassed for weeks by a gull after his van killed its' baby.'

The couple looked at Betty enthralled.

The man said 'only a gull? I'm sure he got harassed by a few people as well.'

'Yes, but they wouldn't poop on his windscreen.'

'Betty!' Gemma said, trying not to roll her eyes, turning to the couple she told them that the corner shop was the best place to find Battenberg as it was more of a supermarket cake but pointed out Sindy's home-made spiced fruit cake that they could purchase by the slice.

The couple took her advice and left, still chuckling about Betty.

Oliver slouched out from where he'd been hiding in the back, phone in hand, eyes half closed, looking as if he'd only had about an hour's sleep. Gemma, trying to make conversation, asked him if he'd had a late night.

'Mates came round. Watched a couple of movies then played old video games. Do you like C.O.D?'

Gemma chuckled, 'I guess it isn't fish,' she said, trying to be witty. Oliver didn't smile.

'Um, no, I don't play computer games very often. When we have friends over, we might play cards or board games.'

Oliver looked at her as if she was an alien then said 'you're not very busy, are you? I think I'm going to be bored.'

Gemma handed him a broom and told him to sweep outside, in front of the shop.

Betty put in 'and watch out for the dead gull. I would sweep it into the gutter and move it about 2 shops down, outside that cheap shop that thinks it can charge High Street prices.'

Oliver took the broom, keeping hold of his phone and walked out, dragging his feet.

'You look nice today, love,' Betty told Gemma, 'That black blouse and skirt looks smart. I love the red poppy scarf you've tied your hair back with too. I've got a black jersey dress I'll wear next week, it will be like our uniform, like waitresses in a proper old-fashioned tearoom.'

Gemma laughed and said loudly, 'okay, why not, let's dress to impress. We've had a couple of bitchy reviews on social media, one said our cakes stay in the window for days and must be stale. Our cakes are always fresh, you know that nothing stays in the window for long. It was anonymous of course.'

'Who would do that? That's being a troll, that's what that is, wonder if it's someone in this street?'

'Who knows. Perhaps it's someone who sells cakes locally, I'll find out eventually. Just trash talk I expect, there are always bored people out there who want to spoil things for someone else.'

'Don't let it get to you,' Betty glared at the doorway, where Oliver had his head down looking at his phone, before she could shout at him, one of her friends came in for an apple Danish and a chat. Gemma called for Oliver to come in, then answered the phone to a customer wanting to order a whole fruit cake.

Betty fiddled with her hearing aid as she chatted to her friend, 'so I said I don't want to go abroad at my age, I'd rather go to Cornwall for a few days. I love Cornwall.'

'Whereabouts?'

'St. Austell or Truro maybe, stay in a caravan park.'

'When are you going?'

'Eh? I'll finish about 12.' Looking at her watch, 'which is any minute now.'

Gemma finished with her telephone order and said 'Oliver! Will you put your phone away please?'

He glanced at her before saying 'I can't, it's my dad.'

Gemma reached the end of her tether, 'well tell him to come and pick you up, you can wait outside. Leave the apron in the kitchen, you haven't done a stroke of work since you got here. This is not the job for you.'

Oliver shrugged, 'got a job in an ice cream place in Paignton if I want it anyway.' He slouched out, pushing past a customer who was coming in.

Betty stopped chatting to her friend to give her attention to the customer, 'where's that boy gone? I swear I've seen so little of him I wouldn't recognise him if he popped his head round the door. Now, what can I get you, my lover?'

The customer asked for a chocolate flapjack and Gemma served him before Betty could say 'pardon'.

The customer left as Betty said 'I thought he said backpack! Have you seen the price of them in the so-called cheap shop?'

Gemma raised her voice, 'just think logically Betty, a customer wouldn't be asking us for backpacks.'

Betty shook her head, 'customers are always asking for odd things, someone asked for a balaclava the other week, remember? And in my old job a person came in and asked if we could do a ticket to Italy. I thought I must have misheard him, but it turned out that he knew the owner's wife worked as a travel agent. Nowt as queer as folk, so they say. Anyway, I'm going to get off, is it all right if I take a slice of Sindy's spiced fruit cake and an apple Danish for my friend?'

Gemma sighed, 'I wish you'd take some money Betty. Yes of course, you take what cakes you want. I'll see you next Saturday.'

After Betty and her friend had gone, Gemma tidied up, checked her list again, wrote out another Saturday Staff wanted sign and put it in the window, just as a young woman with shoulder length pink hair walked past. She stopped to read it and came in and told Gemma that she would like to give it a go.

'What's your name?'

'Clova Cooper-Dent.'

'Clover. What an unusual name, how do you spell it?'

Clova spelt it out. 'I was born in Clovelly, but mum wasn't sure how she should spell it as a Christian name, so she decided on Clova plus we didn't want dad to have the same trouble as he did with Antney (also spelling her brother's name out) when he went to get tattoos of our names on his arm. Mum wanted our names spelt just the way they are whatever anyone else might think about it. She said she likes to be original. Antney was named after a character in a comedy show, that's how they used to say his name 'our Antney', mum liked it, she could have spelt it Anthony if she'd wanted, she's not bad at spelling most things.' Clova gave Gemma a look as if she was expecting a comment, when Gemma stayed silent, Clova went on 'Then after all that, dad decided to have them done in Chinese script, but it could say anything, we wouldn't know. Sweet and sour chicken and pork balls probably.' She laughed.

Gemma smiled, 'all right then, Clova, my name's Gemma, we'll have a trial day next Saturday and see if it suits us both.'

'That's brilliant, my mum will be over the moon that I'm working here, she loves this shop. Shall I take down the sign for you? You don't want to be inundated.' Clova ripped the sign down and put it in her bag, presumably so that Gemma wouldn't be tempted to change her mind. She waved, saying 'see you next week', unhooking the door as she went, so that it closed.

Gemma moved about the shop talking to herself 'I bet she's a control freak. Betty will be hooking the door open every 5 minutes and she'll be closing it. I can see it now and they'll both be bossing me about.' She looked at the door wondering if it was worth hooking it open again for the last ten minutes, when she noticed a person behaving oddly, in front of it. The young person, who looked like a foreign tourist, was taking 2 steps up to the door, then 2 steps back.

2 steps up, 2 steps back.

Gemma frowned and opened the door, 'everything all right? Can I help you?'

The student smiled and walked in, taking her time perusing the cakes. Eventually she made her choice and paid then said, 'in my country, doors automatic.'

Gemma chuckled, 'Ah, I get it now, you were waiting for the doors sensors to pick you up. We're a bit behind the times here, still in the dark ages.' She held the door for the student and said goodbye, then closed it and locked it but couldn't resist copying the student, she walked forward then back a couple of times, snickering, before realising that Carl from Tollys was walking past, giving her an even dirtier look than usual.'

Still talking to herself she picked up her bag and let herself out, 'he probably thinks I'm nuts now, oh well, who cares, phew, what a morning, what till I tell the gang.' Gemma was meeting Sindy and some of their friends at a clifftop café, it was a 20-minute stroll along a quiet country road, still quite cool but dry after a shower had passed over and the sea mist had drifted away. It was pleasant to wind down in the fresh air after her shift, she walked along, listening to the birds singing and some dogs barking on the nearby beach, and soon spotted Rosa, Bee and Sindy sitting outside, with a view of the countryside behind them and the sea in front, the dogs lying under the table, having had their walk. They were talking about the people they fancied, Bee was always drawn to dark haired men Rosa observed.

'Poodie is so your type, dark hair, green eyes, outdoorsy, gypsy looking, you could imagine him standing on the back of a waltzer car at the fair,' Rosa was saying, 'whereas I prefer blonds, like that vet in Australia, everyone loves him, yum.'

Sindy and Bee looked at each other, 'nope, no clue,' Bee said, 'she's living in the past and watching old re-runs of reality shows. Oh good, here comes Gem, we can order now.'

They placed their order, calming the dogs down, as they had excitedly jumped up to greet Gemma, who sat down with a sigh of relief and told them all about her day, the food and drinks arrived as she finished recounting the tale of the non-automatic door. Bee laughed as her phone rang, it was Rosa s mother, Bee passed over her phone.

'Yes, I've met up with the girls … on the headland…I didn't hear my phone, it's at the bottom of my bag… I'll be home in an hour, yes, what would you like?' Pause as she listened, 'what advert? No, it's too complicated and too much for lunch. I'll pick up a cake for later and a cheese and ham slice and salad for tea, how about that?' She paused and listened, 'I know but the doctor said you must eat more fruit and veg… um a Chelsea bun doesn't really count as one of your five a day

Pause … the others were laughing quietly, 'okay, bye mum.'

Rosa gave Bee back her phone and told them that her mother had got mixed up with the 'all you can eat' restaurants and the delivery services. She wanted to order a banquet because it looked delicious on TV.'

Gemma said 'Hilarious', she always pronounced it hil AIR ious, which made her friends laugh and parrot it back.

Bee sipped her coffee, 'I analyse the ads now, how they even use music to manipulate you, that plink plink music that accompanies the ad to persuade women to buy products related to bladder weakness. Winds me up. Why is it aimed at women? I wonder if men have the same problem?'

'I'm sure they do, an older friend of ours, John, can't go anywhere unless he plans the route according to where the public toilets are.' Bee sighed, 'growing older sounds such a joy.'

Sindy said, 'it's not just older people, you've had a few close calls, won't be long before you need special pants.'

'What a cheek, I've just waited too long, and someone has made me laugh.'

'How is your mum settling in to her new flat?' Rosa asked Bee.

'Oh, she loves it, she'd had her eye on one of those warden-controlled flats for ages. Sea views, company if she wants it, she can eat what she likes without me bossing her around, knit, do her painting, whatever she wants, when she wants to do it, and I'm not all that far away if needed.'

Gem glanced across the table at her partners plate, 'I know you're a fast eater Sind. But have you finished that already?'

Sindy looked for her 2nd slice of garlic bread and groaned. 'Harley!'

It was always Harley, he was like a food Ninja, faster than lightning, he knew the second someone was not paying attention.

Bee started to say that Sindy could have hers as she wasn't that hungry, and Sindy swiped it before she finished speaking.

'That's where Harley gets it from. Like his owner.' Bee grumbled. 'I was being polite really; I didn't expect you to say yes.'

'I'm doing you a favour, you said none of your clothes fitted you.' Sindy responded.

'Fine, well I can squeeze in another coffee, anyone want a top up?'

Sindy said, 'half a cider.'

Gemma said, 'can you ask if they do a Virgin Mojito, I'd better not have alcohol, I'm driving later.'

Rosa rarely drank alcohol as she had a few health problems. She said, 'any non-alcoholic cocktail for me. Surprise me.'

Bee shook her head and said sarcastically 'I'm so glad I offered to go and get some more coffees.' She stomped off to place the order.

The others laughed, 'she's so easy to wind up.' Gemma commented.

'And so easily irritated, she's a gift to us all.'

Rosa said, 'one of you say something about staying alert, then I can say 'your country needs lerts, she hates that, it drives her mad.'

Sindy said, 'great, more ammunition.'

She went on to tell Rosa that she had won a small prize from the last village show, it was a bottle of talc. She had had to go and collect her mystery prize and was disgusted with it.

'Who uses talc these days? It's so last century. It's in a nice box though, perhaps I can re-gift it.'

Rosa gave Sindy a look; 'as long as I don't get it for Christmas, it's so old fashioned, even my mum doesn't use it.'

Bee returned and sat down.

Rosa turned to her, 'random question Bee, do you use talc?'

'yes, who doesn't? Why?'

There was a long pause with a few stifled snickers.

Bee gave a slight shake of her head and craned her neck to try to see the back of her skirt in case she had talc on it, glanced at her friends as if to ask, what the heck? then said, 'all drinks ordered, although I don't know why I'm paying for them all, I'm sure I'm owed drinks at the very least, I made cakes for Sins, gave Sindy my last piece of garlic bread ..'

Sindy got some notes out of her purse and gave them to her, saying she had been planning to pay anyway, which threw Bee off her stride, but she took them and put them in her purse quickly in case Sindy changed her mind.

….'only joking,' Bee said, 'but thank you.'

'My pleasure and glad to see you put the money away safely. You need to be alert.'

Rosa said, 'Yes because your country needs lerts.'

Bee groaned, pulled a face and went red with the effort of not replying.

'Worth every penny.'

Sindy glanced across at the next table, Marks friend Gabriel was sitting there with his girlfriend, who had recently moved down from Wales to join him. Gabriel was a 6-foot-tall black guy, and his girlfriend was a petite blonde, they made a striking couple, he was wearing jeans and a long-sleeved shirt, and she wore a very short sun dress with yellow flowers on, even though it was quite a cool spring day. They had always got on with Gabe, he worked in the kitchen at one of the nearby pubs in the evenings and worked in I.T with Mark at the college during the day. Gabe loved their dogs and usually came over to make a fuss of them and give them a treat but today he seemed a bit harassed and wasn't looking in their direction. Sindy called out a greeting and waved. Gabe looked up, waved then went back to his veggie burger.

'Woo, did you see that? The girlfriend gave us the death stare,' Gemma said, 'I was going to go over and have a quick word, but I don't think I'll bother.'

Gemma was a bit of a mother hen, always checking to see if her friends were comfortable and warm enough which was why Bee said, 'don't go offering her your scarf either, let her freeze, give it to me instead.'

They laughed and finished their second round of drinks, Rosa said her goodbyes, Gemma had an appointment at the hairdressers, so Bee and Sindy walked the dogs home, taking a short cut through a park. Bee trod on something which turned out to be a plastic crab, she picked it up to put in the bin and they talked about how many plastic items were in the window of the cheap shop. Crabs, lobsters, fishing nets, bottles with corks in so kids could write a message and throw the bottle in the sea, which they agreed was a bad idea and not environmentally friendly but supposed that they might just play at being castaways in their gardens at home. Children were much more caring about their environment than in Bee s youth, she started humming a song from the late 70's.

Sindy put words to it, 'message in a bottle, message in a bottle,' Bee joined in, 'I saw you so many times today, I guess it's all true what your girlfriend says,'

'that's not 'Message in a bottle.'

'Isn't it?'

They were quiet for a while, running through the lyrics in their head before Bee had to concede that Sindy was right. Neither of them could hold a tune but loved singing, loudly and often.

Bee sang, 'I can't stand losing you OOOO' ending on a high note that sounded like a howl, just as a man with an exceptionally large dog came round the corner, the dog looked at her, she crooned 'hello big boy,' in a seductive voice. The man gave her a startled look.

'Not you!'

Sindy gave the man an apologetic look, rolled her eyes. Glanced at Bee as if to say, don't worry about it, it's her.

'I texted Ro ...'

'Poodie! Stop calling him Rohan.'

'Whatever, he's picking me up on the corner, so I'll catch up with you in the week, unless we can give you a lift? I bet Blue Ice will grow as big as that dog, his paws are huge.'

'No, I'll walk, thanks. Are you sure you want to keep him? Rosa was saying she wants a dog again.'

'No way. We're keeping him and even if we weren't, that's not the sort of dog she would want. She hankers after a corgi or a dog that looks just like Mac. Blue Ice is going to be a big dog who'll need a lot of exercising.'

Bee left the park to find Poodie waiting, she got in the van and made a fuss of Copper and the puppy, Mac wriggled himself between the two dogs and went to sleep.

4.

Friday afternoon, Bee met Sindy after her shift at work, Sindy had Mac having taken him for a walk with her two and Bee was giving her a lift home. They had the poo conversation, Bee always asked if Mac had been and needed a description of it to check that his digestion was working as it should.

Sindy sighed theatrically, 'yes, he did a nice firm poo. A perfect Linda McCartney sausage.'

Bee said laughing, 'other brands are available.'

'I've got to call in the shop on the way back to pick up some cheese scones, you can have some if you like.'

'Yes please, as if I don't eat enough carbs already but I'll have them, Poodie likes them too,' she was quiet for a second then said suspiciously, 'what's wrong with them?'

Sindy tutted, 'nothing but they've been frozen once so I can't re-freeze them.

Want to come to the beach with us tomorrow after Sins is closed? The gang fancied a walk and a late lunch at the new place in Goodrington.'

Bee parked the car in a side street about twenty minutes away from the bakery, as she explained to Sindy, she was working off the calories of the cheese scones before she ate them.

Inside Sins, Mark and Kay were minding the shop for the afternoon.

'My only day off and I'm working plus we don't know what we're doing.' Mark moaned.

'Of course, we do, we've helped out before, and you've got the whole weekend off.' Kay said, as she cleaned behind the counter and brushed up crumbs.

'Do I still have to come with you in the morning and do the big shop? I hate shopping and you just say I get in your way, then we end up having words.'

'I'm not your mother Mark, I'm your partner, you eat more than me so yes, you do have to help with the shopping. I'm not carrying it all, It's my day off as well, we're a partnership.'

'Sindy and Gemma do it separately. Gem drops Sindy at the supermarket then goes and does her own thing for an hour, they end up having a row if they try to shop together. Besides I hate shopping and you love it.'

Kay ignored him, going into the back and returning with a tray of cakes, making room for them on the counter.

The phone rang and Mark picked it up. It was a rude phone call which cheered him up immensely, 'Sorry, we are only a bakery, we don't offer any other services. If you want, you could come in and buy 10 cakes and pick Gluttony as your Sin of the Day. Goodbye.'

Mark and Kay exchanged looks; Kay wondered if it was the same person who kept ringing, and should they tell the girls to report it?

'Perhaps they should change the name of the shop? Though that would cost time, money and effort. It is a new business, whoever the person or persons are, they will get bored with the joke soon, if not, Gemma should tell the local paper and get a free write up. All publicity's good or whatever the saying is, at least the name is getting them noticed.'

'That might increase the silly phone calls tenfold.'

Mark laughed, 'I'll give up my day job and just answer the phone.'

Harley charged in the open door, his lead trailing behind him, running behind the counter and jumping up, he snaffled something, ran back out and gobbled it up greedily. Sindy followed, panting and gasping for breath and grabbed his lead just as Clova stumbled in the door nearly falling over, stopping herself from falling by grabbing Sindy s arm.

Sindy steadied Clova while rubbing her arm where she had been grabbed.

Clova glared at everyone en masse. 'Bloody hell, are dogs allowed in here? He's eating something as well.'

Sindy looked at Mark and Kay, 'he got away from me. Bee's outside with the other two. I'm getting more stressed by the minute, he nearly ate a plastic crab the other day, but Bee managed to chuck it away before he spotted it, last time he ate plastic he was ill for 2 days. What did he eat?'

Mark said, 'a cheese scone, I think.'

Clova pulled a face, 'You'll have to throw the rest away now, you don't know how many he touched,' turning to Sindy she added, 'you should offer to pay for them and leave him outside.'

Mark and Kay watched the drama with smiles on their faces, trying not to laugh.

Sindy glared at Clova, 'who died and made you boss?'

'I work here.'

Sindy raised her eyebrows as high as they could go, 'since when?'

Clova looked defiant, 'tomorrow.'

'So you say, none of us here, know you. Who are you?'

'Clova.'

Mark scratched his head, 'Clover? Like four leaf, or margarine? Or a cow?'

Clova bristled, as Kay told Mark off for being rude. They heard Bee outside getting restless, shouting for Sindy to hurry up.

I wasn't being rude, I was just thinking of cows being called Daisy and Buttercup, it was the first thing that came into my mind, sorry.'

Clova, sounding a bit sullen said, 'It's spelt differently.'

Kay said, Bee and Mark ought to be a couple, they're both guilty of 'open mouth, disengage brain' syndrome, perhaps they should do a DNA test, they might be distantly related,' she chuckled adding, 'besides I would imagine cows are probably given numbers, like B12.'

Clova, not being one to hold a grudge said, 'My mum has those, B12 injections, once every 3 months, perks her up a treat. Also, a lot of people still name their cows, especially those with smallholdings, where they don't have large herds.'

Sindy interrupted the farming chat, announced she was off, asked if Mark and Kay were okay to lock up and requested the rest of the cheese scones, putting 4 in a separate bag.

Clova watched her suspiciously as she left the shop, commenting that she had just handed the small bag to her friend.

Mark told her not to worry. Sindy and Bee were both 'doggy people' and wouldn't worry about Harley possibly brushing his whiskers on some of the scones.

'I still think she should have paid for the one he ate and binned the rest. I would have. Come to think about it, she didn't pay at all, did she?'

Kay changed the subject, asking Clova what she wanted.

'I came in to see Gemma, I wanted to ask her what I should wear tomorrow. Is she giving me a uniform?'

Mark advised her to wear a short black skirt with a frilly apron, as Kay told him off for being sexist but with a half-smile on her face.

Clova gave them both a wary look. 'Do you work here on Saturdays?'

Kay took pity on her, 'Not usually. Look, wear what you feel comfortable in, Gemma will give you a hairnet and an apron.'

Mark said 'Oh look, I missed one of the scones, it dropped on to the tray with the flapjacks. Clova, fancy a cheese scone?'

'No thanks and I hope you're going to throw that one away.'

Mark picked it up and raised it to his mouth before he noticed Kay glaring at him. He sighed and put it in the bin.

'Who was that woman anyway?'

'The owner.'

'I thought Gemma was the owner.'

'That's the other owner, Sindy.'

The light dawned on Clova s face, 'Oh, is that why the shop's called Sins? That's clever, mum will be relieved that it's nothing to do with cream. See ya.'

Mark looked at Kay with a bemused expression.

She grabbed her anti-bacterial spray and started cleaning around the counter saying, 'don't ask and don't speculate.'

'What am I allowed to do?'

'Make us a drink. I'll give the shop a good clean before we go.'

Saturday: Gemma had just finished serving her builder customer with his fairy cakes as Betty and Clova arrived . Betty hooked the door open and said hello to her boss.

'Morning all. Betty, this is Clova, she'll be joining us as our new Saturday girl.'

Betty turned to look at the young woman, who was wearing combat boots, a dark green skirt and a top with faint red polka dots on a white background, which didn't clash with her newly died orange hair at all.

'Sorry, what's your name?'

'Clova.'

'I'm sure you are, love, cleverer than that gormless lad we had last week. I like your orange hair. If I were younger, I'd be changing my hair colour every week.'

Clova beamed and said enthusiastically, 'I'm thinking of going bright purple next week,' adding in a louder voice, 'and my name is Clova because I was born in Clovelly.'

Betty said, 'If I'd been born in Botswana, they'd be calling me Botty instead of Betty.'

Clova giggled, clearly delighted with her new workmate and Betty showed her into the back room/kitchen/staff room, Gemma could never decide how to refer to it, where they could leave their bags, wash hands and put aprons on, they returned just as two customers walked in, Clova watched as Gemma served them and she and Betty walked behind the counter.

'It smells lovely in here,' Clova said, 'freshly baked bread and cakes, it must attract everyone who walks up the street. What time do you start baking?'

Gemma told her about their semi-retired baker Jack who came in at 4 or 5 and did most of the baking. 'He sometimes holds the fort if I want a day off. Sindy and I do some baking at home and bring them in with us. I do most of the cupcakes and various other things. If you want, you can just watch us for a while before you serve.'

'I came in yesterday. Was that Jack?'

'That was Mark and his partner Kay, friends of ours. They help sometimes too. Mark can have an odd sense of humour and be a bit tactless. Did something happen? You're frowning.'

'No, no, it was fine. I came in to see if I needed a uniform. I've used a till and card machine before, so I don't need to watch. Oh good, people are coming in now.'

Clova excitedly served the first customer with four cakes and Gemma showed her how to make up a cake box. The second customer had been perusing the cream cakes and said to Betty, 'I fancy a cream horn.'

Betty glanced at Gemma with a slightly puzzled look on her face.

'You could try the chemist.'

The customer looked at Betty blankly as Gemma hurriedly put a cream horn into a bag, leaned across and gave it to him, leaving Clova to take his payment using the card machine, once he'd gone Betty said 'that was odd, all he said was, I want to put cream on. Cream on what? I thought it was going to be like your dirty phone calls.'

Clova said, sounding delighted, as she looked at the phone obviously willing it to ring, 'what dirty phone calls?'

Then Gemma and Betty between them, explained about the calls and some of the requests, saying they weren't sure if it was someone playing a practical joke or if they really thought the shop was a front for other services.

'Never a dull moment,' Betty told her, just as a gull hopped through the open door, Betty threw it a broken corner of a cake which had fallen on the counter.

'Betty!' Gemma said, raising her voice, 'you know better than that. Don't feed the seagulls, we'll be inundated, they'll all come in, pinch stuff and poop everywhere.'

Clova added, 'mum says they are vermin. People are always giving them chips down by the harbour, suddenly there are hundreds of them, and they swoop down and steal your whole fish supper.'

A man coming in shooed the bird out and added his opinion, saying darkly, 'that one will be back with his friends.'

Betty told them about the seagull on the local news, who had walked into a shop and taken a packet of crisps from the shelf. It came in every day, and they filmed it. Then Clova told them about the time one had flown past her holding a fisherman's knife in its beak, adding if that had been caught on camera, she thought the tourists would disappear, knowing the seagulls in Torquay were now armed and dangerous.

Gemma chuckled at the mental image Clova's comment had evoked. The customer looked up from his perusal of the savoury shelf and told them that there was no such thing as a seagull and to look it up. There were all types of gulls but no such thing as a seagull; then informed them that most of gulls in Torbay were Herring gulls, they were a protected species, but best not to feed them. Adding that he would like a large sausage roll.

Clova picked up the tongs and deftly put the sausage roll into a bag, handing it to him with a smile, then went into the back to get her phone and google it.

'He's right. There are Herring gulls, black backed gulls and all sorts, so there you go, every day's a school day, as my mum always says. I often see cormorants when I am out kayaking. I love watching them.' Betty shook her head, 'how did we manage without mobile phones in our day, you youngsters can't go two minutes without texting or googling or whatever.'

'You should try it, Betty, especially as you're a bit deaf. You could communicate instantly with your friends.'

Betty said, 'What?'

A couple entered the shop before Clova could reply, she turned round to put her phone away and bumped into Betty who was eager to get to the customers first, between them, they knocked into a glass shelf behind the counter and it fell to the floor with an ominous crack, everything on the shelf crashed to the floor but the glass only broke into three pieces.

Clova and Betty started talking over each other, panicking, apologising and generally making things worse. Betty was stressfully rubbing her hands together and Clova looked tearful.

Gemma shrieked and said 'nobody move, stay away from the glass in case it cuts your legs. My list! My list was on that shelf, I can't lose that.'

She looked up and saw the expressions on the faces of her staff and calmed down saying in a soothing voice, 'don't worry, accidents happen, we'll sort it out. At least it didn't shatter into thousands of shards. Clova, carefully pick up the broken pieces and put them out the back, then have a sweep up just in case. See if you can see my list. Betty, go and make us a nice cup of tea,'

Gemma turned to the customers, who had looks of horror on their faces, told them everything was fine and served them with their cakes. Once they had left, she picked up the phone and rang a local handyman, leaving a message on his voicemail. Then took several deep breaths.

Clova and Betty came back out with the tea.

Clova asked if Gemma was going to let her go.

'Go where?' Gemma asked, genuinely puzzled.

'Give me the push?'

Betty put a consoling arm around her shoulders, 'it was as much my fault as yours.'

Gemma said, 'these things happen, forget it. Perhaps the shelf was loose, we'll never know.'

'But disasters seem to follow me around and it's my first day. Yesterday, when I came in to try to see you, I hadn't even started working here and a dog ran in and pinched a tray of scones! I hope I'm not going to be a jinx.'

Gemma tried not to smile, 'Yes I heard about that, a dog running in and pinching **one** scone.'

'Is Sindy your partner?'

'Yes.'

'So that dog is yours too?'

Gemma had been hoping not to have to acknowledge her relationship with Harley, paused for a second or two before replying, 'Harley, Bless him. He is a terror; he must have run in looking for me. He's very loving.'

'Well, he certainly loves scones.' Clova took a sip of her tea as she recovered her usual sunny disposition. 'I'm going to bring my own mug in here to use next week.' Giving the plain white China mug a slight scowl. Clova had found Gemma s list and informed her that she could do lists on the phone.

Gemma, who had been reading a text from the handyman, looked up and said, 'I get satisfaction from crossing things off a list.'

'You can cross it off using modern technology.'

'I like the physical act of writing a list then crossing things off when I've done them. Now let's double check that everything is clean behind here. Help me measure the shelf so I can send the measurements to Matt.'

The rest of the morning passed without any dramas then around lunchtime a man dressed in workworn jeans and a faded khaki t shirt, carrying a tool bag, came in.

'Matt, so good of you to come so quickly. I didn't realise how much we use that shelf until it wasn't there.'

Matt laughed, 'It's always the way, you don't miss these things until they're gone.'

Clova had been surreptitiously eyeing him up at the same time as she wrote a text on her phone and showed it to Betty.

Betty narrowed her eyes, trying to read the small text. 'What kind of break? You haven't even finished your tea, why do you want a fizzy drink? We haven't got any, you'll have to go to Tollys.'

Clova, going a bit red, shushed her saying to Matt, 'you used to go to my school, I used to watch you play football, I mean, I was watching my brother, but you were on the same team.'

'Really? You must only have been about ten.'

'I'm 19, you're not much older than me.'

'I'm 23. You don't look 19.'

Clova snapped, 'well I am. Nearly 20 actually.' She had just turned 19.

Betty announced she was going and told Gemma she didn't want any money but would take a couple of cakes.

'Betty, you can't work for nothing. Please let me pay you.'

'If I think I've got a real job I'll start resenting it. I like to think of this as a hobby, the thing I do on a Saturday, like a reading group or an exercise class. If I don't feel like coming in, I don't have to.'

Gemma looked a bit concerned, 'No of course you don't but I would appreciate a phone call if you decided you don't fancy it; I'm starting to rely on you.'

'You've always got me though,' Clova said to Gemma, before turning to Matt and announcing 'it's my first day, bit of a dramatic start. Shall I make you a drink?'

Matt nodded and Clova hurried into the back saying goodbye to Betty, who already had her coat on and had chosen her cakes, rushing out of the shop as if she was on a mission.

Gemma gave a slight shake of her head and a chuckle as Betty disappeared.

Clova came back with Matts drink and tried to engage him in conversation, 'what's your accent, it's nice. Where are you from?'

'Torquay.' Matt mumbled, as he double checked the measurements for the new shelf.

'No, originally, I mean. Your family were refugees, weren't they?'

'Clova, don't bother Matt while he's working, and you were going to finish at half past one. Why don't you get off now?'

'No, I'm staying till we close to make it up to you for breaking the shelf.'

Gemma started to say, 'don't be daft,' just as Bee rushed in at her usual breakneck speed. Like a bull in a china shop, her friends usually said, which Bee felt was appropriate as her star sign was Taurus the Bull. She was carrying a large tin. Gemma narrowed her eyes at her friend.

'Don't look at me like that, I forgot to drop these off this morning. I've made some Millionaire Shortbread; will you try and sell it for me?'

Gemma sighed, 'Bee, it's no good bringing them in at this time on a Saturday, we close at half 2, beside I don't really need them.'

'Please,' Bee wheedled, 'I made them on a whim, now what am I going to do with them?'

'Oh, go on then, I've got a gap at the front of the counter, and I suppose I can freeze them. How much do you want?'

'Nothing. It's an experiment. If people love them and you want a regular order, then I'll charge. Did the others sell?'

'We sold a few and I think we took the rest home, they got eaten eventually.'

'What happened to the shelf?'

'It was an accident, Betty and Clova got in each other's way and the shelf came off the worst.'

'Betty's in Clova? What are you on about?'

Gemma sighed and introduced her new assistant. Just as Clova was explaining her name, the burly regular customer came in for his second visit, so Gemma went to serve him, purposely phrasing her question to wind Bee up with the answer she knew would be forthcoming.

'Hello again, how are you?'

'Not 3 bad.'

They all turned as they heard Bee make a very strange noise which sounded like a growl.

The customer turned back to the cakes as Gemma asked her if she had growled.

Clova said, 'it sounded more like a rawrr,' trying to do a quiet roar.

Bee widened her eyes and glared at the customers back, as he perused the cakes trying to find his favourite eventually asking Gemma, just in case she had secreted them in a cupboard.

'Only one left? Don't you have any more in the back?'

'No sorry.'

The customer resigned himself to just the one remaining cupcake then decided to have 2 slices of shortbread as a consolation prize.'

He left the shop looking a little disconsolate, muttering about Sins not having enough stock.

Gemma said, 'that man is addicted to cupcakes, he should have placed an order but yay, at least I've sold 2 slices of your shortbread.'

Bee glowered. 'I don't want anyone who says that to have something I made.'

Matt piped up, 'what did he say?'

'Not 3 bad. Bee hates it.

Matt and Clova laughed.

Bee said, 'and you had to say it again, didn't you? It's so annoying. If he comes in at this time of day, I'll only visit in the morning.'

Gemma said sweetly and with the knowledge that the man was usually her first customer, 'yes, best come in just after nine.'

Bee narrowed her eyes at Gemma, suspiciously.

Matt stepped back from the newly fitted shelf, dusting his hands off and declaring it finished.

'Matt, thank you, you're a life saver and so quick, I can't believe you are finished already. How much do I owe you?'

Matt told her and she got the money out of the till as he wrote out the receipt.

'You haven't finished your tea, would you like a cake?'

Matt looked at Bee and winked, saying he would have a piece of her Millionaires Shortbread as it was freshly made.

Gemma said, 'three pieces gone already, that's a record, in fact … that's not 3 bad.'

5

Sindy and Bee had taken the dogs to their favourite country park and the dogs were having a great time. The weather was favourable, there was a pleasant breeze, a gardener had just finished mowing and they could smell the pleasant scent of newly cut grass. After 40 minutes they sat down on a bench and gave the dogs a drink. Bee absently stroked Harley as they enjoyed the peace and beauty of the local park. Sindy produced a packet of cheese and onion crisps which they shared. Bee licked her fingers divesting them of the last traces of the crisps then rubbed her hands briskly and wiped them on her trousers.

'By the way, did you know that Harley s fur is quite matted around his neck?'

'Oh yeah, he rolled in something, shit of some kind, maybe fox, he'll have to have it washed out when I get home.'

Bee shrieked. 'What? You've just been letting me eat crisps and lick my fingers, ugh and I was fingering that lump for ages.'

A smooth voice came from behind them. 'What were you fingering?'

Bee and Sindy both jumped.

'Poodie!' Bee admonished, then to Sindy, 'he's like a silent assassin, I swear he does it on purpose, he's always sneaking up on me.'

Poodie raised his eyebrows, 'you're going deaf, that's what happens when you get older.'

Bee ignored him and stood up to make a fuss of Copper and the puppy, who had doubled in size again and was now bigger than Copper. Blue Ice was very reserved and un puppylike, standing next to Poodie and watching everything and everybody out of his silvery blue eyes. Bee stroked him and kissed the top of his head which he accepted as his due but continued his slightly un-nerving scrutiny. Poodie and Bee had concluded that he had been badly mis-treated but were hoping that with their love and care he would come out of his shell. He was good with their other dogs but even Harley didn't try to play chase with him. Whatever they sensed, they were content to let him be. Poodie asked if he could leave the young dog with Bee to save him going back home as he wanted to get into work early. Bee agreed so Poodie gave her an affectionate kiss on the lips, calling Copper, who usually accompanied him to work as was his habit. She was a very obedient dog who would stay by his side or on her blanket in the van, he said goodbye and agreed to meet later.

'I couldn't trust you off lead, could I Mac? You'd be off chasing squirrels.'

Mac immediately started to look around. Bee had unwittingly said the S word and Mac was looking for it, preparing to give chase. He had a good understanding of language and recognised a lot of what was said around him.

Bee suggested to Sindy that they pop into the village pub so she could wash her hands and have a drink. ' Are we having a bit of lunch? I might get a slimline tonic or something as well, I fancy a soft drink.'

'Bit late for that, luv. All right, keep your hair on, I was only joking.' They put the dogs on their leads and went to the pub which had an outside area, and sat at one of the round tables, putting the dogs underneath. Sindy offered to walk up the 21 steps and order, while Bee stayed with their animals, she'd found a dried-up wet wipe in her bag to wipe her hands with and had declared that was enough to ward off the germs, even though it wasn't wet and didn't wipe. Sindy came back 10 minutes later, carrying the drinks and moaning that the staff would not bring their order as she had forgotten to look for the table number. 'I told her we were the only ones here and we had 4 dogs, but she wouldn't have it. Jobsworth.' She paused, waiting for Bee to offer to go back but it wasn't forthcoming, so she trudged back up the old stone steps to inform the waitress that they were at table 48.

Bee said, when she returned, 'that's a waiting staffs pet hate, people not knowing their table number but even so ...' she took a sip of her drink and did her usual thing of jumping from subject to subject, expecting her friends to follow her train of thought, 'I think he'll be dark grey when his puppy fur grows out. I love the little white tip on his tail and on the tops of his ears, he'll be a handsome boy, but I wish he would come out of his shell, he doesn't show much emotion, barely even wags his tail, although he has started to greet me and Poodie. Do you think puppies can be depressed?'

The waitress arrived with sandwiches, plonking them down harder than necessary, with a bit of a glare at Sindy, making Bee smirk.

'Give him time, you don't know what he's been through.' Sindy ran her hand over her newly shaved head. It was noticeably shorter than her usual cut due to an error with the clippers, Bee, who was not very observant and hadn't even noticed until Sindy asked her what she thought about it, assured her it would soon grow but was a bit upset that she couldn't call her Sparkle anymore.

Sindy asked her how she and Poodie were getting on after their six month separation.

'Great. He was holding himself back a bit emotionally before he went away. I was worried that he was going to find another woman on the Isles of Scilly, women seem to be drawn to him and chat him up. I felt very insecure. I'm hardly the catch of the day am I?'

Sindy laughed, 'where did that expression come from, you old trout? I'm joking!

Don't start with the 'I don't know what he sees in me' business again. I'm surprised I got through your enforced six months apart with all your angst.'

'Charming. That's what friends are for. Actually, we're getting on really well. He's almost more committed to our relationship than I am. Now I'm holding back a bit in case it suddenly falls apart. I have to pinch myself every day when I look at him. I can't believe he's mine.'

'Are you still talking about Poodie or the puppy?
Don't look for problems when there are none and if you want help
with the pinching …'

Sindy leaned over and pinched her friends arm hard.

Bee frowned at her, rubbing her arm.

'Ow. You're stronger than you look, that hurt.'

'Wuss.'

Bee took some cheese out of her sandwich and shared it with the
dogs.

Harley quickly reached up and snagged half of the sandwich dragging
it on the ground. Bee grabbed it and brushed it off.

'Did you see that?' She said incensed, 'he's fast as lightning. I can't
eat that now.'

'Waste not, want not,' her friend said, grabbing the half of the
sandwich, giving it another quick brush before eating it.

'Don't glare at me, think of the calories I've saved you. Poodie will
love seeing you in that new dress I found for you and now it will fit
better.'

Bee licked her lips.

Sindy pounced, 'just talking about Poodie and you subconsciously
licked your lips. Imagining a steamy evening?'

'wasn't.'

'Yes, you was.'

'yes, you **were.**' Bee replied, correcting her grammar.

'Knew it. We'll call into Sins on the way back, I need to pick up some stuff and Gem wants to give me a 'to do' list.

Midday and the bakery had been busy, a couple with children were just leaving so Betty followed them to hook open the door, complaining that someone kept shutting it and that it wouldn't look welcoming unless the door was open.

'Much better if we all freeze,' Clova said, as Gemma told them it wasn't even cold.

Betty, mishearing said 'what's free? Is somewhere giving away free stuff? Well, it won't be in the cheap shop, they wouldn't give you the time of day for free.'

Clova rubbed her arms, as if cold but laughed at Betty who added that the door kept sticking anyway.

Gemma said, 'I know, must get round to fixing it.'

Clova beamed, 'You should call Matt. If you give me his phone number, I'll call him for you.'

'I wouldn't dream of bothering him on a Saturday.'

'You bothered him last Saturday.'

'That was an emergency. I'll do it in the week. What was all that about last week? You texted something about a drink to Betty when Matt walked in.'

Clova gave a tut, suggesting she thought Gemma and Betty should have been on her wavelength. It's an old advert, they showed it on that programme that just shows the best adverts from the past. When a hunky builder arrives in an office, all the girls say, 'it's time for a cola break', they get their cold drinks and stand at the window looking at the hunk as he takes his shirt off.'

'No don't remember that one,' Gemma snorted, 'they wouldn't be allowed to do that now, too sexist. Unless they made about 5 different versions to please everyone. Now who's fa coffee?' Gemma always said it in that way to pretend she was swearing, just as Betty was going to tell her off, Kay, Mark, and Gabriel came in and Clova and Betty both rushed to serve them.

'Careful,' Gemma said, remember what happened last time, they probably don't want anything anyway.' She looked at Kays face, sensing an atmosphere.

'What's up with you two, you look like you've had a falling out?'

'Over nothing as usual.' Mark informed them.

Kay rolled her eyes. 'In my limited experience with men it appears to have been genetically programmed into them to leave dirty clothes on the floor and when they have a shower, to just drop the wet towel wherever they happen to be at the time and then guess what happens?'

Clova widened her eyes, 'what happens?'

Kay said sarcastically, 'the magic wet towel/dirty laundry fairy whisks them all away. Then they re-appear at a later date, washed, dried, ironed and put away.'

Mark muttered to Gabriel that he would pick them up eventually.

Kay said, yes, next week or next month or if you had run out of towels or clothes to wear. I bet Gabriel doesn't do that, do you?' Gabriel, who was very tidy, looked away and asked Gemma how his cakes had been selling and brought out a box of individual chocolate swirl cheesecakes. His cakes had proved very popular, so Gemma took his next batch and paid him, as Mark and Kay popped up the road to the corner shop, saying they would call in on the way back. Gemma talked to Gabe about his baking and asked him to bring them in first thing in future. Why her friends thought that mid-morning or later was the best time to bring in cakes, she had no idea. Gabe nodded, half listening but distracted by a cake he didn't recognise.

Gemma told him it was a lemon and lavender pound cake. 'Tell you what, I'll cut some slices and put it on the counter for people to try.' Deftly cutting small, even slices and cubing them before putting them on a plate and passing them round.

They all made pleasing noises and Clova asked why it was called a pound cake. Gemma told them that all the main ingredients roughly weighed a pound before metric. She had found the recipe in an old book.

'It's delicious but it needs promoting. It won't be the customers first choice. We'll push it, won't we Betty?'

Betty, hearing Clova correctly the first time started singing 'we'll push it, push it good …' hummed a bit and finished with another 'push it good.'

Gemma and Gabriel laughed, and Gemma said she couldn't believe Betty knew that song and asked her if she had been a podium dancer in the nineties.

Gabriel joined in singing 'Salt n Pepa's here…' humming the rest while Betty wiggled her hips and danced a bit, telling them that they used to play it in her exercise class.

Gabriel looked at Clova and raised his eyebrows, 'Clova doesn't know what we're on about do you?'

As Clova was about to explain that she thought her mum might have played it, Gabriel s girlfriend came in, looking for him. They all said hello and Gabriel introduced her. Toni grunted then turned to Gabriel urging him to hurry up, commenting that it was a bakery not a meeting place. A customer came in and Gabriel made way for him as Clova held out the plate.

'Free tasting today, please try some.'

The customer took a piece, then another. Clova frowned and moved the plate out of reach as the customer asked if they had a Rum Baba. Betty said 'I wasn't a bad dancer but never did ballroom. Would you like to buy some of our pound cake?'

The customer, obviously racking his brains for his second choice asked if they had any banana cake.

Betty said, 'did you call me Nana, my lover?'

The man looked at Gemma and asked her.

'No, we haven't, I'm sorry.'

The man started to look a bit desperate 'well have you got anything *moist*?'

Clova pulled a bewildered Betty into the kitchen and a few muffled snorts could be heard.

Gemma raised her voice calling to them 'while you're out there, make us a drink,' turning back to the man she said 'how about this fruit cake? The raisins are soaked in black tea overnight which makes it a lovely moist cake. That's about the best I can offer.'

The customer sighed but agreed then suddenly pointed to the pound cake and asked for two slices of that as well.

Gemma gave a sigh as the man left and put her head on the counter, she and Gabe exchanged a knowing look as Clova came out with drinks for herself and Gemma, she put them on the back shelf and picked up a cleaning cloth.

'That was funny, have you got anything moist? Like that Peter Kaye sketch. My dad still watches his stand up on DVD. Can't wait to tell him.'

She turned to Gemma, a slight frown on her face and waved her cloth.

'I'll have to clean the counter now; you've had your head on it.'

Gemma shook her head, 'how did a nineteen-year-old get so bossy? I'm wearing a hair covering.'

Clova ignored her and started spraying and wiping, 'you've got a Hygiene rating of 5 and you don't want to lose it.'

Gemma raised her eyebrows and looked to Gabe for backup, who laughed and told her he was keeping out of it.

Clova finished her job with a flourish and went on to the next matter in hand, asking her boss if she had phoned Matt about the door yet, suggesting that she ask him to pop in next Saturday to fix it.

Gabriel said 'what's wrong with the door? Want me to take a look?'

Gabriel s girlfriend started tapping her foot impatiently as Clova looked horrified and asked him if he was a builder or handyman and if not, he should leave it to the experts.

Gemma said, 'I don't want to hold you up, we'll get Matt in, besides Clova fancies him, got to keep the staff happy.'

Clova went a bit pink, 'no I don't, well maybe a bit. I had a crush on him when I was at school. I like exotic looking men, he looks a bit like that cricketer from the old days than my Nan used to like. I wonder if he's single.'

Toni gave a loud sigh and grabbed Gabriel's arm, 'come on, before she decides she likes the look of you, we've frittered away most of this morning.'

They left the shop just as Clova was trying to explain she wasn't desperate and Mark and Kay came back with their shopping and Sindy, Bee and the dogs came in.

'Ye Gods, there's hardly room for customers. Shouldn't dogs be left outside?'

Gemma secretly thought she might have a point but felt she had to be loyal to her partner and friend said, 'Clova, it's a nice big shop and well-behaved dogs are allowed in.

'It's not that big and isn't that the dog who pinched the scones?'

'one scone.'

Kay pushed her glasses back to rest on the bridge of her nose and turned to Clova, 'a word of advice. I've noticed that dog owners and parents react defensively to any criticism of their offspring or pet, however justified.'

Sindy bristled, 'Harley just likes food. He probably had to fight for his share when he was young.'

Kay raised an eyebrow and said, 'I rest my case.'

Clova tapped her foot as she pondered the dogs and tried to think of a persuasive reason to have a 'no dogs allowed' sign put up.

'Shouldn't we be concerned about their hair getting on the food?' Gemma said firmly, 'they don't moult, they are all Poodle crosses, apart from the puppy and he's still got puppy fur.'

Clova raised her eyebrows about to grill Gemma some more, so Bee explained about mixed breeds and how people were crossing poodles with all kinds of different breeds and calling them Cocker poos or Cava poos and even Bullshit and Jackshit. A bulldog crossed with a Shiatsu and a Shiatsu crossed with a Jack Russell.

Clova gave Bee a sceptical look, 'very funny.'

'Honestly, I'm not joking, that's what they were.'

Mark asked her if the Kennel Club knew, then noticed that the shop answerphone was flashing, 'hey, look at your phone, don't you check it first thing?' He pressed play and they listened to a male voice gruffly telling them that his fantasy was to have 3 ring doughnuts on his dick and have a sexy woman nibble them off. Adding 'Is that a Sin?'

Mark hurriedly deleted the message.

'Oh no, not another one. That's the last image I want in my head,' Gemma said, going a bit red and screwing her face up.

Bee, whose sense of humour bordered on the filthy, said 'only 3?'

Mark frowned, '3? I would say that was adequate, if not generous.'

Sindy said, 'I'm so glad Betty has taken herself off to the kitchen, she'd never work here again if she could hear you.'

'Don't be so sure, she might have led a very colourful life.'

Clova said, 'I've had boyfriends, but I don't really get what would be sexy about what that man said.'

Gemma agreed, 'sticky sugar and greasy cake over everything, yuk.'

'You lot have no imagination. I bet I could eat the doughnuts without my mouth touching any flesh. Although I don't think that was his point. Wait till I tell Rohan.'

'Bee! Stop calling your fella Rohan and that was not a challenge but if it was, I'm verbally patenting it for an X Rated TV programme so if my business falls through I can be on Channel 5 in a heartbeat, also, I wouldn't mention it to your boyfriend, remember what happened with the fruit and veg man. Now let's drop the subject cos I'm getting fed up with dirty phone calls.'

Clova said to Bee, 'what fruit and veg man? What happened?'

Bee put her head down and mumbled, 'an ex-boyfriend and I don't want to talk about it.'

Mark said, 'Your answerphone is the highlight of my day, I'm visiting every Saturday just to get to it first.'

Unnoticed Harley had pulled to the end of his lead to reach one of the shopping bags on the floor. He pulled out a bag of sausage rolls and began gobbling them up as fast as he could.

Sindy belatedly grabbed Harleys lead and pulled him away, 'Mark, what was in that bag?'

Mark and Kay looked at each other, embarrassed.

Kay told her it was an impulse buy by Mark; sausage rolls on offer.

Gemma rolled her eyes, 'you knew you were coming back here, yet you bought sausage rolls from another shop, how could you?'

'They were reduced.'

'Reduced to nothing now,' Bee muttered.

Gemma looked a bit hurt, 'you're lucky Harley ate them, they were probably poor quality and full of all the horrible bits, you're our closest friends, I thought you would stay loyal.'

'Don't over-react Gem, it was a spur of the moment buy for me, we are allowed to buy stuff from other shops.'

Mark said, 'anyway, Harley shouldn't be going in our bags and pinching stuff. I love him guys, but he's a nightmare.'

Clova decided to put her two pennies in, saying that with Harley's reputation they should have left the dogs outside.

Sindy turned a darker shade of red as Gemma said hastily, before Sindy could explode, that they didn't believe in leaving the dogs outside in case they were pinched, dognapping was big business and cocker poos were highly sought after. She widened her eyes daring Clova to contradict.

'Now please go in the kitchen and have a tidy up and try to remember this is our shop and our dogs.'

Clova took herself off into the back room, head down, with the mug she had brought in from home which said, 'Little Miss Awesome'.

Betty looked at her retreating back and said 'aw, she means well and she's really trying.'

'You can say that again,' Sindy huffed.

'She means well and she's really trying.' Betty said louder.

The rest of them snickered and the tension lifted. Kay mouthed 'sorry' to Gemma and Gemma mouthed 'it's okay,' back. Kay stepped to the side to allow a woman to come in. She made a beeline for the small pieces of free cake and asked if she could try some.

Gemma went into sales mode, telling the customer that they were just a taster of her new Lemon and Lavender pound cake.

The woman frowned. 'You put lavender in a cake?'

'Yes, it's edible. You can put it in curries too.'

The woman took a sample, closing her eyes to savour the taste. 'Well, I've never heard the like but it's nice. I'll take a piece home for my old man, just so I can tell him what's in it. He'll accuse me of poisoning him but nothing new there.'

Gemma and Sindy exchanged glances, trying not to laugh. The customer left and Mark said 'never a dull moment in here. Is it always like this?'

Gemma had to admit that they got their fair share of eccentrics. Mark said, 'and that's just the staff.'

'Mark. Stop it, get your money out and buy a sausage roll before they kick us out.'

Betty went out the back to grab her coat, saying she couldn't believe it was nearly closing time. 'That was a good idea to put samples on the counter for people to try, you've nearly sold all of that lavatera cake. You should do it every day,' adding craftily, 'pretty sure it was Clova's idea Gemma.'

'Um … think it was mine, but Clova backed me up, don't worry about her, she's fine. Now what would you like, Betty?'

'A slice of the spiced fruit cake and something else, oh I don't know, surprise me.'

'BOO!'

Betty jumped and Mark added 'surprise!'

Kay shook her head, 'Mark, for heaven's sake. Poor Betty, you'll give her a heart attack.'

Mark looked chagrined and put his arm around Betty, who didn't really know what was going on, thinking she had missed a central part of a conversation so didn't take offence just saying that he had given her a bit of a turn, 'though I dare say giving me a start is good for the heart.'

Bee said, 'that sounds like an advertising slogan, but I don't know what for.'

'Whatever rhymes with heart.'

'Cart? Part? Fart?'

Mark and Bee were on a roll, 'Beans. The more you eat, the more you fart, which they say, is good for your heart.'

Gemma said 'don't give up your day job Mark and it's a good job there are no customers in.'

'It's all right for you,' Kay said, 'I've got to go home with him.'

They all said goodbye, Sindy collected her list of errands, leaving Clova and Gemma to finish off and Bee hauled Mac and Blue Ice up trying to get them out. The puppy didn't want to leave. Clova gave a slight shudder commenting that he was staring at her without blinking and gave her the creeps.

Bee became quite defensive and said she couldn't believe someone was frightened of a puppy, to which Clova replied that she wasn't scared just not that keen on dogs in general, wisely not adding 'and the puppy in particular.'

Bee shook her head and managed to get the dogs out, waving to Gemma as she left.

'Another day at the crazy cake shop, looking forward to next week.' Gemma said to her assistant. They finished their shift without any more dramas and walked up the road together, Clova chatting about finishing college and having the summer off before deciding what she wanted to do, apart from her Saturday job which she loved, she hurriedly told Gemma. Spotting her friends up ahead she said goodbye and ran up the road to catch them up. Gemma smiled ruefully at her young assistant's energy, she just wanted to go home and put her feet up. Clova was on her way to a Spin class.

10 am the following Saturday Gemma, Betty and Clova were drinking their first cup of the day as Bee came in clutching a big cake tin. Gemma gave her a wary look and said that she hoped it wasn't more cakes for them to try to sell and if it was, why hadn't she come in as soon as they opened?'

'I didn't want to bump into that guy. He might have decided to come in early.'

'What guy?'

'You know, the one that says the thing that I hate.'

Gemma pretended she didn't know what Bee meant.

'the how are you thing' Bee said with a glare.

Gemma and Clova said in unison 'not three bad.'

Bee groaned, 'just for that, please put these out for sale.'

Gemma took the tin, trying not to sigh and they all peered into the container. It was half full of over baked big, thick biscuity type things. Bee said quickly, 'they taste nice.'

'They need to look nice too, else a customer won't pick them. What are they?'

'Longue du chat. I saw them on the telly. They're French. It translates as cats tongues.'

'I know what Longue du chat is/are, but these just look like hard biscuits. They are meant to be small and delicate and melt in the mouth.'

Betty helped herself to one and dunked it in her tea, saying, with her mouth full, 'hmm, good dunkers.'

Clova twisted a strand of her newly tinted dark purple hair under her hairnet from where it had escaped, then followed suit.

Bee frowned, 'oh just help yourselves, why don't you? You can't deny that they are different, no-one else has got any like that.'

Gemma shook her head saying, 'not this time Bee, sorry.'

Bee shrugged, taking it in good heart and offered the tin round again.

Clova said, 'I hope a customer doesn't come in now, it looks bad, us all standing around eating and drinking.'

'Clova, you've barely been working here 5 minutes and you sound like you're the owner and I'm the Saturday girl, but I appreciate that you have the best interests of the shop at heart.'

Betty brushed the crumbs off the counter, dusted her hands off and took her cup into the back room telling them as she went that Clova was an 'old soul.'

Bee told Clova wistfully, that she had the mind of a 40-year-old with a teenager's body and energy.

'I have a bit. Changing the subject, I asked my brother if he remembered where Matt had come from originally. He said Albania. His dad is Albanian, and his mum is Scottish. She had gone out there on her gap year, met him on the second day of her travels and stayed until they came over here.

Matt's got a lovely voice, don't you think? Traces of both accents in there. His exotic looks are from his dads side I expect. I had a bit of a crush on him in school.'

'Yes, you said.' Gemma said, raising her eyes and trying not to roll them.

'Do I know Matt?' Bee asked.

'I think you've met him,' Gemma told her, 'very good carpenter/handyman.'

'My college course has finished now, and I wouldn't mind working here full time,' Clova said hopefully, looking at Gemma.

'If our finances improve, I'll keep you in mind. You can always do overtime and cover for now until you find something you'd rather be doing. You're so sporty I'm surprised you didn't do something along those lines at College.'

Clova smiled and shrugged, telling them that she had considered sports physiotherapy and a teachers course in physical education amongst other things but by the time she had decided, the only course left was media studies.

'I'll take this year out to think about my options and possibly go back to college,' she told them, taking the other two mugs into the back room to wash them up, squeezing past Betty coming back in. Bee took her tin back, fitting it sideways into her shopping bag, 'better get off, loads to do before tonight, see you later.'

Two customers came in as Bee left. Betty smiled at the man wearing a football shirt, 'what can I get you, my Lover?'

'4 macaroons.'

'I used to follow football in the nineties. Manchester United. I liked that David Beckham and Keano. What were you saying about Wayne Rooney?'

Obviously not a fan, the man grimaced, 'I didn't say anything about Wayne Rooney.'

Mickey Rooney? He was in old movies but that was before my time. In the days of black and white but I have seen them on that channel that does old films.'

Gemma leaned across Betty and handed the man a box of macaroons.

Betty was still oblivious but nodded sagely, 'good choice Sir, you can watch the footie, eat macaroons and watch Rooney ... well, you could if he was still playing. I think he might be a manager now, I'm

not sure. Or in America? They all end up going to America, don't they?'
The man pulled the best anti Rooney face he could do but said nothing, handing the money over with a grunt. The lady with him asked if they did coffee to take out.

Clova came back to the counter as Gemma told the lady no. Once they had left the shop Clova commented that they should sell coffee adding that they could get one of those big catering urns and sell hot drinks and maybe home-made soup in the winter. She narrowed her eyes and turned slowly around then pointed, 'I reckon a new shelf would fit over there, you could ring Matt and get an opinion and a quote.'

Gemma looked very thoughtful, 'A smaller tea urn would fit on the shelf that we already have but you might be on to something there. I'll think about it.'

Clova said eagerly, 'if they buy a coffee, they'll probably buy something to eat as well and there isn't a café in this street.'

'I'll run it past Sindy and see what she thinks.'

'Change is good, you should get in there before someone else thinks of it.'

Betty had got the gist of most of the conversation for once and raising her eyebrows, she told Clova what a goer she thought she was. Clova looked taken aback as Gemma said 'Betty!'

'What? Do I mean a doer? A get up and go … er, always coming up with new ideas.'

Clova smoothed her apron down and snorted before suggesting that she might mean innovative.

Betty nodded. 'You should go on Dragons Den, or do I mean The Apprentice?'

Clova laughed, 'don't get carried away Betty, I only suggested selling coffee and soup. I haven't invented the instant pancake.'

'Instant pancake! Whatever will they come up with next. How does it work? How instant? I mean, pancakes are quick to make anyway. I wonder if it's like those pop tarts, remember them? They used to be so hot they'd burn your mouth.'

'Betty, you're getting hold of the wrong end of the stick.'

'Bread stick?' Betty huffed, 'I'm losing the thread of this conversation, you should stick to talking about one thing at a time. I can't keep up and you youngsters all mumble, my mum would have told you to speak clearly and enunciate. I'm going to sort out the pastries.'

'Good idea,' Gemma said, rolling her eyes discreetly in Clova s direction, 'I think they already do microwave pancakes; someone beat you to it, Miss Innovator.'

Clova smirked, 'by the way, they call macaroons 'macrons' these days.'

'Wasn't he president of France? My mum always called them macaroons.'

Gemma had a lightbulb moment, 'I'm going to call them Macsins, we'll be original, change the filling each time we make them, they can be a speciality of this shop.'

'Good luck explaining that to Betty.' Clova said, raising an eyebrow. Gemma waved her pen in the air, picked up her pad and wrote Betty a memo.

'Always good to go back to the eighties.' Clova muttered, shaking her head.

6

They had a busy rest of the day and after saying goodbye to her staff, Gemma bagged up some of the cakes to take to Bee s, who was having a soiree on her patio or as she called it, a pack get together. They all, apart from Poodie, lived within walking distance of Bee's terraced house set in a private road halfway up a hill. Rosa lived across the road with her mum, who had declined the invite saying she didn't want to miss her soaps or the reruns of Judge Judy and asked her daughter to bring her home a doggie bag.

Poodie was already there, his van emblazoned with P.R Ross, Tree Surgeon and Landscape Gardener, was parked in the carport behind Bee's rusty old Honda.

'The neighbours will be placing bets as to which tree she is having taken down, they don't like you messing with their trees here, they'll be ringing the council to see if she has got permission,' Mark said, as he walked up the drive with Kay at the same time as Sindy, Gemma and Rosa arrived. Harley was already barking with excitement, inside, Mac responded with his very loud, for a little dog, bark. Chilli whined and squealed as Bee opened the door and stood back to let all the dogs in to run around and greet everyone, claws skittering on the hall floor, tails wagging. Copper charged up the stairs to say hello, followed by Blue who solemnly sniffed everyone, gave a quiet wuff and went back downstairs to continue his observation of the back garden. Bee went into the kitchen to feed the dogs, singing her soppy 'calling Mac for dinner' song. 'Dinner, dinner, dinner, dinner Macman.' Harley. Chilli and Copper hurriedly joined him and ate heir food in seconds. Poodie had fed the puppy earlier with his special puppy food. Then they followed the humans on to the patio in front of the garden which Bee had decked out with tables and chairs. Helped by Gem, Bee carried a tray of drinks out and an ice bucket with a bottle of wine nicely chilling, drops of condensation on the glass, with a couple of beer bottles squeezed in, in case someone didn't want to try her cocktails, which were a variation of a Pimms with a celery stirrer and seemed to contain a lot of fruit.

Mark looked at them dubiously and grabbed a beer, declaring that he didn't do fruit or celery and thought the drink looked like something from a bygone era, adding, 'no offence, Bee'.

The sun was just setting, and the sky was glowing with shades of pink, orange, yellow and a deep rosy red. They paused to appreciate it, Bee commenting that it looked like a cream egg.

Mark laughed, 'cream egg? Trust you!'

'It's a known fact that anyone born under the sign of Taurus will mention food at some point in any conversation, at least once a day. I'm just getting it out of the way, also, I don't eat cream eggs, ugh, far too sickly, I've lost my sweet tooth I think.' Bee said, sounding a bit mournful.

'What do Sagittarians do?' Mark asked.

'Run their hands through their hair a lot,' Bee answered, just as Mark was about to pat his ponytail, making him withdraw his hand rapidly.

'Don't believe in all that rubbish,' Mark said, 'but Sagittarians are known for being cynical.'

They laughed, accused Mark of pinching the quote from somebody famous but no-one could remember who, laughing again when he denied it and surprisingly Bee stuck up for him, saying Sagittarians didn't believe anything until it had been proved to their satisfaction.

They discussed the weather and the sunset for a while remarking on how the nights draw in so quickly and they should make the most of the light evenings, even though it was nowhere near the longest day. Rosa watched the insects which were drawn to some Sweet Williams. 'Look how many butterflies are on those flowers, your wild area really attracts the insects, it's lovely.'

A Buddleia had self-seeded amongst the Sweet Williams and shot up like a weed, reaching six foot and it was also attracting insects. The sky darkened and the solar lights came on, Bee had left the radio on, and an eclectic mix of music was playing, Sindy trying to sing along to Scatman whilst complaining that little flies or gnats seemed to pester her more than anyone else, waving her arms over her head trying to get rid of them to no avail. 'Why me?' She moaned as Bee said, 'body heat' at the same time as Mark said, 'shit attracts flies'.

'Very funny. Not. You and Bee should be a double act or a couple,' Sindy told Mark, you've got a similar sense of humour and both of you have a case of 'open mouth, disengage brain' syndrome.

'Why does everyone keep saying that? I don't think I'm like that at all. No way, Mark's much worse than me and at least I try to think before I speak.'

Mark took a long swig of his beer before saying, 'Bee's not my type. I like the prim and proper school mistress sort of woman, don't I, love?' Immediately proving Sindy right and managing to upset his partner and Bee at the same time.

'The last thing I am is prim and proper,' Kay said, frowning. Her glasses had slipped down her nose and her dark brown hair was coming loose from its' topknot. She was wearing a loose blue blouse which was perfect for her habit of, when merry, lifting her top and flashing her boobs, usually encased in a lacy item of lingerie.

'I know,' Mark winked at her, 'but you look it sometimes.'

Poodie put an arm round his girlfriend who was looking a bit put out.

'The important thing is, you're exactly my type.'

'Ah,' Rosa said, 'that's really romantic.'

'You told me you didn't have a type,' Mark said, inserting his foot into his mouth yet again.

Just as Bee was about to glare at the pair of them, Poodie told her that that was before he'd met her.

'Back of the net.' Mark said, using a football metaphor, even though he wasn't into football at all.

'Stop trying to be clever,' Kay said, telling him off.

'You mean I'm the woman of your dreams,' Bee said giving Poodie a wink, her good mood restored, turning to Mark she added, 'and if you say, 'nightmares more like', I might have to kick you where it hurts, never mind, back of the net.'

Mark laughed. 'Didn't enter my head.'

Watching the little gnats above Sindy's head circling round and round made Bee scratch her scalp in sympathy, she commented, 'flying ant day must be due soon. It was so hot last year it happened twice. I hate it but the birds love it, they gorge themselves and act like they're drunk staggering about on the road and on the pavement trying to get every single one. They don't move for cars either I think they go into a food coma. I got caught out last year and got loads tangled in my hair, ugh.'

'What, birds?' Gemma asked, deliberately mis understanding. Sindy, wildly waving her hands over her head like a demented dancer, agreed, 'you've just got to stay indoors and shut all the windows to keep the flying ants out. Wow there are some old tunes being played', she digressed as the strains of Mack the Knife was heard.

'Mac and Harley in one song' Bee said thrilled. Harley's nickname being Harley Shark. She hummed along as she went to and fro bringing out food. Dips, salad, salsa, crudities joined plates of sticky chicken wings and mini kebabs along with vegetarian sausage rolls, a variety of sandwiches and cheese scones. Keeping a close eye on the dogs to make sure the buffet was safe before she offered the animals a long chew each and they retreated into the garden to enjoy them in peace.

'I want a dog,' Rosa whined, 'if I could get one the same as Mac, I'd definitely have one, or a corgi. I love corgis.'

'You could get a rescue corgi,' Kay suggested.

'I couldn't afford a dog,' Rosa said in an immediate turnabout, 'vets bills and vaccinations and flea treatments, cost the earth these days.'

Bee said, 'You can walk ours whenever you want.'

'That would involve you actually walking, Rosa.' Mark muttered but loud enough for her to hear.

'I've got bad knees, you know that. I'd love to do a long walk. I used to love it. I might start off by doing some light exercise down at the gym.'

'You could join our Saturday girl's Spin class, that's cycling.' Gemma suggested.

Rosa sniffed, saying she would think about it, she used to like cycling but it was so hilly in their area, she needed to start slowly, find somewhere flat or do the class that Gem suggested.

Bee changed the subject saying that she had been going to make some Espresso Martinis but then thought they might keep everyone awake all night.'

'Yeah, she doesn't want us too lively, she likes her visitors to leave by half 9,' Sindy put in, making them laugh.

Bee bit. 'I don't, anyway you're even worse. Whenever you invite us to yours you say something like 'we won't make it a late night' or 'what time were you planning on going?'

'You do, you know.' Gemma told her partner.

Bee continued, getting into her stride, 'sometimes Sindy will give an exact time, she'll say 'so if you get here at 5 and leave at 10, that's all right, isn't it?'

Rosa nodded, 'I've heard you tell people to book a taxi in advance for no later than 10.30.'

Sindy raised her eyebrows, 'taxis are few and far between. I don't want my friends to have to wait or walk home. It's called being thoughtful.'

Rosa said, 'thoughtful as in thinking of yourself and not wanting people to outstay their welcome.'

'I have to be up early to let the dogs out.'

Mark started singing 'who let the dogs out …'

The others joined in with the 'who, who, who … who let the dogs out…'

Some of the dogs started barking, thinking it was a game so, Mark chased them round the garden for 5 minutes before he doubled over wheezing and panting. When he could speak, he declared that he was not as fit as he used to be, giving Rosa a sidelong glance in case she suggested he joined her at the gym and asked for another beer.

Bee said 'they're in the fridge, help yourself. Um ... what time are you thinking of going?'

Sindy pounced, 'Huh, told you, you were worse than me!'

Bee said 'impossible, I just want an approximate time in case I have to do an Off Licence run.'

'You're such a bad liar,' Sindy said, helping herself to some mini veggie sausages and falafels.

'Okay but I must be up early for Mac as well. Half 10 finish is all right for everybody isn't it?' Turning to Gemma before anyone could reply, she asked her how things were going in the shop.

Gemma began telling her their new ideas but was interrupted by Harley who appeared from out of the bushes carrying something grey with a long tail hanging out of one side of his mouth.

Gemma looked horrified and Kay screamed to Sindy to do something. Sindy, not being a fan of rodents, insects or much else relating to the fauna of Great Britain backed into the house calling for Bee to sort it.

Mark and Poodie analysed the creature still in the possession of Harley and argued over whether it was a mouse or a rat but not actually doing anything about it. Rosa, always good to be relied on in a crisis, calmly walked over, offered an exchange, a biscuit for the rat. Harley happily dropped his prize and took off with his biscuit. Sindy made a grab for him and put him on the lead as most of the others hastily gathered their belongings and made a dash for the door, calling excuses as they went.

Sindy shuddered as she put Chilli on the lead, 'Oh Bee, I really hope it's not from inside the house, you might have an infestation.'

Gemma added 'I run a Bakery, no offence but I can't be near rats.'

'It was one mouse from the garden, it's not going to be avenged by a hundred of its family and follow you to work. This is all Harleys fault.'

'He just found it. Don't take it personally but rats make me shudder.'

'It was a mouse. Don't go. And I am taking it personally.'

Kay shoved her arms into her jacket as she pushed past, 'it's been a lovely evening, but I've just remembered someone is ringing me on the landline at 9. It's important I get it.'

'Who's ringing at 9'?

Kay glared at Mark and hit him on the arm pulling him out of the door as she did so, closely followed by Gemma and Sindy.

Bee shook her head as she looked at Rosa and Poodie, 'we live in the countryside, talk about an overreaction.'

'You've got to remember they are townies. It was just the shock of seeing Harley with that furry grey body in his mouth, ugh, just as I was taking a bite of a ham sandwich.' Rosa pulled a face.

Bee flopped into a chair calling Mac to her for a cuddle she stroked his ears as she looked at the abandoned drinks and plates, 'there are rodents in towns too. Harley's a nightmare, much as I love him.

Remember when he found that dead squid on the beach, ate it and puke all the way home? What am I going to do with all this food?' Rosa peered short-sightedly into the dusk trying to work out what the puppy was up to near the magnolia tree, he was digging with a focussed intent.

'Yes, I do remember, it was my car he was in. Do you have to talk about Harley and food in the same sentence? Also, I think the puppy is burying the remains of that rat.'
Bee squeaked, 'what do you mean, remains? Never mind, I don't care, and I don't want to know.'
Poodie returned from seeing everyone out and passed Bee her drink, squeezing her arm in sympathy, he sat next to her, dipping crisps into the hummus, Mac and Copper by his legs in case hoovering up was required.
Rosa poured herself another drink from the jug on the table and sat down next to them, bending slightly to stroke Macs ears. They sat quietly for a while, listening to the music and watching the moths fluttering around the solar lights. Rosa cast her eyes over the spread of food remaining before declaring that they had all had a nice evening, it had just ended a bit prematurely and she would be happy to take some of the food home to share with her mum. 'It'll keep us going for a couple of days,' she said gleefully, practically rubbing her hands together.
Poodie said 'we'll sort it out, that'll be my sandwiches for work for

the next few days and we can have a picky meal tomorrow, take some over to your mum and give the rest to Rosa when we've divided it up.'

Rosa saw her chance at having the pick of the buffet disappearing rapidly so got up announcing that she would help clear up and they could sort it out in the kitchen then Bee wouldn't be faced with the chore in the morning.

'Honestly,' Rosa said, grinning from ear to ear, 'I don't mind. Cheer up, everyone had a lovely time, and you wanted an early night. Look on the bright side, and it didn't rain.'

7

A couple of weeks later, Betty and Clova arrived at work just as Gemma was carrying a bucket, broom and cleaning products back into the kitchen, she informed them that Jack had texted to inform her that it looked as though someone had chucked a takeaway curry over the shop window and door entrance, it had stuck like glue and smelt rancid. She'd had a job to get it off the window and the smell was stuck in her nose.

Jack had come in at 3 a.m. and it hadn't been there then. He left at 5 but hadn't had time to clear it up for them. He hadn't heard a thing but said it must have happened between 3 and 5.

Betty and Clova sniffed and screwed up their noses in disgust.

'It smells of pee as well, I bet a drunk pee'd in our doorway. I'll fill another bucket with disinfectant and swab it down.'

'I despair of people sometimes,' Betty said shaking her head, she took her coat off, put her apron on and passed Clova an apron and a hairnet, as she continued 'it's vandals or more likely some drunks. Perhaps it was vomit? I'll make us a nice drink.'

Gemma looked at Clova and pulled a face, muttering that the thought hadn't occurred to her, she didn't do bodily fluids first thing on a Saturday morning and thanks Betty, for putting the thought in her mind. She told Clova that there had been another rude message on the answer machine which she had deleted as soon as she heard the heavy breathing.

A young woman dressed in lycra cycling gear, ran in as Gemma was putting the cleaning gear away, she asked for as many Blueberry muffins as they could spare to take for a lunchtime picnic in the park. Clova packed them into two boxes for her, which the woman said would fit in the basket on her bike and jogged out. Clova went into the kitchen about to help Betty with the drinks.

Hearing a customer coming in, Gemma and Clova came back into the shop greeting the man who enquired if Gemma was the owner.

'Yes, how may I help you?'

'Your co-owner Sindy said that if I came in and mentioned her name, I could have a box of cakes on the house.'

Clova frowned, 'Really? That's an odd thing for her to say.'

Gemma glared at her Saturday girl, 'Clova! Please leave this to me.' Addressing the man, 'Did she say why?'

'Her dog tried to eat our cream tea.'

Clova rolled her eyes, 'Harley, of course, it had to be Harley. How many scones did he pinch?'

'Clova! Go back into the kitchen and help Betty,' turning back to the customer Gemma said, 'yes, I heard about that, we're so sorry, have anything you like.'

The man perused the goods on offer, taking his time before choosing some cakes which Gemma put in a box for him. He was thrilled and said with a smile, 'let me know the next time Harley is in the park and I'll make sure we're there with something in a bag for him to pinch. Your cakes are far superior to our very ordinary cream tea. Thank you.'

Gemma laughed as the man went out, holding the door for a woman to come in. Betty and Clova returned holding 3 mugs of coffee which they placed carefully on the back shelf then Betty hurried to hook the door open, sniffing like a hunting dog all around the entrance, to make sure all she could smell was disinfectant.

 The next customer was looking a little fraught, she was flushed and had a slight sheen on her face, Gemma asked if she was all right. The woman wiped her face with a tissue, panting and gasping to the point that all the staff started looking concerned, the woman gasped and panted as she said 'I'm all right, just trying to catch me breath. I suffer with me chest, it used to be just when it was damp,' she paused, gasping 'now it's all year round. Do you have 4 blueberry muffins?' Betty glanced at the counter and apologised saying they had sold out.

   'Already? I tried to ring you first thing this morning and left a message. Didn't you get it?'

Betty looked at Gemma, who was looking shifty, obviously she had mistaken the asthmatic woman for a dirty phone call. 'Um ...' she began unsure how to answer.

Clova said quickly, 'the machine's playing up, isn't it? What about those new muffins you made. Blushin muffins.'

The customer laughed, coughed, panted and gasped 'oh don't make me laugh love, what are they then?'

Gemma pointed them out, the raspberry muffins looked as if they had red cheeks, hence the name. The customer thought they looked very cute and asked for 4, chuckling and gasping as she left.

Clova immediately turned to Gemma and said, 'that was your dirty phone call.'

'All right, well done for covering for me, I guess I'll have to listen to the whole message in future.'

They picked up their drinks, Clova looking pleased with herself, taking a sip of her hot coffee, she asked what their plans were for the afternoon informing them that she was going to play netball. Betty said she was going shopping with her friend Iris before going back to her house for lunch.

Carl, the manager of the corner shop walked past, he looked in and made eye contact with Clova in a slightly creepy way, she turned her head and went a bit pink.

Gemma wrinkled her nose, 'that was a bit odd, do you know him?'

'He's an ex-neighbour. He told mum I shouldn't work in here for a pair of … um …sorry Gemma, I wasn't going to say anything, people shouldn't say things like that especially in this day and age. It didn't go down well with mum, she informed him that our Daniel is gay, she said she was very proud of her nephew, he was a wonderful human being unlike some, and Carl wouldn't be welcome in our house if he had that attitude. Not that he was welcome before, she just felt sorry for him.'

Betty had missed the gist of the conversation and said 'eh?'

Gemma said 'he's homophobic. I'm not at all surprised, the slimy little git.'

Betty said a little querulously, 'what's slimy?'

Clova and Gemma said loudly 'Carl'!

'Wouldn't surprise me if he threw up on your window.'

Gemma laughed, 'I'm not going to get paranoid, I'm sure even Carl can't produce vomit on tap.'

'Bet he could,' Clova said, adding that she didn't like him, and her mum couldn't get rid of him if he ever called round, 'mum felt sorry for him, he's had no luck with relationships or with his various businesses. He offered me a job in Tollys but no way, I didn't want to work for him and I'm not a spy.'

'I didn't think you were. What have you got to spy on anyway, which are our most popular cakes?'

Clova went red.

'What?'

'Mum asked me, she said Carl was curious. I didn't know it was industrial espionage.'

Gemma shook her head in disbelief, 'even if you knew, which I don't think you do ...'

Clova interrupted, 'maple and pecan slices.'

'Nope. It changes every day. This week it's Sindy s spiced fruit cake, with the Lemon Drizzle tray bake running a close second. Let's not talk about that twonk anymore.'

'Twonk, is that a word?'

Gemma said 'I've picked it up from Bee, who picked it up from her manager at work, the pair of us are always picking up other people's quirky words and phrases. Mrs Kahn is coming in shortly; she wanted a box of macsins and the coffee cake that is on the back shelf. Clova, can you get it ready please?'

Clova hurried to do so, relieved that she'd got her so-called relationship with Carl out in the open. The morning flew past with a steady flow of customers, Betty left with her cakes and a cheery 'see you next week' and Gemma wiped down the counter saying to Clova 'in answer to your question of about 3 hours ago, this afternoon I'm meeting friends on the beach. We are going to have a nice relaxing dog walk followed by a coffee at the beachside café.' Glancing at the sky, 'well I hope so. Enjoy your netball.'

They finished clearing up, Clova grabbed her jacket and took off up the road, leaving Gemma to lock the bakery, enviously watching her assistant, who'd started to jog up the road with as much energy as she had started the day with. It had started to rain but the weatherman had assured people that it would only be a shower, promising good weather for the afternoon.

An hour later Gemma and Sindy had met their friends on the dog friendly beach in Paignton. The tide was out, and the beach seemed to stretch for miles, strands of seaweed on the shoreline adding streaks of green to the slightly red Devon sand. the sea glinting and sparkling in the bright sun, the shower had passed, and the weatherman had been proved right.

 The dogs had enjoyed a long walk and a swim and now they were sitting under a big table outside the café, a big bowl of water beside them.

'It was so busy at work this morning,' Bee said, 'I'm shattered, I could just sit here, soak in some sun and listen to the sound of the sea and the gulls, so peaceful.'

Under the table Mac was twisting himself around trying to clean himself.

'What's that noise?' Sindy asked

Bee bent down and looked at the little pretzel shape that was her dog and told Sindy it was Mac cleaning himself.

'I've never heard anything like it, he sounds like a truffle pig.'

Gemma laughed 'when have you ever heard a truffle pig?'

Sindy said quickly, 'on T.V, it sounded just like that.'

Their friend Rosa, who had passed on the walk and had commandeered a table for them all, commented 'I remember a time when me and Bee had gone out in the car and Jess was on the back seat. Jess was Bee's dog before Mac, there was a strange noise. I couldn't work it out, it sounded like a typewriter...'

Bee carried on: 'Jess was frightened of kites and had seen one out of the window and it was her teeth chattering.'

Rosa said, 'it was hilarious, not that she was scared but that noise, I've never heard a dog do that; it really did sound like a typewriter. Mind you, how many people would know what one sounded like these days. I've still got an old Olivetti in a cupboard somewhere, it's bright red, probably worth a bomb. It's practically an antique. '

Rosa tried to make the noise of a typewriter complete with the ding, with hand gestures thrown in.

More snorting and snuffling sounds emerged from the black shape under the table. Chilli decided to use the waiting time to groom herself and was making loud rasping noises as she used her tongue to smooth her fur and clean her private parts.

Gemma told them 'Chilli s got a new game,'

Sindy added, 'Rebound'

'Did you see her?' Gemma continued, Sindy threw her ball against the sea wall and Chilli caught it on the bounce back, she was going crazy and just wanted to keep playing the ball, wall, game.'

'The Rebound game, luv, hence the name.'

Gemma pulled a face as Rosa yawned and said 'fascinating,' in a bored tone.

Gemma ignored her, 'she loved it, we played it for ages.'

Bee said 'yeah, I was watching Sindy and counting how many people sitting on the wall and next to the wall that she narrowly missed hitting. In fact, the minute my back was turned she *accidently* hit me on the back with the ball.'

'It was an accident.'

'Sure it was.'

'You're paranoid.'

'That's probably because I'm always getting hit with the ball.'

'I've told you a thousand times not to exaggerate.'

The waitress came out and placed 3 halves of cider and a non-alcoholic cocktail in front of them.

'I thought we were having coffee,' Bee remarked.

Sindy said gleefully, 'nothing like an ice-cold drink on a warm day, isn't that right Harley Shark?'

Harley looked up, sniffing, hoping for some food, finding nothing being offered he started to clean himself, his teeth clicking busily through his curls.

Bee said, 'I need to go to the loo, but I can't get out, I'll have to go round the outside.'

Sindy started singing Buffalo girls by Malcolm McClaren. 'Buffalo gals go round the outside,' she crooned loudly and tunelessly as Bee started moaning about another annoying song getting stuck in her head to join Baby Shark.

'You're so easy to wind up.'

Bee told them that she had watched Farming Life on T.V the previous night.

'Really? You're so rock and roll.'

'Ha-ha, it just happened to be on, and I got into it. A farmer had bought some female buffaloes but due to financial problems had to sell them almost straight away. When the lorry came, to get on it they had to go round the outside and I thought, literally, buffalo gals go round the outside. You've brainwashed me.'

Sindy, unable to help herself said 'Gigolo' in a loud voice.

Rosa frowned then gave a slight shake of her head, 'I'm not even going to ask. I suppose it's in the song but it's well before my time.'

Gemma said, 'when we watch quizzes that's our pet hate, contestants saying 'it's before their time. Who was Sir Francis Drake? Don't know, before my time, or it will be a music question and they'll say 'I wasn't born then' about a classic hit from the 90's.'

Bee eventually managed to squeeze her way around the table to go to the loo. The others sat quietly, people watching and enjoying the scenery. A baby Herring gull had perched on the low roof of the building just above their heads, it was making continual begging sounds 'ack, ack, ack, ack, ack, ack'.

Bee returned and shuffled back into her seat glaring at the bird.

'What a racket, they must drive their parents mad.'

Gemma looked around not having noticed the gull .

Rosa hadn't noticed either until Bee pointed it out and commented on her low tolerance to noise.'

'I can't help it; I've got fan shaped nails.'

Sindy groaned 'don't start her on palmistry or we'll be here all day. Besides I hate it when people eat noisily, crunching crisps or popcorn (giving her partner a sideways glance) when I'm trying to watch a film and I haven't got fan shaped nails.'

Bee studied her friends hand carefully and found one vaguely fan shaped nail on her ring finger. 'There! You've got one but I've got four.'

Under the table came the loud sounds of snorting, snuffling, rasping and clicking but Bee didn't mind dog noises, she found them cute. Overhead the gull continued his begging 'ack, ack, ack, ack.'

Bee said 'Flippin' eck. All we need is a pigeon to join in and my misery would be complete. They are so clumsy and noisy, have you ever heard them trying to fly out of a tree? They sound like someone shaking a paper bag, my friend spent half an hour under a tree last week, thinking that a pigeon had got trapped and was trying to free itself, but it was just shifting about trying to get comfortable, and I don't like pigeon song, it's monotonous and gets on your nerves.' Making a credible attempt at a pigeon impersonation.

Rosa and Sindy start singing 'I know a song that'll get on your nerves ...'

'Stop it, now I'll have annoying songs stuck in my head all day.'

Gemma said 'now now children ...' just as a real child nearby set up a piercing shriek, hurting their ears. Harley perked up recognising a 'food dropped on the ground cry ' and crept to the end of his lead stuck out his long tongue and obtained half a sausage.

Everything got noisier, Mac and Chilli continued their grooming, the child carried on screaming, the gull begging. A helicopter passed overhead, and the steam train merrily chugged it's way along the train line behind them, blowing its whistle. The noises from inside the café got louder, glasses clinked, and the coffee machine churned. Bee sighed as Gemma said 'so nice to relax and enjoy the serenity of the seaside after a morning at work. We're so lucky to live here.' Bee said through gritted teeth, 'that's what I love about you, Gem, your positivity.' She tipped the rest of her drink into Sindy's' glass and said she was off to meet her mate Angelique who she had given the nickname 'last minute.com' but not to her face, due to the fact that she would start a text with ' I know it's short notice, but can you meet up now?'

Bee said goodbye and grabbed Mac. Angelique picked them up in the car park and drove to a hotel they liked in Torquay where they could sit on the large patio and have an uninterrupted view of the sea.

'Thanks for meeting me. I know it's always last minute but when my last client cancelled, I texted on the off chance you were free. My treat, what would you like?'

'No probs. I haven't seen you in ages. I'll have coffee with cream please with some of their homemade biscuits. You look great Annie, are you enjoying being a Personal Trainer?'

Angelique wore cream linen trousers and a floaty cream top with very pale primrose stripes, her dark hair was short and shined with health or good grooming products. Bee on the other hand looked as if she had just got out of bed, fallen in the sea, dried in the sun and been on a trek. Her cheeks were red, her nose was starting to peel even though the sun hadn't been that strong. Her thick blonde hair had come out of its grips and was flying all over the place, her clothes were creased but she was clean, at least nobody could fault her personal hygiene.

'Love it,' Annie said, 'and I'm helping to run the health club, so many different types of people, it's so interesting. We had a couple of jockeys in today, looking for a new training regime. They have to keep themselves really fit.'

Bee rummaged in her bag for a gravy bone to give Mac, who assumed that every time she sat down, he would get a treat, which to be fair, he usually did.

'I used to walk Jess on Walls Hill most days and often walked round with an old chap who used to be a jockey. He was Devon through and through and always coming up with country lore, like pointing to the trees and saying that the leaves had turned upside down which meant it was going to rain. I couldn't see any difference to be honest but then my eyesight's not that good, or he'd say, the ants are scurrying about faster than usual – also a sign of rain. Don, he was called. I think he knew about a hundred different signs of approaching rain and repeated most of them to me daily.

He told me that when he was a young lad all the stable boys used to wrap horse manure in paper and put it in their Wellington boots in the winter to keep their feet warm.'

'Ugh, that would be the worst case of smelly feet ever.'

'You look nice. I never wear linen; it creases so much and I hate ironing. I bought a really nice dress last week from that posh shop down on the harbour but I think I look like a bag lady in it, it will probably end up straight in the charity shop.'

Annie chuckled and told Bee she was sure she didn't.

The waiter brought their drinks over, a coffee with cream and a skinny latte and the expected complimentary biscuits. He patted Mac on the head and left with a warning to watch out for the grabby gulls.

'Grabby gulls? Keep those biscuits out of reach,' Annie said, moving the plate closer to Bee, 'I love people watching, don't you? That couple over there are obviously on a first date, she keeps touching her hair and laughing and they're gazing into each other's eyes, aah.'

Bee discretely indicated another couple, sitting in silence, both on their phones and not communicating with each other at all, unless they were doing it by text, 'and that couple have been together for a long time,' she whispered adding in a louder voice 'look at that woman with the big dog, he just jumped up and put his arms around her waist, holding on while she got a biscuit out. How funny.'

Angelique laughed, 'arms?'

Bee laughed and snorted coffee from her nose, she looked up from dabbing her face with a tissue as someone nudged her. Of course, it would be Poodie. He patted her and Mac on their respective heads and said hello to Angelique before joining another man at a table near the entrance.

'He always appears when I'm making a show of myself, it's like he has a sixth sense. I forgot he was meeting a client.'
Annie gave her a quizzical look, 'he patted you on the head.'

'I know. He usually nuzzles my hair and sniffs it. I think he's got a fetish.'
Annie snickered, 'could be worse I guess, remember the fruit and veg man?'

'Don't remind me. Damn, now I can't have a biscuit. I'm on a diet, I go to a slimming club now.'

'Poodie likes you as you are, don't be daft. If you want one, have one.'
Bee didn't need telling twice and took one of the buttery shortbread rounds, biting into it with a sigh of pleasure, considering Annie s job and all-consuming hobby was fitness she never suggested any form of exercise or diet to her friend. In fact, in the early days of their friendship Annie had been the manager of a Health food shop yet used to buy Bee bacon sandwiches for lunch and sit outside with her as Bee had been a smoker then.

 Bee told her she had started sea swimming or to be more accurate, bopping up and down while periodically screaming about the cold. She had been once with Gemma. The sea temperature had been 12 degrees, she had stayed in the water for too long and nearly got hypothermia but not to be put off she was trying to go once a week and maybe soon she would do some actual swimming. Her target was going to be 400 strokes each time, if she could stop screaming when the cold water reached her nether regions.

'Good for you', I couldn't swim in the sea, I hate cold water. I enjoy going out in the canoe wearing my wet suit but that's my limit as far as the sea goes. We saw some dolphins the other day, did I tell you? Made my day.' Annie said. They carried on, catching up on what had been happening since they had last met. Bee told her about the puppy and said it was being looked after that afternoon by Poodie s friend. The waiter delivered sandwiches and drinks to Poodie s table. Poodie thanked him absentmindedly, he was staring at Bee.

The man, who knew Poodie from years ago, noticed him looking and said 'not still single are you mate? Fancy her? Yep, your type, dark hair, could be a model, looks a bit like your ex.'

Poodie raised his eyebrows, 'I don't have a type and my girlfriend is sitting over there … the blonde.'

'What? Can't picture you with her at all, no offence but she looks like she's been dragged through the undergrowth by her hair for about an hour, then dumped in a ditch.'

Poodie frowned at the rude comment, wavering between wanting to punch his friend and finding the remark slightly funny. After a few moments glaring, he saw the funny side and chuckled. 'She would probably agree with you but a bit harsh mate. There is nothing about her that I would change, she is just how I like her, the complete opposite of Dawn and ready to get down and dirty.' He laughed again, 'God, she would kill me if she heard me say that. It's not even true but she'd go for a walk with the dogs any time whatever the weather if I suggested it, without complaining or needing to put on her special 'walking outfit' and taking five hours to get ready before we could leave the house.

I had two years of being bored rigid by the beautiful Dawn. I look below the surface now, all that glitters is not gold and all that.

In my eyes, Bee has a more natural beauty, lovely complexion, gorgeous hair. She's loyal, kind and makes me laugh.

She's much more me than Dawn was. Dawn was all style and no substance.'

His friend sat back in his chair and raised his eyebrows, listening to Poodie's passionate defence of his girlfriend.

'All right calm down, I apologise for my thoughtless remark and If you're quoting Shakespeare, it's 'all that glisters is not gold' but fine, whatever turns you on. I'll have the one that looks like a model then, cheers.'

'I don't know her that well, but I think she is married. I've seen them jogging round the village. She's into her fitness.'

His friend shrugged, 'fair enough, I'm not into running, a walk to the local pub is enough for me. Now on to business, I'm here on behalf of a friend, he's got quite a bit of work, just moved into his new house. It's near that big garden centre, a bit out of the way. He's got about an acre of garden that he wants landscaping with some trees to sort out. His house is called Llamekcuf.'

Poodie repeated what he thought he had heard, 'Lamb e cuff?'

'Look at the card and read it backwards.'

Poodie laughed, 'he's had enough of everyone then. Thanks mate, I'll give him a ring.'

Hearing a sharp gasp from the table behind the men, they all turned round in time to see a gull fly off with two tuna sandwiches.'

Bee said to Annie 'two sandwiches in one swoop that's terrible, even Mac is looking impressed.'

Mac snorted and lay down, patently disgusted that the bird hadn't even dropped a crumb.

8

Gemma pulled up outside Sins. It was Jack's morning off, but he had baked enough for two days to see them through. Gemma and Sindy had risen early and done extra baking too. Gem began to unload the car as Sindy unlocked the shop door for her, bending down to look at the letterbox which was damaged.

'Look at this, someone has broken our letterbox. How on earth did they do that?'

Gemma frowned, pushing the door open with her foot and then gagged, someone had pushed a rotten fish through the letterbox with some force, breaking it in the process. Harley jumped out of the car, grabbed the fish and ate it. Sindy held her nose and waved her arms in the air as if that would dissipate the odour, they both shouted at Harley who promptly brought the fish back up then tried to clear up his own mess.

'Ugh, I'm going to be sick.' Sindy grabbed Harley s lead and shut him up in the car, taking as much time as she could away from the stench in the bakery.

Gemma tried to breathe through her mouth, still waving her arms. Carl from Tollys walked past, glancing in he pulled a face and said 'very hygienic, I'm sure. How nice. Just what you want to start your day in your posh little cake shop.'

Sindy walked round the side of the car glaring at him, 'oh shut up, you probably did it to sabotage us.'

'Got better things to do with my time. Upset a fisherman, have You?' Carl walked off jauntily, whistling.

Sindy said to her partner, I'll leave the dogs in the car until you're ready to open, then I'll walk them home. You finish bringing the stuff in.'

Gemma stood looking at the floor, 'um...'

Sindy waited but no sentence followed.

'You often do that.'

'Do what?'

'Say, um. As if you're going to say something then don't say it.'

'And you say, 'not being funny, but' all the time but I don't bring that up, do I?'

'Don't mention bringing it up, it makes me want to gag.'

'Which one of us is going to clean it up?' Gemma asked hopefully, her mouth and nose screwed up. Sindy gave her partner a long look before taking a deep breath, which she regretted, then said, 'all right. I'll do it.'

Gem edged out of the shop, wafting the door to and fro to get some fresh air in, thanking her partner, telling her that she was a perfectionist when it came to cleaning, so she was the best person for the job.

'Is this a normal part of being a shop owner do you think? Or has someone got a grudge against us. We were in a bit of a bidding war for this shop when we bought it, maybe it's someone who hopes we will sell? I might have a word with the other traders to see if they are having any problems.'

Sindy went and got the bucket and mop and commenced the clean-up. Gemma finished unloading, mumbling to herself that all the cakes would stink of fish which Sindy overheard and counter mumbled, 'no they won't, they'll stink of bleach and disinfectant.'

'Lovely. Just want you want in a cake.'

Sindy said, 'if you're that worried, put the oven on and make something quickly, not to sell, just so the shop will smell of warmth and baking. We'll leave the door open, and I'll put some more disinfectant down before I take the dogs for their walk. I hope Harley's stomach will be all right.'

'We'll have to start bulk buying disinfectant at this rate.' Gemma moaned.

They just managed to get ready for opening at 9 and Clova walked in, sporting some new blue tips on the ends of her purple hair. She sniffed a few times and looked around, before saying 'is there a funny smell in here?'

Gemma and Sindy exchanged glances.

'Is there?' Gemma replied, 'what can you smell?'

'It's a little bit fishy.'

'Oh God. We've cleaned it up. Someone put a fish through the letterbox, breaking it in the process.'

Clova looked horrified, 'that's awful. Not the kind of smell you want in a bakery.'

'That's what your mate Carl said.'

'He's not my …'

Clova was interrupted as an official looking man carrying a briefcase, walked in.

'Good morning, my name is Mr Edwards from Environmental Health. We've had a complaint that we need to check out. A person claimed to have got an upset stomach from one of your products, nothing remained of the item for us to check but we must follow up any complaints of that nature. I'm sure you have nothing to worry about. I just need to have a quick look round.'

Gemma looked aghast but showed him into the kitchen where he spent 20 minutes carefully scrutinising the work surfaces, fridge, freezer and ovens. He asked a few more questions before shaking her hand and leaving.

Gemma looked at Clova and gave a deep sigh, 'Oh God, what a start to the day, at least he didn't have your sense of smell.'

'What did he say?'

'He couldn't fault my hygiene, so we won't lose our 5-star rating. He said the person who complained could have picked up the bug anywhere, but he had to investigate it. I'm glad Betty is late in today, don't mention it to her. I can't handle trying to explain it to her 5 times then dealing with her bad mood on my behalf.

Clova nodded and they got on with their jobs as the customers began to come in. Betty arrived mid-morning and made them all a cup of tea as they had a brief quiet moment.

Betty said, 'I know I made it, but this is a good cuppa. Where do you get your teabags Gemma?'

'The Pound shop.'

Betty looked surprised: 'Really? How much were they?'

Gemma s mouth twitched, and Clova giggled. Betty looked a bit annoyed then realised why they found it funny.

'Not everything in that shop is a pound.'

Gemma said, 'well these were and you're right, they do make a good cuppa. Bee was here just before you arrived, Betty. She made those little angel cakes over there and 'Not Three Bad' came in, it was brilliant, the faces she pulled, perfect timing.'

'Doesn't she like him?'

'She doesn't like people saying that, it drives her mad. Bee's got quite a low tolerance level, lots of things irritate her, it's hil air ious, makes me laugh. Also, she's easy to wind up, always a good trait to have in a friend.'

The others chuckled. As Gemma put her drink down, a customer came in.

'Remember me?' she asked, 'I bought the lavender cake the other week.'

Gemma said' 'oh yes, the lady who is poisoning her husband.'

Betty said, giving a nervous laugh, 'I must get my hearing tested again, the things I think you're saying, well, I wouldn't like to repeat them.'

'I'm not poisoning my husband; he's just accusing me of trying to poison him. Anyway, the lavender cake kept me amused for days. Have you got anything else weird?'

Gemma said 'this week we have some chocolate and courgette cupcakes with chilli in the frosting, giving them a kick of chilli heat, or the red velvet cake which has beetroot in.'

The lady wrinkled her nose, 'they both sound horrible. I'll have 2 of the courgette ones please.'

After she had gone, Betty said, 'it's so strange in here sometimes. I'm sure she said the cakes sounded horrible; she pulled a face then she bought two. I'll say again, nowt as queer as folk.' Betty gave a slight shake of her head as she gathered up the cups and took them into the kitchen.

Matt the handyman came in, he looked straight at Clova and winked. 'Like your hair, what colour would you call it?'

Clova looked a little flustered but smiled and said, 'It was supposed to be duck egg blue, but it went purple, I wasn't keen, so my mate tipped the ends with the blue, do you really like it?'

Betty returned getting the wrong end of the stick as usual, 'what's that about eggs? My neighbour rescued some chickens a few months ago, she's put them on her allotment, they were those battery-operated ones ...' a snort was heard in the background, but Betty didn't notice, she carried on, 'They had no feathers hardly, when they first arrived but they're plump and happy now. Proper posh chicken house they built for them. I could live in it; it's even got heating. In fact, I'm going to visit it a lot in the winter. Sometimes she brings me half a dozen eggs but not lately, I think she's forgotten me, perhaps I'll take her a cake round, that might jog her memory. Those eggs taste better than any I've bought in a shop.'

Gemma said she'd always wanted chickens, but Sindy wouldn't let her, said it would attract rats and foxes and drive the dogs up the wall.

Matt turned to Clova again. 'I remember where we know each other from. We did that charity rock climb last year. Your hair was flame red, easy to spot you on the cliff face.'

Betty looked puzzled as if wondering what that had to do with chickens or eggs.

Clova smiled and nodded, 'I remember that. It was a biting Easterly wind, I thought I was going to be blown off the cliff face. Then we all went down and stood on the rocks talking about doing the cliff dive, rock leap, or whatever it was called. Tombstoning, all the kids at school used to call it and most of them tried it in the summer holidays. I know you from school though, remember, and the footie team, you used to play with my brother.'

'What's his name?'

Clova told him.

'Of course. Nice lad. I still see him around.'

Betty said wistfully, 'you don't see them much these days, everyone used to make them, you'd make them in Domestic Science at school.' Gemma had started wiping down the back shelf, but she was listening and asked Betty what she meant, at the same time as Clova asked what Domestic Science was.

Gemma said, 'I think it's called Home Economics now.'

'If you're talking about learning to cook in school, it comes under Science and Technology.' Clova and Matt exchanged a glance at the lack of knowledge from the older generations.

Betty sniffed loudly, 'as I was saying, you don't see rock cakes anymore. They were the first cakes I learnt to bake at school but when I tried to make them at home, I put the gas oven on, forgot to light it. Mum bent down with the matches and boom … no eyebrows, could have been worse.'

'Hmmm,' Matt said, as clearly no-one was going to investigate the matter further, they enjoyed it when Betty rambled off into her own version of what she thought they had been talking about. Although Matt did add that they sold rock cakes in the café at the caves nearby.

'Oh, that's appropriate,' Gemma chuckled, 'probably why they do it.'

Matt took his toolbox over to the door and began working, stepping aside for a customer to enter.

Betty got to the man first and gave her customary greeting, 'morning, my lover.'

He asked for four Nuns Puffs. Gemma pointed to the tiny doughnuts on display under the counter and told Betty they were 4 for a pound. Betty served the man without comment and Matt stepped aside to let him out, laughing as soon as he'd left.

'Nuns Puffs? Never heard of them.'

Betty looked relieved that it wasn't her hearing.

Gemma told Matt that she had made them once as a special order for a customer, told Gabriel who, fancying a challenge had made some and brought them in.

'They look better than mine.' She added ruefully.

Clova took a pound from the back pocket of her trousers and served herself with 4, giving them all one to sample.'

'Mm mm, they melt in the mouth.' Gemma said, licking her fingers before remembering where she was and grabbing a wipe.

Betty said, 'very cinnamony.'

Matt had practically inhaled his, saying that you would want at least four to yourself if you were buying them.'

'Matt, I've just remembered, our letterbox is broken, could you fix it sometime? Also, could you give me a quote for CCTV.'

'I'll measure it before I leave and get one for next week, I'll block it off for now, letters can still be slid under the door, and I'll look into the camera for you.'

Clova said, flirting, 'Would you look into the camera for me?' Pointing her phone at him and taking a picture.

Matt laughed. 'Right, I'm done.'

Clova looked horrified, 'What? Already? I was going to make you a drink. You were quick.'

He winked, 'I'm a fast worker.' Matt opened and shut the door several times to show them that the door didn't stick, measured the letterbox and told Gemma to settle up with him the following week. He had to dash, he said, as he'd promised a mate, he'd sort his fence out for him.

'Bye, Blueberry, thanks for the Nuns Puff.'

Clova hooked the door open, watching Matt hurry up the road, muttering 'Blueberry' to herself and huffing in a pleased sort of way.

'Can't change your hair colour now that your not-so-secret crush has given you a nickname.' Gemma teased.

Clova ignored her, looking around the shop.

Gemma raised her eyebrows, 'I can practically see your brain ticking over. Everything in here is fine, apart from the letterbox. I can't make up a list of jobs just to keep you happy. If you can't wait until next Saturday to see him, I think he drinks in the Eight Bells now and then, if you're out with your mates. Oh, nice work with the photo, quick thinking.'

Clova took her phone out of her pocket and looked at the picture before putting it away again. 'I know, I try to be ready for any opportunity, that's my motto, Carpe Diem. Look how I got this job? Walked past at the right time, just as you were putting that sign in the window.'

Kay and Mark came in, after saying hello, Kay told them that Mark wanted to buy something to make up for the other week.

'No need. You cooked us dinner, although then you took all my spare change after fleecing us at cards.'

Clova looked shocked, not expecting her boss to be a gambler.

'It's not high stakes. Still, I'd rather have been up a fiver than down.'

Mark and Kay laughed, and Mark said, 'So I'll spend my ill-gotten gains in here, what shall we have?'

Clova, obviously associating Harley with Mark said, 'Is that dog coming in today as well?'

Mark gave her a mock frown, 'that's no way to speak about Sindy.'

Kay nudged him with her shoulder, as Gemma said, 'I'm telling her you said that.'

Mark held both hands up, 'okay, okay, she gives as good as she gets. Clova, don't you like Harley? He's a sweetheart.'

Clova said darkly, 'he's a pincher.'

'Dobermann?'

'Eh?'

'Stop teasing my staff, now what do you want?'

Kay said, 'Rosa calls Harley Fagin and sings 'gotta pick a pocket or two.' When she sees him. He's such a tea leaf. He literally picked Marks' pocket one night, extracted his scarf without anyone noticing, and put it in his basket. Another time he managed to get Bee's purse out of her handbag and was just about to make off with it when she spotted

it in his mouth. He's very good at it and seizes every opportunity.'
Mark smiled thinking about Harley, 'he's the exact opposite of
assistance dogs, but we love him anyway, he's such a character.'
Clova was looking at him, askance, with a dubious look on her face,
she didn't understand the appeal.

'Watch the wind doesn't change, as my mum used to say, else your
face will be stuck like that. You should spend some time with the dogs,
get to appreciate their finer qualities.' Mark told Clova, before
choosing some Tiramisu slices and saying a friendly goodbye.
Gemma put her cleaning cloth underneath the back shelf saying that
she hoped the rest of the day would be free of stress and no more
dramas or breakages.

'And no naughty dogs,' Clova muttered under her breath.

9

It was a Friday, Bee and Poodie had time off work and had done a long walk with their dogs. Blue Ice had doubled in size again and was now a bit bigger than a German Shepherd. For a young dog, he was very well behaved and hardly ever pulled unlike Mac, the 8-kilo crossbreed who was weaving from side to side, sniffing and weeing at every opportunity. Bee had hoped he would copy Blue Ice but no, he was a stubborn little dog who thought he was at least the same size as Blue and therefore should be leading the pack, in Harley's absence. They had just walked down some steep steps and finally Mac looked tired, the man-made steps, which had been dug out of the earth, were uneven and had been a bit high for his little legs. Bee sympathised, she'd found them hard going too, whereas Copper had bounced down and Poodie and Blue took them at speed. Nearing the village shops they called into Sins and Poodie bought a couple of cakes, sausage rolls, fresh bread and 2 pizza slices.

'What are you having, hon?'

Bee looked dolefully at the luscious goods on display, 'nothing. It's my slimming class tonight, weigh day but I'll pop in tomorrow and treat myself.'

Gemma looked horrified. 'I didn't know the slimming club had started up again, we'll be inundated Saturday morning. I must double up on everything.'

Bee snickered.

'I'm not joking. It used to go mad after slimming club, I'll ring Jack …oh hi, Clova, everything all right? Please don't say you want tomorrow off.'

'No, I was passing and just popped in to say hello and to buy some lunch.'

Clova tried to edge past the dogs, but Blue was ecstatic and shoved his nose between her legs, sniffing with delight. Forcing Clova to take two steps back and steady herself against the door.

'My, he really likes you. He doesn't show that much interest in us.'

'I'm flattered,' Clova said in a distinctly insincere voice, as she unsuccessfully tried to push Blues' nose away from her crotch. Glancing up, she said, with surprise, 'Uncle Poodie, I haven't seen you in ages, since before you got Copper and now look at you, casually dressed, much less formal than your previous style, you look a lot more relaxed. Mum said you'd been working on the Isles of Scilly. We knew you were back, mum said you'd called in to see her a few weeks ago. I didn't realize you and Bee were an item.'

Poodie, who had been engrossed in looking at the goods under the counter, and hadn't noticed his niece, seemed genuinely pleased to see her, introduced Bee properly, chatted about the family and college before saying goodbye.

Walking back to his van Poodie explained that his dad had a daughter from a past relationship, his half-sister Mary, Clova's mum. They didn't see much of each other as she was quite a bit older than him, but he was fond of them, especially his niece.

'Now that I know she works in Sins, I'll pop in more often.'

'I wonder if that explains Blue s fascination with her,' Bee pondered, 'perhaps he can scent the family D.N.A.'

Poodie snorted, 'He's not even that fascinated with me, who knows what's going on in his head. He certainly has a marked preference for certain people.'

Bee moved to Blue's side, keeping herself between them as Carl was walking up the road. Blue knew who he didn't like, and she didn't want to risk an incident with the dog lunging and possibly nipping his ankle. True to character, Carl muttered under his breath and glared at the dogs, as if they shouldn't be allowed to walk on the same bit of pavement as himself.

Bee gave a slight shake of her head but declined to comment, reaching the van she put the dogs in the back and got in the passenger side with a sigh, Mac's legs weren't the only ones who were tired.

'Do you think we walked far enough for me to have a pizza slice?'

'You always do that,' Poodie complained, 'I asked you if you wanted anything and you said no, now you want to eat all my lunch.'

'Don't exaggerate and don't be a pig. You bought more than enough. You can stick your pizza slice, wouldn't have it now if you offered it to me served up on your naked body.'

'Really?' Poodie laughed, his eyes twinkling, 'I've just thought of a way you can work off some calories. I'll even sacrifice one of my pizza slices.'

Clova hooked the door of the bakery open and watched Poodie and Bee walk off towards Poodie's van before going back to order her lunch.

'Huh, fancy them two being an item, I couldn't have pictured it but now I see them together they seem really well suited. Uncle Poodie's got a dry sense of humour that matches Bee's. Mind you, I never took to his last girlfriend, none of the family liked her, although we tried. She used to give me fashion advice and was so critical. We thought Uncle Poodie changed when he was with Dawn and not for the better.' Clova flicked her blue tipped hair away from her face. She was wearing low slung cream culottes and a short candy-striped blouse which she had tied under her bust, leaving her pieced bellybutton on display. Gemma complimented her on her look but told her that her first thought was, it wasn't that warm.

'I'm turning into Bee,' she said, 'or I'm getting old. What age do people start obsessing about the weather?'

'Your age,' Clova laughed, 'although it's a British thing, innit? Talking about the weather, even I do it but not as much as you oldies.'

'Charming. It's nice to see Bee happy, they make each other laugh.'

'Uncle Poodie didn't laugh much when he was with Dawn. Just watching him with Bee walking up the road, you could tell he was comfortable with her and more content. He always seemed on edge if

I met him out with Dawn.

I should text him and meet up, we used to see each other quite a bit, go for coffee or lunch. Can't wait to tell mum I bumped into him, I don't think he told her he was seeing anyone, they spent most of his visit talking about his job. That's men for you, avoiding any chat about emotions.' The nineteen-year-old said, sounding jaded.

'See you tomorrow.' Clova paid for her lunch and left. The next day she and Betty turned up together just as Gemma was turning the Closed sign to Open. Betty hooked the door open and hurried out the back to get ready.

'We're going to be busy, better have a drink now,' Gemma called and heard Clova put the kettle on. The Golden Rule for most people who worked in retail was, make a drink at every opportunity. Tucking her hair more securely under her red and black poppy headscarf, she served two of her regular customers before the women returned from the kitchen carrying 3 mugs. Mark and Kay came in to say hello on their way back from a walk. Mark said instantly, '2 sugars in mine.' Clova turned to Betty, ignoring Mark and said loudly, 'My friend texted me this this morning, this is funny, to find your rockstar name you have to say the colour of your underwear and the last thing you ate. Mine is Black banana muesli.'

Betty frowned as her brain tried to process the conversation. Gemma said, 'Red Popcorn.'

'Who has popcorn for breakfast?'

'That's the last thing I ate, didn't have time for breakfast.'

Mark said, 'Kamikaze bacon sandwich.'

Kay rolled her eyes, 'he means 'commando', and honestly, Mark too much information.'

'Oh, I get it,' Betty said gleefully just as 2 women came in, 'Orange Polka dot Toast'.

Clova and Gemma looked at each other then turned back to the customers who were looking puzzled but more interested in picking out 6 cream cakes, paying and disappearing up the road at speed. Mark asked hopefully if they were still getting dirty phone calls as he wanted to stay to answer the phone. Gemma told him that they'd died down although she'd had one in the week, a man who'd wanted to scrub their floor with a toothbrush to atone for his sins.

'I'd take him up on that on that one, if he calls again give him my number.' Kay said, being very keen on cleaning of any kind. 'We can't stay today anyway, Mark, too much to do.' They said their goodbyes, moving out of the doorway to let in another regular, looking for his cupcakes.

As Gemma had predicted, they were very busy and the early morning drinks had been left to go cold. Gabriel and his girlfriend had called in with more tray bakes, both sweet and savoury. Clova had smiled and said that they would go down a treat, arranging them on trays under the counter and passing Gabe his tins back. His girlfriend seemed to sneer, pulling at Gabriel's' sleeve to hurry him out of the shop.

'She's a cold one,' Betty commented.

'It might be shyness,' Gemma said kindly, some people can't deal with small talk.'

'Humph,' Betty began but was distracted by another steady stream of customers. They carried on until closing when Gemma offered them any of the remaining baked goods to take home. Loading themselves up with treats, even Clova looked tired, and Betty declared she was going straight home to collapse in her armchair, make a big pot of tea, eat her cakes and watch rubbish T.V.

Gemma locked up, saying goodbye to her staff and watched Clova walk quickly up the road in pursuit of Matt who had exited the corner shop with bags of shopping that clinked. She heard Clova offer to share her cakes and scones with him, if he fancied sharing his beer, heard Matt reply that he was going to watch the match with mates, but Clova could join them if she wanted. Gemma was impressed at Clovas' confidence, and her willingness to grab an opportunity when it presented itself. Good luck to her she thought.

The next working day, Clova came into Sins mid-morning and offered to make Gemma a drink, she was bursting with excitement and Gemma correctly assumed that the previous evening had gone well. It was a slow day, so Gemma accepted the offer.

'Guess what?'

'England beat Germany.'

'Gem ma. Guess again.'

'Matt asked you out.'

Clova looked deflated, 'how could you guess that? Anyway, he sort of asked me out. He's doing a walk with some of his rambler friends on Sunday and asked if I wanted to come along as he knew I was into outdoor pursuits. Obviously, I said yes. I think we're going to Dartmoor, so he'll have to give me a lift. We'll be able to talk all the way in the car.'

'I don't mean to put a dampener on your joy, but he might be giving some of his friends a lift too. You might be sitting in the back squashed between a couple of his beefy mates.'

Clova screwed her mouth up, 'it's a start, I don't care. He might start to see me in a different light, rather than a kid. I was going to change my hair colour, but he called me Blueberry again so I might leave it as it is for now, See you Saturday, er, I don't suppose I could have an advance on my wages, the Vintage shop downtown has got a sale on.'

Gemma smiled saying 'who am I to stand in the way of romance, go on then.'

10

Poodie drove Bee and the dogs to the outskirts of Torquay where he thought he had discovered a new dog walk. It was near their favourite haunt, Cockington, so they parked in the village and started walking. It was a lovely sunny day with a slightly cool breeze. The dogs were excited. New territory, new smells, their tails were wagging. Copper and Mac pulled, trying to get ahead, Blue stayed next to his owners, remarkably well behaved for such a young dog, though his ears were twitching and the white tip on his tail trembled like an exotic insect caught in a trap, as he moved his tail back and forth.

'Even Blue Ice is excited.'

Poodie glanced at his girlfriend and gave a slight shake of his head, 'do you have to call him 2 names? Pick one already.'

Bee gave an exaggerated sigh, 'if you insist, *Rohan*. I'll stick with Blue.'

Poodie raised his eyebrows, 'I'm not biting and good, Blue it is.'

They walked for 20 minutes with the dogs on leads, along the narrow country lane before they came to a gate leading into a field, checking first that there were no farm animals in the near vicinity, they let all the dogs off their leads to start exploring. It was quiet, they could only hear birdsong and the distant sound of occasional cars, they could feel the tensions of the day slowly evaporating.

Both being nature lovers they enjoyed any new walk in the countryside with their animals. Bee and Poodie were wearing shorts and t shirts. Poodie had good trainers on, Bee had a well-known brand of plastic clogs on.

'They are no good for your feet, you know,' Poodie couldn't help commenting.

'why do half the nurses wear them in hospital then?' Bee countered.

'Let's go into town and I'll treat you to some decent trainers.' Bee wanted to say no, she loved her footwear, but Poodie s offer was too good to resist, so she mumbled an assent slightly ungraciously. She could wear the trainers when she was with him and her clogs the rest of the time, besides she'd been tempted into ordering some sports clogs online, which were the same as she had on, except they had a chunkier sole, they sounded perfect for muddier walks despite the fact that if it was muddy then it was probably wet and the sports clogs had the same trademark holes in the top. Bee decided she was only going to wear them when she was on her own or out with Sindy.

'Blue's pooing,' Bee pointed out, concluding that it was Poodie s job to pick it up.

'Find me a stick, we're in the countryside, no poo bins. The country rule is hit and flick, off the path into the hedgerow.'

'Hit and flick, as if,' Bee snorted but inwardly thought it was more environmentally friendly than gathering it up into a bag. They reached the end of the field, coming to a stile. Over the stile they could see a dusty dirt path with grass, bracken and bushes on either side, wending its way into another field, up a grassy hill and into woodland. It looked charming but first the obstacle had to be negotiated. It was high and awkward for Bee, and she struggled to see where she could put her foot to get her first step up. Without being asked, Poodie obligingly put his hand under her bum and heaved. Bee clung to the top of the stile and edged her way backwards to get down, finally landing on terra firma. Poodie, Blue and Copper jumped over with ease and Mac crawled underneath.

Poodie put his arm around his glaring girlfriend. 'It'll get easier each time we do this walk,' he assured her, 'It reminds me of our first date. That was a walk which started with a stile as well. I asked if you wanted a leg over.' He chuckled, 'you got very flustered, told me I meant leg up and went bright red.'

Bee got over her hump at being shoved arse first on to the stile, with the pleasure of remembering their first date.

'I remember exactly what you were wearing, that tight tee that shows off your muscles. Do you remember what I was wearing?' Poodie hadn't a clue so countered with, 'it was a beautiful day that ended with you falling in cow shit and you still insisted on going to the pub. I had to breathe through my mouth for the rest of the date and we had to sit outside as far away from the rest of the customers as we could. In retrospect, it was a clear indication of your ability to fall into things, over things, or spill stuff down you.' He chuckled to himself.

Bee narrowed her eyes at him. 'I was just going to say, I remember thinking how nice you smelt, a mix of masculine heat and the outdoors with a touch of that expensive aftershave, you only wear on special occasions, a bit like now except you're not wearing the special aftershave, familiarity breeds contempt, eh?'

'It was our first date. I wanted to make an impression, even on a dog walk. You should be honoured; it *is* very expensive. I dabbed a bit on last night and we weren't even going out.'

Bee snickered, 'I noticed, and I noticed where you dabbed it as well.'

Poodie laughed and bent down, kissing her thoroughly, putting his arm around her again and giving her a squeeze.

'I can't believe the main thing you remember about our first date is me falling into a cow pat. I remember everything about that day, I even remember the jokes and the puns in the pub,' Bee said darkly, let's hope this walk doesn't end in disaster too.'

Poodie gave her another kiss, told her he remembered every detail of their first date as well, crossing his fingers behind her back and hoping she wasn't going to quiz him.

They'd reached the small copse of trees and surprised a pheasant which flapped away in a panic, giving its trademark call.

'I keep hearing that sound, now I know what makes it. I think we'll call this The Pheasant Walk, to differentiate between all the other walks we do near here.' Bee said, looking pleased.

'Did you see how Blue reacted? He's got a wolfs instinct, we nearly had pheasant for dinner, then we would have had to name it the

'Death on the Mile' walk.' He paused, adding 'In honour of Agatha Christie who came from Devon.' In case his clever remark had gone over Bee's head.

'Yes, very funny and if Blue had caught it, I'd like to have seen you try to get it off him.' Bee scoffed. She bent down to pick some wild garlic to take home, although it was everywhere it was nearing the end of its flowering season and she enjoyed a bit of foraging. Poodie was very knowledgeable, and he knew so many of the wild plants and flowers they spotted on the walk. Bee was constantly asking him what this, that and the other were.

They'd walked past Dove's foot Crane's Bill, a small pink flower, the purple Bush Vetch and Common Vetch, Hogweed, which looked nicer than it sounded, Poodie said he thought it was poisonous to dogs, nettles with their companion dock leaves and lots of grasses that Mac especially, felt the need to eat. As long as he didn't eat the Hogweed, Bee let him alone. The dogs seemed to know when their diet needed supplementing with greens.

As she often did, Bee would impart an item of useless information she had heard or read, telling Poodie that rubbing Dock leaves on a nettle sting did not relieve the pain, contrary to popular belief.

'Fascinating.' Poodie said, meaning it.

A tiny blue butterfly flittered around the nettles. Bee identified it as the Devon Blue. Five minutes later they saw a very small yellow butterfly. Bee wondered what it was, having never seen one before.

The Devon Yellow?' Poodie suggested, quick as a flash.

'Nice try,' Bee said, making an eh eh sound which was supposed to sound like the wrong answer buzzer from a popular quiz show.

The sky which a few moments before had seemed to be devoid of clouds, got darker and darker.

'Look at that!' Bee said, in a disgusted tone, 'not a cloud in the sky when we set off now it looks like rain, we're going to get soaked. I asked Alexa if it was going to rain today, and she said no. She's such a liar, sometimes she says it's not going to rain when it's actually raining. I say something like 'but it's raining now' but she never replies.'

'She's a computer, she answers questions, she doesn't get into an argument about the weather. Let's turn round, we might make it back to the van if we're lucky.'

Poodie grabbed her hand and pulled her along, 2 minutes later the heavens opened. Bee s plastic clogs became very difficult to keep on and walk in and she made squeaking, squelching noises with each step she took, glancing at Poodie out of the corner of her eye to see if he would say 'I told you so.'

The dry, dusty, dirt track turned into a mud bath and with each step more of it covered Bee's clogs, which being plastic, with holes in the top, meant her feet as well as her clogs were turning dirty and red due to the colour of the Devon soil.

By the time they had got back to the van they were all soaked, Mac, who hated the rain, looked the most miserable, his long beautiful bushy tail drooping on the ground. Bee grabbed a towel out of the van and gave all the dogs a quick rub down. She eyed Poodie, observing the way his wet t shirt clung to his sculpted chest and noting that his wet shorts didn't leave much to the imagination.

Caught out ogling her boyfriend, Bee informed him primly, that his shorts were nearly indecent, and he ought to bear that in mind the next time he wore them.

He winked at her, not falling for her prissy tone, 'I can see you eyeing me up, Miss Wet T Shirt, you know what they say about rain being a gardener's friend, well I'm feeling very friendly just now,' he leered at her, making her laugh, then said,

'Hurry up, let's get back to mine and you can do something to warm me up.'

'Yeah, I'll stick the kettle on.'

'It wouldn't suit you.'

'You're not as funny as you think you are.'

'Am'

'Shut up and drive, clever clogs.'

'Oh yes, talking of clogs …'

11

'I think it's going to be foggy on the moors tomorrow,' Clova told Gemma, as she scuffed one foot backward and forward. Clova was wearing a short, pleated skirt, her favourite combat boots and an oversized purple jacket that clashed with the red and green tartan of her skirt but curiously looked fashionable rather than odd.

'Are you still going to go?'

'Of course. I'll just have to stick closer to Matt for safety. I'm pretty certain he's single, though have you noticed how his hair always looks tousled, like some woman has just been running her fingers through it.' she laughed, 'Oh hiya Betty, just in time for a cuppa, shall I make it?'

Betty, who was under the impression that nobody could make tea or coffee the way she did, declined and went into the kitchen to get ready and make the drinks, coming out she was just in time to relieve Gabriel of a large tin of Salted caramel frosted cakes, unpacking them and handing him the tin back. His girlfriend Toni stood in the doorway with a disapproving look on her face as she looked Clova up and down, turning to Betty, she said, 'nice black dress and white apron, very appropriate for a bakery.' Glancing at Clova out of the corner of her eye, to see if the dig had hit home.

Betty frowned, and said 'why do you need my address?'

Which cheered Clova up no end.

'Oh, never mind. Come on Gabriel, we've got things to do.' Toni flounced out of the shop, Gabriel raised his eyebrows and gave them a slightly apologetic look saying he thought Toni was a bit homesick for Wales.

'Maybe she should go back then,' Clova muttered under her breath, while Betty was still asking Gemma why they needed her address.

'She liked your dress,' Gemma said loudly. 'Look, here's that lady that wants to buy unusual cakes, wonder what she'll have today?' The lady in question approached the counter, 'have you got anything burnt?'

'No, Bee hasn't been in yet.'

'Clova! Why do you want something burnt'? Gemma managed to remonstrate her employee and speak to the customer at the same time.

'It's the latest trend. Cakes that taste of burnt caramel. I wanted to get some for my husband, so he'd moan and wonder why I'd paid good money for an over baked cake.'

Clova and Gemma between them had managed to explain to Betty about their unusual customer, and Betty had thought it very funny.

'What's your name, my lover?'

'Christine, you ought to write a book. 1000 things to do to wind up your partner, I bet it would be a best seller.'

Gemma now had her older employee to glare at and willed them both to go out back. Naturally neither of them moved, too interested to see what Christine was going to buy.

'I think the trend you're thinking of is salted caramel but if you want a burnt sugar taste, the Toffee Apple slices have that sort of effect,' Gemma suggested eventually, ' the sugar is burnt on the top like a Crème Brulé.'

'Lovely. I'll take two, thank you, on second thoughts make it 3, that'll make Geoff demand to know why I would buy an extra one when there's only the two of us.'

The morning passed with no dramas except for Carl walking past glaring and Betty getting the wrong end of the stick a couple of times.

Clova was upset that Matt had fixed the letterbox and installed a CCTV camera on a day she hadn't been working.

'I don't want him in on our busiest day unless it's an emergency. You'll see him tomorrow anyway,' the phone rang just as Mark and Kay walked in and Mark leapt to answer it before any of the staff could get there.'

'Do they what?' pause, as he listened.

'You want what?' Mark held the phone away and tried to speak quietly. 'He either wants you to give him a bath or he wants a bath filled with buns or he wants a Bath bun, is there such a thing?' Gemma snatched the phone off him and glowered, while she dealt with the enquiry.

Mark shrugged, 'I couldn't believe my luck, I thought it was a dirty phone call, what are the odds, just as I walk in the door?'

'Obviously not good,' Clova told him, 'as it wasn't.'

Kay gave a slight shake of her head as Gemma put the phone down.

'Are we meeting tonight? Mark wants to go to The Eight Bells, it's live music night but we could sit in the garden with the dogs and still hear it. Bee and Poodie are coming.'

'Do you mind if I come?' Clova asked, 'Poodie is my uncle and I'd like to see more of him and get to know Bee a bit better.'

'Of course we don't mind,' Kay said kindly, 'the more the merrier.'

They said goodbye with a cheery 'see you tonight then.'

Gemma was looking at Clova with one eyebrow raised.

'What?'

'You're not fooling me, lady. I know why you want to come.'

Clova shrugged and held her hands up. 'Guilty as charged but I really do want to see more of Uncle Poodie. Shall I wear this tonight or change?'

'I don't think Poodie will mind one way or the other.'

'Gemma.'

'Wear something warmer.'

'Forget it, I'll ring Tamsin, see what she thinks, maybe my white crop top and those hipster trousers, or just a white t shirt bra under this jacket, yeah that'll look good.'

'Clova, I think you're getting pretty hung up on Matt, but you don't know much about him, what if he's with someone in the pub tonight? I don't want you to get hurt.'

Clova scoffed, 'I'm not that into him. You worry too much. I just fancy him a bit that's all.' She turned to Betty to deflect the subject, saying, 'Betty, you're looking tired, why don't you sit down for a bit and drink your tea.'

Betty looked surprised and said to Gemma that for a young girl, Clova was very intuitive, she was feeling her age, but a few minutes sitting on the stool would remedy that.

Clova looked sheepish, she hadn't noticed anything, just wanted Gemma to change the subject. She obliged by telling them that Harley was in disgrace. Last night he'd eaten half of her dinner when she'd got up to get the vinegar. It was hake and it wasn't cheap either.'

'I bet he had an upset stomach after that,' Betty remarked.

Gemma frowned, 'actually, fish is good for dogs.'

'Fish! I thought you said cake.'

Gemma and Clova said 'Hake' loudly, trying not to chuckle.

Later that evening the friends had pushed together 2 long tables in the beer garden, Poodie and Mark came back from the bar with all the drinks and proceeded to produce bags of crisps which they had concealed in their clothes and up their sleeves, throwing them into the middle of the table.

Kay and Bee exchanged exasperated looks.

'He's just the same when we're shopping, anything to avoid buying a bag.' Bee said.

As Kay said, 'What are they like? I would have gone back for the crisps.'

Harley put his paws up on the table, not adverse to the odd crisp.

'Watch Harley,' Kay warned, knowing the cocker poo would snatch a whole bag if they weren't careful.

Clova stood up about to pronounce her opinion on the thief, and to say that he shouldn't be allowed to put his paws on the table when she gave a very unladylike shriek. Blue had shoved his nose into her crotch again. She backed away, trying to repel Blue to no avail. He was a very big dog.

'Hey, Blueberry, I see you've made a conquest, he's a handsome big boy, what's his name?' Matt appeared in the doorway with a pint in his hand, as Clova answered him.

'Blueberry and Blue, you two are made for each other. Be still my heart, a girl who loves animals, that says something about a person.' Clova gave a weak giggle and pretended she wasn't pushing Blue away, giving him a pat on the head, sitting down quicker than she had intended and crossing her legs.

'Good dog, go and lie down.' She hissed under her breath.

'He must really like you,' Poodie said, 'he can take or leave most people apart from me and Bee.'

'Who, Matt?'

'Blue of course,' Poodie replied, looking puzzled.

'He likes me,' Sindy insisted, taking a sip of her rum and coke. 'He wags his tail and gives me a kiss when I pick him up for a walk. Blue is coming out of his shell and starting to show affection.'

'We need 10 minutes at the start of every walk for all the meet n greet that the dogs do. They're very loving, they kiss each other, then us. Harley stuck his tongue down my throat last time. I had just opened my mouth to speak when he went in for a kiss.' Bee told them.

'Ugh. That's gross.' Clova said, glancing quickly around to see if Matt had heard her, but he had gone back inside to join his mate at the pool table.

'I can play pool,' she announced to them all, 'I'm going to go in and watch, maybe play the winner.'

'I don't think you should be bending over a pool table in that outfit,' Poodie said, the comment falling on deaf ears.

'Um … I thought you wanted to spend some quality time with your Uncle?' Gemma called at her rapidly fleeing form.

'Ah, did she say that? That was nice.' Poodie said.

'I expect she meant it, in theory until something better came up.' Bee said.

'Something or someone.' Gemma pointed out.

'The joy of teenage hormones,' Bee laughed, picking up a packet of crisps and trying to open them by pushing the air inside the bag to one end, squeezing hard and popping them, which had the unwanted result of most of the crisps landing on the ground and being snaffled up by Chilli and Harley – the other dogs not being too bothered about crisps.

'Bee.' Sindy snapped, 'Harley better not get the squits now.'

'Sorry, he'll be fine, I hardly lost any crisps.' She lied, hurriedly emptying the remains of the packet into her mouth, in the hope that Sindy couldn't see how many had fallen on the floor, losing a few into her cleavage as she did so.'

'I'll save those for supper,' Poodie quipped.

Bee rolled her eyes.

'You won't starve while you're dating Bee, have another packet, you can be the entertainment before the band starts. What flavour do you like mate?' Mark, high fiving Poodie as Poodie replied 'salt and vinegar.'

Mark picked up a packet and threw it at Bee, who impressed them by catching it one handed.

'Very funny, not,' she said, putting the packet back on the table.

'You're brave, wearing a white top,' Sindy said to her friend, 'bet you a fiver you get something down it before we go home. Mark added that he would have a fiver bet too.

'I don't always spill stuff down me,' Bee said indignantly, 'I'll take those bets.'

'Good job it's only a fiver,' Poodie said to Mark sotto voice, who laughed.

Rosa appeared puffing and panting, blaming her mother for the fact that she was late, even though time keeping wasn't her forte, she sat down, putting her hands under the table to stroke all the dogs.

'What have I missed?'

'Paying for your round. I'm sure you do it on purpose.' Sindy said.

'I'll get the next one.' Rosa said, not rising to the bait and helping herself to a glass of Kays wine, which was on the table in an ice bucket with several spare glasses next to it.

'I thought you were on soft drinks?' Sindy said

'I am. I'll stick to Ginger Beer after this. Oh great, I love this song,' Rosa started singing along, she had a good voice, and her friends were always telling her she should join a choir or a band, but she wasn't interested.

They had a good evening. The music was great, the conversation flowed along with the wine, the dogs were reasonably well behaved apart from barking at any non-pack member that dared to enter their territory. Clova came out at closing time to say goodbye, tripped over Blue, who'd got up to greet her, and spilt her drink down Bee s crisp, white top. She was mortified and apologised profusely. Mark was thrilled, 'That's a fiver you owe me.' he said at the same time as Sindy said, 'I'll let you off.'

'No way. You can't count that. I didn't spill anything down myself.' Bee spluttered, glaring at Mark.

'That's not how the bet was worded, if you recall. Hand it over.'

'I don't recall. Rohan, give him the damn fiver.'

'Me? Why have I got to pay?'

'I'll pay you back,' Bee said, glowering and with no intention of paying him back. She'd noted the high five and it was, so to speak, payback time.

Clova was asking Gemma why Bee was calling her Uncle, Rohan, as Sindy and Rosa said 'Poodie' in unison.

'The more you tell her to stop, the more she'll do it,' Poodie reasoned, 'and I don't mind really. It *is* my middle name.'

'I'm right here you know,' Bee said, still frowning.

Poodie laughed, putting his arm around her and nuzzling her hair.

'Did you just sniff my hair?'

'I love the smell of that shampoo, told you before.'

'and I told you, you've got a fetish.'

'Could be worse,' Kay piped up, 'remember the ...'

'Come on,' Bee interrupted, flustered, 'let's get these dogs home and give them their last walk, I've got to be up early.'

12

A few days later, Clova went into work. Gemma had asked her to do a few extra hours and she was glad to oblige. Gem was becoming more of a friend and a confidante than her employer. The young woman was wearing smart black trousers, a blue blouse and a loose dark blue jacket, which she took off to take out the back.

'I'm early,' she announced, unnecessarily, 'I'll make a drink. There's a commotion going on up the road, Carl is shouting at an elderly driver who is trying to park, and Carl's delivery lorry is due, I understand but his language is atrocious, no need.'

Gemma popped her head out of the door but went back in when Carl glared at her, she decided she had enough to put up with, without getting involved, provided no-one was getting hurt. From her brief glimpse, the elderly gentleman was giving as good as he was getting. Clova came back and placed their mugs on the back shelf.

'We're low on milk, I'll get some later,' she told Gemma. Wanting to avoid Tollys until the drama had died down.

'How was your walk?'

'Awful. It was Matt and 6 of his buddies, all male and super fit. A couple of women had been going to come along but they pulled out, I was the only girl. It was thick mist and drizzly, and they all walked faster than me, I had to keep asking them to slow down. I'm fit and I can easily do a 6-mile hike, but their one stride was like 3 of mine, I felt like I was almost running to keep up, plus my sense of direction isn't that good on the moors and I didn't want to get separated from the group, I was worried that I might have got lost.'

'How did they know where they were going? I've only got to set foot on Dartmoor and within minutes I don't know where I am. It all looks the same, gorse and heather and rocky tors. I'm exaggerating, I know it's beautiful, but I could easily get lost.'

'One of the guys with us, Lem, knows Dartmoor like the back of his hand, even in bad weather, he was in front.
Matt barely spoke to me. I was slowing them up but that wasn't my fault, I was doing my best, the miserable pig.' Clova gave a half laugh, drawing her finger in a spiral on the glass counter where some icing sugar had been spilled.

'Saturday night in the pub he was calling me Blueberry and flirting, Sunday it was as if he had had a personality transplant. I felt like he thought of me as an annoying kid. Don't get me wrong, he kept looking back to make sure I was bringing up the rear,' She paused, thinking about it, then said,

'I suppose he is quite caring, he looked out for the slowest of the guys as well, but I didn't feel welcome. Why suggest that I come in the first place, it's not as if I asked him if I could tag along.'
They stopped talking when a customer came in. Gemma served the man, and waited for him to leave before she went on,

' As you said, I expect he thought some more women would be

going, I'm not sticking up for him, he sounds like he was being a bit rude but perhaps you were oversensitive, if he was checking you were still with them; he wouldn't have let you get lost. You read more into his offer than was there, whereas he probably thought it was going to be a pleasant hike with his friends.'

Clova sighed, 'well I didn't enjoy it at all. It wasn't pleasant, you could barely see any scenery, and I felt uncomfortable and a bit embarrassed that I couldn't keep up.'

She became aware of what she was doing with the sugar and picked up a cloth to wipe the counter.

'He wouldn't have expected you to keep up, he probably thought it was going to be a mixed group of people who enjoyed rambling. I think, in your head, you were thinking of it as a date, but it wasn't. Cheer up, forget about it and try to ignore him, that might work. You've made it very clear that you have a bit of a crush on him so play it cool for a bit, some men like a challenge.'

Clova took a sip of her tea and sighed, 'you might be right. I expect he realises I fancy him, and he probably thinks I'm easy. Which I'm not,' she added with a flash of her eyes, 'I don't know what's wrong with letting a person know when you like them. Some of my friends play games and pretend they're not interested when they've got the hots for someone and of course, they follow them on social media. I've looked up Matt but he's not really into anything. He's got a profile on one of the usual sites but has barely posted anything in months.

The trouble is, he sees me as Ant s kid sister rather than a grown woman. I didn't want to act like the rest of my mates but maybe I should.' Clova made a face, You're right, I'll pull back and try to ignore him and be cool when he's around.' She took a deep breath and changed the subject.

'How did you and Sindy meet?'

'In a nightclub. She fell up a step and nearly knocked me over. She bought me a drink to make up for it and that was that.'

'Ah, swept you off your feet, that's nice.' Clova said, only half listening.

She pointed under the counter and asked, 'What are those things that look like pies?'

Gemma resisted a sarcastic reply such as, if it looks like a pie, it probably is one, merely saying, 'I'm doing a few more savouries this week. I asked Jack to make some individual Homity pies. I'm expecting them to do well. We've got another tray in the freezer. Sindy and I visited the farm shop on Sunday and so many people were buying them, I texted Jack on the spot.

Just as a heads up, Sindy and Bee are walking the dogs this morning and may call in on their way back, so try to resist your usual sarky comments about the dogs, it winds Sindy up.'

'Deep joy.' Clova said, mournfully. 'Sorry. They are just full on, and I was bitten by a dog when I was young, it's not that I don't like them but I'm a bit wary of them.'

'and that's just Bee and Sindy,' Gemma joked, then seeing Clova s face, quickly added, 'the dogs are a bit boisterous, but they would never bite you. Lick you to death, more like. Here comes 'Not Three Bad, your challenge today is to get him to say it and to persuade him to try a Homity pie.'

The regular came in and told them about the commotion outside Tollys, rolling his eyes at the state of the world especially his little part of it, said he was 'not three bad', picked up his cupcakes and declined the Homity pie.

'Oh well,' Clova said, 'I tried'

The next people in were Betty and Iris. Betty's friend was short, plump, usually smiling, with the same short, white permed hair as Betty, she reminded Gemma of one of the artist Beryl Cooks' fat ladies that featured in all of her paintings.

Iris beamed at Clova, telling her that Betty was always talking about her. Complemented her on her hair, saying she wished she could be more adventurous with her own. Iris was very chatty and didn't seem phased when Betty didn't hear her but carried on regardless.

 Betty spotted the new addition under the counter immediately, pointing them out to her friend, talking quickly before Iris told Clova her life story.

'Oh, Homity pie, Iris, we haven't had that since we went to Totnes, let's get a couple for lunch. We'll pop into Tollys and get some salad to go with them.'

'Sold. To the lady with the lovely permed hair,' Clova teased.

'Pam Ayres? She does those funny poems. Is she on at the Little Theatre?' Betty carried on, without waiting for an answer, 'There's quite a to-do, up the road, some old bloke reversed his car into the back of a van coming in, they're all shaking their fists and swearing and of course, that Carl is sticking his nose in, so give us the pies quickly, my lover, we need to get back up there.'

Clova served Betty, giving Gemma a twinkling sidelong glance as they watched the ladies leave the shop in haste. They had a small queue forming which they dealt with quickly and efficiently, one in every 2 people telling them about the incident up the road.

'Oh well, it makes a change from customers saying the same thing about the temperature 50 times in a morning, 'isn't it cold? We need some sun etc. etc.' Gemma commented as Bee, Sindy and 4 dogs entered the shop, three of the dogs desperate to greet Gem and Blue making a bee line for Clova, who groaned and tried to push him away from behind the counter.

'Just let him say hello,' Bee advised, 'then he'll settle. You should be flattered. Hiya Gem, bit cold for the time of year, isn't it?'

Gemma gave a put-upon sigh, gave Sindy a shopping list and fussed the dogs, keeping them well away from the food.

'Ooh, Homity pie, very traditionally Devonian. Rosa is always on about it; I keep meaning to try it.'

'No time like the present,' Clova suggested.

'Actually, your Uncle asked me to ask you if you wanted to come for tea tonight, he can pick you up at half 5, we could have those Homity pies with new potatoes and a salad.'

Clova looked pleased and nodded.

'Okay I'll take 3, can you bring them Clova? Poodie will collect you straight from work and I'll text Rosa, I'm sure she'll be interested to know Sins are doing them.' Bee said, handing over the right money. Gemma nodded and made a note on her list to remind Clova to take them when they closed.

Sindy and Bee left in a big huddle with the dogs pulling anxiously, eager to continue their walk, just as a delivery man squeezed past carrying a very large box.

'Probably contains a very small saucepan,' Clova said cynically, as she signed for it. Gemma was rubbing her hands with glee, 'It's the Tea Urn I ordered.' She ripped the cardboard off and lifted it into the space she had designated for it.

'We'll be offering hot drinks as soon as I've been to Cash and Carry to get everything else and I've applied to the council to have one small table and two chairs to put outside. Well done, this was your idea.' Clova beamed. 'Why don't you go now? I can hold the fort.'

Gemma didn't need to be asked twice, she grabbed her bags and her keys and dashed out of the door.

Clova picked up the leaflet that came with the urn to read in-between customers, then served the next few people who came in, telling each one that Sins would soon be selling hot drinks.

A very smart couple came in and looked at the cakes. The man was wearing designer sunglasses that he didn't feel the need to remove even though he was out of the sun.

'Clova, fancy seeing you here, surely this is not your career path?' Clova glanced at the pair and inwardly grimaced, 'Hello Dawn, how are you?'

'We're entertaining clients later so if you would put a selection of your best cakes into a box for me. This is my partner Philippe,' she said, introducing the man, saying his name the French way 'Philippay'.

'How is your uncle Paudric?'

'He's fine thank you.'

'We see them around, don't we Philippe? They're more into the, How shall we say, comfortable look now, they don't frequent the same places as we do so we don't bump into them as much, but you're looking very smart, my dear.'

Thank you for being so patronising, Clova wanted to say, wishing she'd worn her tartan ensemble and her combat boots. She dealt with them quickly and went to serve the next people coming in, who turned out to be Gabriel and Toni. They had brought in some Banoffee slices, handing the tin to Clova.

'You'll have to see Gemma about payment,' she told Gabriel, 'I'm not in every day so I don't know what has sold. She'll be back in an hour or so.'

'I'm not coming back again today,' Toni said, 'we're supposed to be looking for a better house.'

'I thought you hadn't been in that house long?' Clova directed her question to Gabriel.

'Toni doesn't like the area, so I said I'd see what was around but it's such an expense, moving, probably costs about three grand, which we can't afford.'

'Oh, here we go,' Toni said, pulling a face, she grabbed his arm and pulled him out of the shop leaving Clova staring after them with her eyebrows raised and the tin she had just emptied half held out to return to him. Clova gave a slight shake of her head and put the Banoffee slices on to the display counter and the tin on the back shelf, then was too busy to think more about it. Before she knew it, Gemma was back, they unloaded the shopping and played around with the urn until it was time to close.

Poodie was waiting outside and drove Clova to his cottage telling her that he had been doing it up for the last 2 years.

'I hardly remember it at all, I might have visited once when you first moved in, I think I remember the view, it was stunning, countryside and sea. You bought it at just at the right time, I don't expect I'll get on the property ladder any time soon.' Clova told him about Gabriel and Toni.

'I'm surprised at Gabriel; he was always a hard worker, laid back and always smiling. Now he just seems tired and miserable. I don't think they are suited at all but when you're the one in the relationship you can't always see what everyone else can see.'

'Relationships, huh, too much hard work. I can't be bothered with dating just now.'

Poodie laughed, 'You're too young to sound so world weary. What happened to that bloke you liked?'

Clova shrugged, commented that he seemed to blow hot and cold, putting an end to the subject by looking out of the window at the fields full of bright yellow rapeseed, next to green fields filled with cows and sheep. Poodie drove down a narrow country lane and pulled up outside his cottage.

'It's a nice evening, I thought we could eat in the garden,' Poodie said as he ushered her in through the side gate. Three dogs came bounding over to greet them, Mac barking, Copper squeaking and Blue dividing his attention between Poodie and Clova. Once the dogs had been calmed down, Clova did a slow full turn to take in the view. It was a big garden with a patio outside the back door, large shrubs and containers surrounded the brown and cream rattan furniture, a swing chair with comfortable cushions faced the sea and the table and chairs faced into the garden which had a small copse bordering it. Bird feeders hung from the trees and solar lights decorated the borders. There was a large hole near the vegetable patch which Poodie blamed on Mac and Bee joked that Mac liked to help with the garden and now it was all ready to plant a new shrub or tree. Bee took the Homity pies to heat up in the oven and brought out drinks, telling Clova she had seen cans of Blood Orange cider and had bought them to try.

'Must be healthy,' she laughed, 'orange and apple, two of our five a day.'

'On a chat show that TV chef said we should be having 12 a day at least but he'd said five because not many people would eat 12. An older actress who was on the show with him said she didn't even eat 2, he looked disgusted.' Clova told her, settling herself on a chair, tucking one leg under herself and sighing with delight, not even fazed by Blues' unwavering attention.

'You look more content and happier these days.' She told her uncle, when Bee had gone back into the cottage.

'Dawn and her boyfriend came in the shop this afternoon, she asked after you; said she'd seen you and Bee around and you looked ... comfortable. I think that word was number ten on her 'insult to fashion' chart.' Clova told her uncle, who laughed, as Bee bustled in and out, bringing plates, salads, condiments, dips, individual golden pats of butter to go on the warm rolls which she urged them to eat first and telling them dinner wouldn't be far behind.

Poodie nodded, 'There's nothing wrong with wanting to look good, but trying to change another person to suit how you think they should act, and dress is not on. I went along with it to placate Dawn which didn't work anyway as she was a very difficult woman to please.'
He gestured to himself in his worn jeans and faded top and said, 'this

is me, comfortable is a good word, it's how I feel around Bee, we hardly ever fall out, share a lot of interests, and have the same sense of humour.'

'I like her, and you act like an old married couple.' Clova announced, tactfully not saying how much she hadn't liked his previous girlfriend, Double D, as she used to think of her, Designer Dawn.

Poodie nodded, saying it had taken him a while to find the right person and suggested that Clova should enjoy being young and not settle for serious dating just yet.

'Perhaps you'll visit more now we're back in touch.'
Clova nodded enthusiastically, she'd always got on with her uncle and felt she could confide in him if she needed to. She'd talked to him when she was in her mid-teens and clashing with her parents, feeling that they let her brother do whatever he wanted but were much stricter with her. The usual teenage stuff. Poodie had acted as a go-between once or twice. Clova was fairly level-headed though and her rebellious phase hadn't lasted. She was very good at seeing both sides of an argument and was lucky to have a good relationship with her parents and brother.

 Bee brought out the homity pies and they settled down to enjoy their al fresco meal, chatting and watching the birds on the feeders, the bees buzzing around the lavender and Mac trying to eat the bees.

'He's a stray from Romania,' Bee informed her, 'he probably ate bees over there, but it gives me bad nerves, he could get stung in his mouth, it's dangerous but we can't stop him, the little shit.'

They chatted until it got dark, Poodie said he would take Clova home, stirring herself reluctantly she began to help Bee clear the table which resulted in the remains of the salsa dip being spilt over Bee's skirt.

'Par for the course,' Poodie said, calmly as Clova flapped her hands, trying to mop up the dip which made it worse, and apologising.

'I think I'm a jinx, accidents always happen around me,'

'It was a joint disaster, we just clashed, and I don't always spill stuff over me,' Bee protested, answering Poodie.

'Yes, you do.

Forget it, Coop, ' Poodie said, reverting to the old family nickname he used to call her, 'you're not a jinx and it's only a bit of salsa, come on, let's get you home.

See you soon, love, don't do it all, I'll help when I get back.' He meant his offer, but he knew it would be done before he returned, Bee could be a whirlwind of activity when she wanted to.

As an afterthought, Poodie called out, 'and stick your skirt in the washing machine, so it doesn't stain.' He realised she didn't have a change of clothes at the cottage and gave a slight chuckle under his breath, knowing she would have forgotten that fact.

Bee waved them off cheerfully and swept off into the kitchen to start the washing up, rather quaintly, neither she nor Poodie had ever wanted a dishwasher. Poodie's kitchen was too small for one and Bee thought they seemed more trouble than they were worth, not that she'd ever had one. She threw her skirt into the washing machine and as it had other clothes in, started the wash; went to look in Poodie's wardrobe where she sometimes left some clothes, before calling him names under her breath. He must have known, and she should have guessed when he started giving her laundry advice.

Bee tapped her foot, muttered one last 'Ro, you perv.' To herself, then picked out one of his shirts to wear, it was loose and covered the essentials, she went to return to the kitchen and the washing up then on the spur of the moment, a secret smile on her face, removed her underwear and shoved them into her handbag, her smile becoming wider as she imagined the look on Poodie's face when he came home. Humming cheerfully, she went back into the kitchen to finish the dishes.

13

The Saturday staff were in and raring to go. Betty had made a drink and oo'd and ah'd over the tea urn, although she did comment that it was nothing more than a giant kettle and hoped Gemma hadn't spent too much money on it. It was easy to use, and Betty couldn't wait to start selling hot drinks.

Sindy came in, followed by Bee carrying a tray. Bee had made Lemon and Poppyseed cupcakes, Gemma was genuinely delighted, they looked very professional, and she told Bee so.

Bee smiled, 'practise makes perfect,' she looked at Sindy and did a double take, 'Sparkle! You're back. You've got that stuff in your hair again.'

Sindy glared at Gemma and Bee, obviously it had been Gemma's fault she had edible glitter in her hair, and she'd just done a dog walk with Bee.

'Honestly, you are so unobservant,' she told her friend, 'we've been out for the last hour, and you've only just noticed.'

Betty turned around 'Oh hello Sindy, did you know you've got some glitter on your head?'

Sindy glowered, 'yes, the seagulls have been having a party.'

'Did you say you're having a party? What's the occasion?'

'She's changing her name to Sparkle.'

'Really?'

'I know,' Bee kept a straight face, 'Grumpy would be more appropriate.'

'I am so going to get you back,' Sindy hissed under her breath, 'now Betty will call me Sparkle till the end of my days.'

'The name of the shop won't make sense if you do that,' Betty said, giving it some serious thought.

Clova had been laughing silently and now tears were rolling down her cheeks, she edged past Betty in a shuffle that suggested she needed the little girls room pretty urgently. Betty looked over her shoulder at Clova, wondering what the rush was, then back at Sindy contemplating her new look with a frown on her face.

'Do come back soon,' Gemma said insincerely, pushing Bee and her partner out of the door, 'you're good for staff morale. At last Clova has a smile on her face, after looking like a wet weekend since last week.'

'What happened last week?'

'Sind, do you ever listen when I tell you stuff?' Gemma sounded exasperated.

'Of course, luv but you'd been waffling on for hours and I was trying to watch that film.'

'Bye.' Gem said, with a final shove, almost dusting her hands off, then stepped aside to let a customer in.

'Hello Christine, did your husband like the burnt cakes?'

'They had the desired effect and comments, thanks but he still ate the third one. Those look nice,' she said, pointing at the cupcakes Bee had brought in.

Gemma told her the flavour.

'Excellent. Geoff will think I'm trying to get him high, he's certain anything with poppy seeds in must be heavy with opium and the first step on a downward path.'

She deepened her voice 'Christine, how can these be legal? You'll turn me into a drug addict. Is that what you want?

It's ironic really, he's on about 6 prescribed tablets that he takes every day for his knees and his back and has done for the last couple of years but never questions whether he should start being weaned off them. Let's have four of those cakes this time.'

Gemma laughed and put them in a box for her. Sindy popped her head back in, 'did you know the jeep has a scratch along the side? It looks like someone has tried to key it.'

Gemma hurried out to have a look, she had washed the car two days before and it had been fine, telling Sindy she thought it must have happened outside the shop probably Friday and she would check the CCTV. Luckily, she had insurance that covered repairs to the bodywork but that wasn't the point, it wasn't nice to think that someone had done it deliberately. She left Clova and Betty to mind the shop and went into the back to check the recorded footage.

An hour later she had eye strain and a tension headache starting and no solid proof .A lot of pedestrians had been up and down the street including the manager of Tollys, her Prime suspect. Carl had been up and down three or four times, brushing past the jeep, it looked as if he might have touched it but if he'd had anything in his hand to drag along the side of the vehicle the camera didn't pick it up. Gemma was sure it had been him though, she hadn't seen anyone who'd appeared to be close enough to her jeep to key it except Carl and it seemed like the sort of thing the nasty minded creep would do. She reported back to her staff shrugging her shoulders and saying they couldn't confront him without proof but at least if anything else happened the camera gave them a chance to obtain evidence. Gemma said she would email the owners of the corner shop to inform them that she felt their manager held a grudge against herself and her business, making for an unpleasant atmosphere in the street, whereas the other traders supported and helped each other. She didn't mention specific incidences but hoped that they would have a word with him, then perhaps he would get on with his life and leave her alone.

'We'll try and be more aware, won't we Betty?'
Betty nodded enthusiastically, 'horrible man,' she pronounced, 'now let's forget about him. I've sold loads of drinks.'
Gemma brightened, 'loads?'
'Five. That's a good start and most of them bought something to eat as well.'
Mark and Kay came in with a big bunch of Sweet Peas that an allotment owner they knew had given them; he'd said his wife didn't like the smell and it was the third bunch he had given them, Kay still

had some in their house, so she wanted to pass these on. Gemma took them into the back to take home later, they were one of her favourite flowers and smelled divine.

'Just checking what time you're dropping the dogs off tomorrow.' Kay and Mark were having Harley and Chilli for a few hours as Sindy and Gem wanted to go to Exeter and would be away most of the day.

'You're brave,' Clova commented, 'lock up your food.'

'They'll be fine,' Mark said, with a glint in his eye, 'you can come and help with the dog walk if you like.'

'I'm going kayaking.'

'Oh well, another time. Let's buy some cakes.'
Kay frowned and patted his stomach, 'you said you wanted to get fit and eat healthily'.

'That was yesterday. We went for a walk, and we had a salad. We're walking to the pub tonight, I need some carbs to sustain me,' he wheedled, giving Kay his puppy dog eyes look.

'That look worked once about 5 years ago. Let's get two of the vegan vegetable slices and a couple of the coconut raspberry twists.' Mark said, in an aside to Gemma, 'worked once, did it? Righto.'
Clova served them then took the mugs out to wash them up.

'Don't do the drinks, leave them for me,' Betty called after her as more of their regular customers started coming in.

'Hello, my lover, what would you like?'

Do you have anything with figs in? Perhaps fig rolls?' The man asked.

'Eh? Figaro? That was an opera, wasn't it? Putin?'

The man gave his partner a quizzical look. 'I told you this was a surreal place,' then to Betty,' I think you might mean Puccini.'

His partner said 'Mozart, John, you should know that. The Marriage of Figaro, Mozart and then there was the Barber of Seville written later by Rossini.'

John rolled his eyes, 'David, really. Of course I know. I was suggesting to Betty that she might be thinking of Puccini, not an insane dictator, who as far as I recall, never wrote an opera.'

'Is it on at the theatre today? I expect you want something to eat before you go,' Betty said, glancing under the display glass ready to recommend.

Gemma said, 'we have a nice Fig and Almond loaf, how about that?'

The men looked disappointed that Gemma had taken over, Betty was the highlight of their week, and they liked to recount her conversation to their friends over dinner. They accepted the suggestion with quite good grace, told Gemma the hot drinks idea would be welcome in the winter and left with a special goodbye and see you next week, to Betty.

'You're their favourite,' Clova said, returning from washing the mugs.

Betty beamed and went off to make the drinks.

Clova smiled after her. 'I wonder if I'm anybody's favourite?'

'Every red-blooded male I would think,' Gemma said.

'Hardly and certainly not with one in particular, naming no names. Matt.'

'Naming no names means just that,' Gemma teased her attractive assistant, 'give it time, you never know what the future holds.'

'no cliches on a Saturday please. I just know your next words were going to be 'there's plenty more fish in the sea.'

Betty came out with two of the mugs, 'what's that about fish? I left your coffee on the side my lover, couldn't carry three. What this street needs is a Fish and Chip shop; I've always said it.

 Gemma, I've put those flowers in an empty milk bottle, sweet peas don't last very long.'

Gemma smiled a thank you then impulsively told Clova to take them home at the end of the shift to cheer herself up, adding, 'maybe Matt will see you and wonder who has given you flowers, get jealous and ask you out on a proper date.'

Clova pretended to duck as she went to collect her drink, 'and mind you're not hit by that flying pig, Gem.'

14

Bee dashed into Sins as soon as they opened, holding another big bunch of sweet peas.

'Hiya Gem, Kay asked me to give you these, shall I put them out the back for you?'

Gemma nodded her thanks and Bee said goodbye as Clova walked in.

'How was the kayaking?' Gemma asked her assistant. It was the following week and Clova was doing a couple more days in the shop.

'It was great, we went down to the cove, had an hour on the water and saw some seals, then we came back to the beach café and had breakfast. How was Exeter?'

'Good. I love the shops, we split up and did our own thing for a couple of hours and then met up at that riverside pub. It was very relaxing, and the food was great.'

'More to the point, how were the dogs?'

'Not too bad I think, apart from when Mark and Kay took them for a walk, let them off the lead and couldn't get them back, they rang Bee, she drove to meet them then managed to bribe the dogs back with biscuits. Chilli had chased a jogger and Harley had eaten something he shouldn't. They took them back to their place, Chilli went to sleep, and Harley sat by the front door looking miserable, until we came to pick them up. He's a softie really. Mark said they were no trouble and loved having them though.'

Clova made a face, 'Mark's a good liar.'

Gemma shook her head, 'they genuinely love them, they wouldn't offer to have them if they didn't. They just worry when they think Harley is pining for us.'

'Probably in a food coma, trying to sleep off whatever he'd pilfered.'

Gemma was saved from replying by a steady stream of customers. One of the shops nearby was having a refit and the workmen piled in every lunchtime, Clova was kept busy making up fresh baps, baguettes, heating sausage rolls and doing drinks. She looked up ready to serve the next customer and saw it was Matt.

'Blueberry, what have you done?' Matt asked her, pretending to look horrified.

'What does it look like I've done? What can I get you?'

Matt placed his order almost absentmindedly, 'you've ruined your nickname. I'll have to call you Blackberry.'

Clova had coloured her hair jet black and was wearing dark jeans and a bright red power shirt.

She served Matt with barely a word and took herself off to the kitchen.

'What's up with her?' Matt asked Gemma, 'she was very off with me.'

'She probably thought you were dissing her hair, never comment on a woman's appearance, it will only end badly.'

'I was just teasing, she knows that.'

Gemma raised her eyebrows in a way that suggested 'really?

'Tell her I thought it looked nice, but I miss my Blueberry'. Matt smiled and left.

Clova came out with their drinks, having heard every word.

'My Blueberry. As if. Now he's going to call me Blackberry. If I dye my hair red again, he'll call me Strawberry and that just sounds like one of those toy ponies with the colourful manes. Perhaps I'll go green, there aren't any green berries.'

Gemma muttered under her breath, 'gooseberry',

as Clova continued: 'I didn't know he was working up the road with the lads.'

'It might work in your favour, do him good to realise that most of the lads fancy you, they come in here rather than Tollys to see if you're working, I bet they sing your praises in front of him. He won't want any of that lot asking you out,' Gemma predicted.

'Sing my praises,' Clova scoffed, 'talk filth no doubt. Don't forget, I've got an older brother, I've been around him and his mates, I know what lads are like.' Clova shushed Gemma even though she had been the one talking, as Matt put his head back round the door,

'By the way, there's a new gym opened downtown, they've got a great bouldering room. Want to come with us and have a go? We're going tonight about half five.'

Clova looked a bit flustered but agreed and Matt left saying he'd pick her up.

Gemma raised her eyebrows, 'So much for him being standoffish on the ramble. He probably had a hangover that day, didn't expect him to ask you out that quickly.'

'It's obviously not a date,' Clova told her, 'and I fancied trying a new sport, can I have a bit longer at lunchtime to nip home and get my gym gear and climbing shoes?'

'Yes to the last question, If you say so, to the first comment, also take the flowers that are out the back in case Matt sees you; and finally, what on earth is bouldering?

Oh, Hello Betty, lovely day, what would you like?'

Betty was wearing leopard print leggings, green top and a brown gilet, most unlike her usual smart skirt and blouse look, she informed them that she'd been to a pensioner's exercise class in the church hall, but it was too easy for her. 'I'm fit for my age, especially since I started working in here, even my knees have improved, Iris wanted me to try it first, said she might join, it'll be just right for her, but I think I'll stick to my dance class, I can't keep up with the young ones but I'm not as bad as some', she informed them. 'You look nice, love, your hair is great, very dramatic.'

Clova thanked her, giving her the pastries she had asked for, after a nod from Gemma, on the house. Betty looked thrilled and said she was looking forward to Saturday. After she'd left Clova asked if she was still paying Betty in cakes.

'She won't take money, said she doesn't want to be an official employee, she really enjoys just being here, she said it beats volunteering anywhere else but I'm going to give her cash and/or a gift voucher on her birthday and Christmas, I feel quite bad not paying her. I'll keep working on it. However, I can now afford to take you on full time if you're interested, until you decide which career you want to pursue.'

'Really?' Clova threw her arms around Gemma and gave her a hug, 'that's brilliant. I love it here. Mum said wearing a red top would bring me luck.'

'It's a lucky colour in China, I believe, and I've heard it said that if you wear red underwear it boosts your energy and creativity.'

'Why underwear?'

Gemma scratched her head, 'dunno, perhaps it gives you a kick up the bum. Oh hello, Mr. Benson what can I do for you?'

Clova snickered at her boss getting caught sounding saucy, however the customer ignored or didn't hear her remark, being more interested in choosing his lunch.

Late morning Bee came in again to say they were meeting at a nearby beach Friday after work for a dog walk, followed by a swim then a visit to their local bistro on the seafront, only she and Gem wanted to swim so far, Rosa was thinking about it, the others said they would sit on the beach and look after the dogs and the bags. After complimenting Clova on her hair, Bee asked if she wanted to join them adding 'If you don't mind hanging out with us oldies, that is.' Clova nodded, waving aside Bee's comment. She was a sociable girl and always eager to do any outdoor activity.

'Thanks, and now I'm working here full time, I'll be able to afford to eat out with you too.'

Gemma paid Bee for her last lot of cakes, telling her they had sold out quickly, before saying goodbye. Bee left the shop nearly bumping into Carl, who sneered at them all and stared into the shop for a fraction too long.

'He's getting creepier by the day,' Clova said with a shudder.

'He is. I'm glad I had the camera installed now. Right, you nip off now and pick up your stuff, will you take the rubbish up to the bin on your way and I'll start on the afternoon orders.' Gemma said.

Clova hurried past the shop that was being re-fitted, just as Matt was coming out, brushing sawdust off his overalls.

'Nice flowers, is it your birthday?'

'Nope, secret admirer. Just taking them home on my lunch break and to pick up my gym stuff. See ya.'

Clova nearly ran up the road, snickering to herself, thinking she wouldn't tell Gem but obviously pigs did fly.

15

Poodie and Bee joined their friends on the beach after an extensive dog walk. Rosa had searched for the menu of the bistro and was sitting on a fold up chair she had brought, reading it out from her phone. She always read every word on a menu from Starters to Desserts, usually out loud, no matter who was interested or not.

'I don't know why you bother, you always have a burger,' Sindy told her.

'Well, I might not today, I'm still deciding,' Rosa huffed and carried on reading.

'I look at the Desserts first, but I don't allow myself to have one, except on special occasions,' Bee said ruefully.

'Me either,' Sindy mused 'but if I was going to indulge, I'd have treacle tart with that sticky sauce and cream instead of custard. What's your favourite pudding?'

'Anything that starts with a 'p' and ends in a 'g'.' Bee said, making them laugh.

Clova had already changed into her swimming costume and put on an orange swimming cap, she sat on the sand near Gemma and tried to push Blue away when he came to say hello. Blue had grown a bit more and started to fill out, he looked a very strong muscly dog and Clova couldn't budge him an inch. Mac began his task of frantically digging a hole right in front of them, covering them all in sand and making Clova squeal and jump up, nearly falling over Blue.

'Are you sure this is a dog friendly beach?' She asked, glaring at the dogs who were oblivious to any negative vibes being aimed their way. Harley and Copper were chasing seagulls on the shoreline and Chilli was growling at a jogger 100 yards away.

'Mac likes to dig,' Bee said un-necessarily,
 as Sindy said, 'no shit Sherlock.'
Gemma asked Clova how her date with Matt had gone.
Poodie's ears pricked up, 'date? You said you weren't interested in dating. You kept that quiet.'

'I told you Gem, it wasn't a date and he treated me exactly the same as his other mates. He was slightly more friendly but not in a flirty way, so I concentrated on what I was doing.'

'You never did tell me what bouldering is.'

'Sounds dangerous,' Bee said.

'Climbing without ropes or harnesses. Outdoors it involves actual boulders but in gyms you climb up a wall, with places to put your hands and feet. Easy, medium and hard routes to the top. As I said, no ropes or harnesses but there is a safety mat.'

'A safety Matt? You mean he stands at the bottom waiting to catch you if you fall? Very romantic.'

'It's a very good, total body workout,' Clova said, ignoring Mark, 'you can do competitive bouldering, where you race against another person, quickest up the wall wins but I didn't do that, as they were all taller than me, with longer legs. I was pretty good at it though, even if I do say so myself.'

'What did you do afterwards?'

'The lads went into the bar for a protein shake or something, I walked home, told you Gem, I'm not chasing after him.'

'Just as well,' Poodie said, 'there's a nice lad working with me. He's about your age. Shall I give him your number?'

Clova glared at her uncle, 'no, certainly not. I'm not desperate. If I wanted to date, I'd put myself out there.'

'Put yourself out there? What does that mean?'

'I've barely seen you for the last two years and suddenly you're trying to orchestrate my love life. For Heaven's sake.'

'Did he ask you to join them for a drink?' Gemma said trying to cool the situation.

'Not exactly. He just said they were going into the gym bar. I told him I'd get off home and would see him around. Playing it cool, I told you.'

Clova smiled to herself as she thought of Matt. He had been friendlier than on their Dartmoor walk, introducing her to his two friends as Clova, keeping her nickname to himself and once or twice she caught him standing at the base of the wall, watching her intently with a certain look in his eyes that she recognised as appreciation, either for her climbing skills or her very short black shorts.

'Hurry up and have your swim,' Mark urged, 'm'ungry.'

'What?'

'He's hungry,' Rosa translated.

Bee, Gemma and Clova started walking to the water's edge as Mark said, 'keep an eye on me, I'll wave you in after 30 minutes.'

'He can't wait any longer than that,' Kay said, who had followed them down to have a paddle, 'eek! It's freezing.'

Chilli, Harley and Copper trotted up and down next to Kay, hoping she was going to start throwing their balls. Chilli loved the sea but wouldn't go in if Gemma was swimming, preferring to be the centre of attention. Harley and Copper would paddle, Mac hated the water and Blue remained further back next to Poodie, sitting up and staring intently towards the water's edge, like a canine lifeguard.

The women hurried into the water, knowing that the sooner they emersed themselves, the sooner they would get used to it. It wasn't that cold if you were used to sea swimming, the sun had been shining all day but the water in the U.K never got warm. The sea temperature might reach 16 degrees in the summer, or even 18 in a heatwave if they were lucky. They always described it as 'coldly refreshing' and 'very good for you' to anyone who asked.

Clova was a good swimmer and swam further out, passing Bee and Gemma who were more leisurely. They swam backward and forward, chatting, taking care not to swim out too far, as the tide was going out, and they didn't fancy being swept to Brixham. The sea sparkled and shimmered in the early evening sun, the gulls were drifting lazily over the water riding the thermals or looking for food. No-one else was swimming but there were a few paddle boarders further out to sea. They could see some white dots on the horizon where the yacht club was practising, and a small fishing boat was heading out towards Berry Head. The girls felt invigorated and relaxed. Bee was telling Gemma about a new work colleague who would ask questions but talked over the answer. There was a lot to learn in a Post Office, but she acted as if she knew it all and always interrupted any explanation before they were even halfway through, with 'I understand', until the post mistress, at the end of her tether, fixed her with a steely eye and said, 'but **do** you though.'

When Gemma didn't respond, Bee said 'I suppose you had to be there, Kate and I found it funny.'

Bee was doing a combination of breaststroke and side breaststroke when she wanted to talk and floating on her back for five minutes when she needed a rest, she wasn't as strong a swimmer as the other two.

'When we swim to the right, we're not moving at all, we must be in a bit of a current, be careful. You can really feel it trying to drag you further out. I can still put my feet down and touch the bottom, can you?' Gem asked, ignoring the work chat.

Bee could but Clova was further out. Gemma waved her in and called her. She noticed and was trying to swim back to them but not getting anywhere. She was slowly being pulled further out, so she changed tactics and started swimming horizontally instead of trying to get back to the shore.

'Don't panic,' Bee called to her, starting to panic on her behalf and waving her arms. Poodie had walked down to the water's edge and was standing with Kay, before he had a chance to assess the situation, Blue jumped in and started swimming powerfully out to sea, passing Gemma and Bee, he reached Clova who grabbed his harness and between them got to where her feet could touch the sandy bottom. They waded back as fast as they could. Blue ran out and shook himself vigorously, soaking the bystanders then turning back to Clova he walked behind her, nudging her firmly with his nose, up the beach.

'He's herding you,' Bee said, 'he must have collie in his genetic makeup. My friend had an Australian cattle dog, I think they call them Blue Heelers, he used to push me away from things that he considered dangerous. He was really strong, so I know what that feels like.' Chuckling as she watched the dog shoving Clova up the beach. 'That was amazing. Blue, you're so clever.'

The big dog was pushing Clova away from the perceived danger, his nose shoving her bottom hard. For once, she didn't protest or push him away. She reached the others and grabbed her towel, sinking to her knees and putting her arms around Blue s neck.

Sindy whipped out her phone and took a photo. 'If we don't get proof, we'll never believe it. Clo, what do you say now concerning dog friendly beaches?'

'Blue surprises me every day,' Poodie said, 'I didn't even know he could swim.'

'Most dogs can swim.' Bee said, 'it's instinct. Blue just adores Clova. She should be his part owner.'

Clova, recovering her poise, stood up, took off her swim cap, shaking her hair out and threw a towelling style dress over her costume, belting it tightly around her waist, observing as Bee and Gemma held towels around each other, changing properly.

'I can't believe Blue reacted so quickly,' Poodie said, drying him off with Bee's spare towel that she was saving for her hair, 'he's very intelligent and still growing.'

'He'll be Prime Minister by next year,' Rosa joked, 'are you okay Clova? Were you scared?'

'I'm fine, I was starting to feel a little concerned when I couldn't reach Bee and Gem. I think we caught a bit of a riptide there'

'we?' Bee said quietly to Gemma.

Clover continued, not hearing the remark, 'and yes; Blue was amazing. I think I would like to spend some time with him, maybe take him out. He is officially my hero.'

'Hear that, Blue? Auntie Clova's going to take you for walks and is going to buy you a steak.' Bee joked.

'Maybe a burger,' Clova said, come on. Let's go eat.'

'At last,' Mark said, jumping up with alacrity, 'before we have another drama and I collapse with hunger.'

16

'I've picked up milk for us,' Betty said, 'but we're getting through a lot more now that we're doing drinks, we should get it delivered, then I wouldn't have to go in and deal with that awful man.'

'Good thinking. I'll get on to it and try to work out how much to order.'

Betty went into the back to put the milk in the fridge and make their initial cuppa of the day and Clova served their first few early bird regulars

'We had another dirty phone call left on the answerphone this morning: I've had enough so I've reported it. Let the phone company deal with it and block the numbers if it's more than one person.' Gemma said, fixing her red scarf more securely over her head.

'I picked this scarf specially, Clova, so if it doesn't make me more dynamic, energetic and forceful I'll be docking your wages.'

'See? It's working already.' Clova laughed, taking her mug of tea from Betty and putting it on the shelf behind her. She just had time to drink it before a steady stream of customers came in. The slimming club members, allowing themselves a day after weigh day treat, the builders, who appeared to have more tea breaks than working hours and seemed to need something edible for each ten-minute break.

Clova walked in front of the counter to check that the cakes were well displayed, leaning slightly forward with a look of concentration on her face, when she suddenly gave an unladylike shriek and jumped sideways. Matt had walked in and playfully tweaked her round the waist.

'Hey Blackberry, did you like bouldering? We're going to try and go every couple of weeks if you fancy it, I'll let you know, shall I? Probably see you later when I come back for my lunch.'

Clova who'd gone a bit pink, waited until Matt left, then looked at Gemma and pulled a face. 'I'm not sure I like being tickled.'

'In Albania, that's the equivalent of a marriage proposal,' Gemma teased.

'Gem ma,' Clova said, exaggerating the last two letters of Gemma's name. She went back behind the counter, completely forgetting the plan she had for re-arranging the cakes. A new queue formed, and they were kept busy for the next 20 minutes.

'Hello Christine,' Gemma greeted the next customer who was the last person in the queue, giving them time to catch up on orders and clearing up.

'What have you got for me today?'

'We have an Orange, Thyme and Olive oil cake, how about that?' Christine pulled a face, so the cake was obviously a hit.

'Ugh, sounds horrible and funnily enough, Geoff has been putting olive oil in his ears all week ready for them to be syringed at the doctors on Monday, he's sick of the sight and the smell of it. So am I, it's all over the pillowcases and cushions but it will wind him up more than me, so I'll take it, thanks.'

Gemma laughed, 'he's going to cotton on to you soon. He must realise that you're buying these cakes to annoy him.'

'Not yet and to be fair it hasn't stopped him eating them and I must say, they have all been delicious. From some of the ingredients you told me they contained I was certain they were going to taste horrible or at the very least, odd but they have all been lovely.' Christine left the shop with a big smile on her face.

'We'll have to think of what we can offer her next week,' Gemma said to her staff, 'it's becoming quite challenging.'

'We could do a bake of the week,' Clova suggested, 'something different and unusual every week and put it on the counter with a sign stating that fact. It could be the Saturday Special.'

Before Gemma had a chance to say yes, Clova went on excitedly, 'We could get a juicer and offer healthy juices, I'm really into juicing at home. I do a vegetable one that I call Swamp juice, it looks like the bottom of a pond but tastes delicious. Then there's a beetroot one that looks like a prop from a horror film but it's so good for you.'

'Nope, you're not selling it to me,' Gemma said, pulling a face. I think I should ban items of red clothing for a while, Clova had on a red skirt, all this creativity is giving me a headache. Betty, you're not wearing anything red, are you?'

'I'm not ready for my bed yet. I told you before, I'm fit for my age, why? Did I yawn?' Not waiting for an answer, she said 'here come my gentlemen.'

The two men in question came in and made a bee line for Betty, who beamed and asked them what they would like.

'Do you have Baklava?'

'Gemma, can you believe it, that's the second time we've been asked if we sell balaclavas, how odd and why would you want one this time of year? Not planning to rob a bank, are you?'

John silently passed his partner £10.

David smiling, raised his voice, 'Betty, my dear, we'll take one of the breakfast quiches and two raisin flapjacks.'

Betty put his items in two bags and advised him to try the cheap shop or the sportswear shop downtown for his headgear, scratching her head as they went off laughing.

Clova said, her mouth twitching as she tried not to smile, 'I think we're in need of our second drink,' reaching for their mugs.

'I'll make them,' Betty said, grabbing them before Clova could get any further, leaving Gem and Clova to chuckle. Betty refused to use the urn saying it was for paying customers only.

'We shouldn't laugh,' Gemma said, 'I'd advise Betty to get new hearing aids, but I love her as she is, and sometimes I think she deliberately misunderstands, for comic effect.

I like your idea for bake of the week, I'll have a couple of signs done on the computer and put one in the window, now all we need to do is find some unusual bakes.'

Gabriel popped in to pick up the tin he had left behind previously, and to say he wasn't doing any more baking at the moment. He had a day job working in the same department as Mark at the college and a part time evening job in the kitchen of a local pub. He said he was too tired for anything else.

'That's a shame, Gabe, your vegan bakes were popular. How's your girlfriend?'

'She's started working in Tollys two days a week, she's there now.'

'Really? How does she get on with the manager?'

'Fine, I think, she doesn't say much to be honest. I think she misses home, she wanted to run her own beauticians, but she didn't finish her college course and doesn't want to start at the bottom in any of the salons here, she could have joined forces with her pal in Cardiff but neither have got what I would call business heads and they won't take any advice, at least not from me, she's taking a lot of advice from Carl.' Gabriel sighed, looking tired and stressed.

'I'm sorry, Gabe,' Gemma, who had a very kind nature, sympathised, 'I know you were looking forward to Toni moving here, maybe she'll settle down if you give it a few more months.'
Gabriel didn't look convinced but picked up his tin and said goodbye. Betty came back with the drinks and then they got busy again. It was manic until closing time, Clova said she was going to research unusual cakes and Betty was meeting her friend who was coming round for an early tea. Sindy and Bee arrived with the dogs to meet Gemma, who

groaned inwardly, hoping she didn't have to do an hour's dog walk before going home then remembered she had the car which she couldn't leave outside Sins all day.

'We'll walk back,' Sindy informed her partner, Bee has invited herself round to sit on the patio and have a glass of wine and a bite of anything you may be bringing home in your bag.' Sindy winked, raising her eyebrows.

Gemma liked friends turning up unexpectedly so was quite happy and told them she had some goodies to bring home.

'Oh good,' Bee said, 'I went to Slimming club last night and I've lost a pound, so I deserve a treat.'

'That's not how healthy eating plans are supposed to work is it?' Sindy queried.

'Besides,' Bee said ignoring her, 'we've walked about 4 miles today so that will have burnt off any calories I might consume.'

'I might have to buy you a Fitbit for your birthday, you have no concept of how many calories you've walked off and we haven't walked four miles. '

Clova slung her jacket on and picked up her bag saying goodbye and asked Bee if she could take Blue for a walk on Sunday.

'But you hate dogs,' Sindy said with a frown.

'I don't. I just wasn't a dog lover. I don't understand dogs, but Blue is special, he's more like a person than a dog and there is a bond developing. I've never felt that affection coming from an animal before, mind you, growing up we only had a very aloof cat who didn't like to be petted. I'm enjoying getting to know Blue, and I like walking.'

'Fine,' Bee replied, 'if you think you can handle him, he's very strong….' As Mac, the 8-kilo mixed breed, suddenly pulled her into the kerb to investigate a discarded bit of sausage roll, nearly causing her to trip.

Clova grimaced but said firmly, 'let's try it, can you drop him off around 2?'

Bee agreed and Clova followed Betty heading home, while Gemma grabbed her bags and locked up.

'I'd go to the foot of our stairs if I had any, Clova wanting to walk Blue. When she mentioned it on the beach, I thought it was in the excitement of the moment and she'd go off the idea in the cold light of day.' Gemma said, watching Clova fast disappearing up the road.

'I know,' Bee said, shaking her head in disbelief, 'but there's no denying Blue does adore her and he's very well behaved, better than all of ours. Right come on, Sind, let's walk off those calories we're going to consume. See you back at yours.'

17

Sins was doing very well, and Gemma and Clova worked nicely together, both being hard workers who just got on with any job that needed doing. Gemma would roll up her sleeves and do the dirty work without automatically expecting her employees to do it, and Clova seemed to anticipate what needed to be done and would get on with it without asking. On Saturdays, Betty was a joy and the regulars loved her. They were a tight knit team and Gemma had finally persuaded Betty to join the payroll, wanting to do things by the book, as explaining to Inland Revenue that she was paying a pensioner in cakes would have been very awkward.

 Clova had drawn up a list of unusual bakes and Gemma had texted Jack their first one which was going to be on display Saturday as their Special of the Day. Gemma opened the till and took some money out, telling Clova she was going to pick up another couple of litres of milk. It was drizzling so she ran up the road, wishing she had grabbed her coat, stepped into Tollys just as Carl threw a bucket of soapy water over his step, soaking her feet and legs, she jumped back, cursing.

'Look where you're going,' Carl said, rudely.

'Unbelievable. Who throws a bucket of water over their step before making sure no-one is coming. You did that on purpose, you small minded, nasty little man.'

'I didn't, you got in my way, you should have been looking where you were going.' Carl mumbled, hurrying back into his shop.

Gemma groaned and manfully decided she wasn't going back without picking up the milk. She squelched into the shop, grabbed the milk and thankfully was served by a shop assistant, Carl having disappeared into the stockroom, presumably embarrassed, possibly gloating.

Stomping back to Sins, seething, she told Clova all about it, who sympathised, called Carl a few names, dried Gemma off with a tea towel that was about to go in the laundry bag and put the kettle on.

'Anyone else would have apologised profusely, and at least tried to make amends. Who can I complain to though? He'll just say it was an accident and he didn't see me.'

Half an hour later, dried and soothed, Gemma felt able to put it behind her and get on with her day.

'How did your first ever dog walk go?' She asked her.

'It was brilliant, we followed the path by the caves and went into the wood and then got on the coast path and on to Preston. I let Blue off the lead in the wood and he didn't stray far from me. When we came across other dog walkers, Blue came back and stayed by my side as if he was protecting me. I must admit, I enjoyed the walk so much more with him than doing it on my own. There's something about watching a dog walking along, tail wagging, enjoying the scents and sights around him that really increases your pleasure in the whole experience. We're already reading each other's body language. I can finally get what dog owners have been on about all this time. I asked

Uncle Poodie and Bee if I could take him out every week.'

'For someone who didn't even like dogs, you've really jumped in the deep end. He's more like a wolf then a dog, how do you even hold him, Harley nearly pulls me over.'

'Blue never pulls. He's very good with me. It was so funny when he was off lead, in the dappled shade of the wood, he blended into the shadows and made a few walkers jump when he appeared, seemingly out of nowhere. This large grey and white monster coming from behind a tree to check in with me.' She chuckled, recalling a couple of people startled into cursing profusely.

'How are you coping with picking up poo?'

'I held my breath the first time, but I expect you get used to it.' Clova had added silver tips to her hair which looked very dramatic, and she felt, it would prevent Matt calling her Blackberry.

'Hello Blackberry Frosting,' said the man in question, coming in with a couple of the other workmen for their lunchtime orders.

'Matt just, no. That's ridiculous. Pack it in before I think of a nickname for you,' Clova stormed off into the kitchen, Matt's laughter following her.

'Stop winding her up,' Gemma said, serving the men with their various sandwiches, quiches and cakes.'

'I can't,' Matt said, with a twinkle in his eye, 'it's my favourite thing to do.'

'It's too busy to have her storm off out back each time. Try to restrain yourself.

Clova!' Gemma called, 'I need 2 coffees and a tea, can you come back please.'

Clova came out and busied herself making the drinks, bringing them over without a word, then started to serve the rest of the people who were in the queue.

Matt started singing a song from the old days, as he strolled out of the shop. 'Blackberry way…' he warbled, leaving the other builders snickering.

'If that's an actual song, it's rubbish.' Clova muttered, to the elderly person she was serving, who heard her mumble and told her it *was* an actual song by a band called The Move from 1968.

'Before my time, I wasn't even born then and nor was Matt. He has no right knowing a song with the word blackberry in it.' Clova looked quite put out.

The customer looked bemused, and Gemma chuckled. Once the customer had left, Clova tried to think of a nickname she could call Matt.

'Handyman Matt?' Gemma suggested.

Clova tutted. 'That's his job. Let's analyse him. He's dark, mysterious, dark brown eyes, olive skin …'

'Olive?' Gemma said. ' Evie?'

'Evie? Don't get it.'

'Extra Virgin. Don't look at me like that, it was clever. Oh, I know,

Door.'

Clova rolled her eyes and tutted, 'Gem, you are rubbish at this. What does he remind you of? I could imagine him in a film playing a dark knight.'

'Lance?'

Clova spluttered, 'I don't get that either, and, if I think about it, it sounds rude. Forget it, I can't think of anything, I don't have to stoop to his level anyway.'

Gemma couldn't help it, 'ador.'

'eh?'

'Mat a dor.'

18

A few days later, Clova went back to the gym after a message from Matt saying they were going to try bouldering again, she was early so went into the main part of the gym and paused for a second, looking at all the equipment available before choosing the running machine. Stepping on, she ran at a steady pace for ten minutes, lost in her own thoughts before being aware that one of Matt's friends was behind her, doing some free weights. He hadn't noticed her.

In-between grunts he told the guy he was with that he was meeting Matt and they were going to do bouldering.

'Matt's made friends with this girl and she came last time, think she's coming again tonight,' The guy, whose name was Harry, said. Clova's ears pricked up.

'Fit, is she?'

'Obviously not my taste although I can appreciate that she is a pretty girl. Just a kid really. Very good at climbing, interesting to see how she does tonight.'

'I'm not a kid.' Clova muttered, too low for them to hear.

Harry moved over to one of the rowing machines, his friend following, still using the free weights to do bicep curls. The men were quiet for a few minutes, concentrating on their exercises. Clova slowed the treadmill down to a fast walk but kept her head down in case Harry looked over and recognised her.

'I might come in and have a go, think I just saw Matt come in. Do you reckon he fancies this girl?'

'Doubt it, I teased him about her the other day, and he said she was too young for him. Right, come on, let's get in there.'

Clova felt her eyes filling up with tears, blinking furiously. She was *not* going to cry over a man. She carried on walking on the treadmill, telling herself that she didn't care, she was being stupid. She couldn't help her age or her feelings for Matt, which were a lot stronger than she had realised. He was only four years older than her, that was absolutely nothing.

He was an idiot, that's what he was. He didn't know a good thing when he saw it. They would have been good together.

They had loads in common, besides, she was in full time work not a bloody schoolgirl, what was wrong with him. What was wrong with her? Why did her stomach give a flip when she saw him?

Bloody man. Her inner monologue was interrupted as Matt poked his head into the gym, spotted her and called, 'hey Blackberry, coming to chase me up a wall?'

'Yes, then hopefully I'll drive you round the bend,' she muttered, before turning off the treadmill and turning to face him, pasting on a fake smile and hoping he'd think any moisture on her cheeks was sweat.

'Just coming.'

Another man who had been on the treadmill next to hers, grabbed his towel, wiping the sweat off his body, smiled and asked her if she wanted to go for a drink when she finished.

'No thanks, not going to undo all my good work with a drink.'

'You could have an orange juice, come on, we could have a good time.'

Clova opened her mouth to give a firmer refusal when Matt appeared next to her. Giving the man a glare, he said, 'the lady said no. Come on, Clova.' He took her arm to pull her out of the gym.

'Don't pull me along, like a child,' she hissed at him, 'and where did you come from? I was handling the situation.'

'Jeez, you're like a lamb to the slaughter, that guy is known for chatting up the young girls that come in, he spends most of his days in here on the prowl. Dirty bastard. He must be forty if he's a day. I'm going to speak to the manager about him. Should have done it months ago.'

'God, you're really hung up on age aren't you? He only asked me to go for a drink.'

Matt glowered at her, 'and the rest. You're not that innocent, he just wanted to get laid.'

'and I said no, so stop it with the caveman attitude. What do you care anyway? Do you want to take me out?' Clova added, boldly.

'I'm too old for you.' Matt said, looking uncomfortable.

'Oh yes, all of four years. For God's sake. It's you who should grow up Matt. Forget the bouldering, I'm going home.'

Clova began to walk out, and Matt took hold of her arm, gently this time.

'Sorry. I'm just looking out for you that's all. I hope he's not your secret admirer.'

'For God's sake, what secret admirer?'

'The one who gave you those flowers.'

'I've never seen him before today and I handled it. I told him I wasn't interested.'

'Of course, and a man like that would take no for an answer, would he? Look, I like you a lot, you're a mate but you've got an innocence about you that draws men like that. You were being too polite.'

'Rubbish. I told him no. I don't have to tell him to fuck off to make my point.'

'Yes, you do. I told you, I've seen him in action.'

They glared at each other.

'Oh, and by the way, do you flirt with all your 'mates'?' Clova said, the term having rankled.

'Only the pretty ones.' Matt said, trying to lighten the conversation. Clova narrowed her eyes at him, waiting for the next line.

'What?'

'You forgot to add a few cliches, 'It's just banter.' 'it's not you, it's me' etc.' Oh, forget it. I'm going home.'

Matt put his head to one side, looking at her. She had one hand on her hip, her eyes flashing, one step away from storming out, like a frightened deer.

'Don't go yet, in case that dick is hanging about outside. Can we just start again and forget it? '

He could tell Clova was weakening and gave her his most charming smile, 'come on, Blackberry.'

'Don't call me Blackberry and stop with the wheedling.'
She glared at him for another second then they looked at each other and laughed.

'Wheedling? Wheedling? The more you say it, the more it doesn't sound like a word.'

'Whatever. All right, I'll come and climb up the damn wall.'
She managed to put her emotions on hold and surprised herself by enjoying the session. She watched Matt and Harry, calling out words of support, then they watched her, doing the same with a little bit of good-natured teasing. It was quite busy, and she teamed up with a woman called Izzy who was very good, encouraging without being patronising, offering advice and cheering her on. She suggested Clova should join a team and think about doing it competitively.
Clova laughed and said she would have no time for work at this rate, with all her hobbies and walking Blue.
Matt, who had been standing nearby, added that she would have no time for boyfriends either. Undoing all his good work and earning himself a glare from Clova, and a quizzical look from Harry accompanied by a nudge in the ribs.

After changing in their respective changing rooms, they went into the gym bar. Clova and Izzy sat at the bar drinking a coffee and the boys had a protein shake.

Matt offered Clova a lift home, which she declined but smiled in a friendly way telling Matt that she expected she would see him the next day, giving a deep sigh of relief as he and Harry left, not realising how wound up she had been, rolling her shoulders to ease them, as she had been holding herself almost rigid.

 She could relax now he'd left the gym and drop the act of pretending not to notice Matt out of the corner of her eye or being aware of everything he did and said. It was a new feeling for her. She had never been that interested in relationships before, even though she'd had several, they hadn't been serious, and she certainly hadn't felt the ups and downs in her moods that she did now.

 She didn't know if she liked the fact that she was thinking about Matt almost all the time or not, but she couldn't seem to stop. Clova felt out of control. She remembered what she had told Gemma. 'Not that into him' huh, who was she kidding.

 Izzy hadn't noticed that she didn't have her full attention and carried on chatting cheerfully. They took their time, finishing their drinks and arranging to meet in a couple of weeks.

They left the gym and walked part of the way home together, before Izzy turned into her road, leaving Clova to continue her journey alone. She walked quickly up the hill, looking forward to getting home and having her dinner, she realised she was starving and chuckled to herself that she had forgotten to have any lunch, blaming it on her hormones. Bloody man, she thought.

A red convertible pulled up alongside her and the older man from the gym leaned across and offered her a lift. She declined and walked a bit faster, the man cruising leisurely beside her, 'Come on Darlin, you know you want to. I've got a nice bottle of champagne in my flat, we could drink it and watch the sunset.'

'I don't want to, I said no, leave me alone.' Clova looked around, not seeing anyone else about. She was beginning to feel isolated and a little nervous then caught sight of her brother being dragged towards her by Blue. Waving wildly, she hurried towards them. Antney dropping Blues' lead with relief as the dog charged toward Clova.

'Hiya Clo, Uncle Poodie came round with the dogs, he said Blue was obsessed with you, so I brought him to meet you. I thought you said he didn't pull. He nearly had me over.' Her brother panted as he caught up with her. The sleaze from the gym, deciding to call it a day, put his foot down and screeched up the road.

'Who was that?'

'Some creep I saw at the gym coming on to me. I'm glad you turned up when you did. He made me feel uncomfortable. You would have had him for breakfast, wouldn't you Blue?'

'More likely, he took one look at me,' her well-built brother said, not overly blessed with modesty.

Clova raised her eyebrows, 'rather than being scared off by an animal That weighs more than me? Sure.'

She squatted down to give Blue a hug, then straightened up and walked home with her brother.

'You should be careful, sis. I would have picked you up.'

Clova shook her head, 'it's not dark or even that late. I should be able to walk home by myself, I refuse to feel threatened.'

'You should always be aware of your surroundings, remember what our Sensei used to say?' They'd both done karate as children, Ant still went now and then.

' have an escape plan, hold your keys ready to use as a defence. Walk into the first house you see, pick up your phone …'

Clova tried not to roll her eyes; she felt her brother was over protective, they didn't live in a city, and she'd always felt safe walking anywhere on her own but she accepted that there were bad people everywhere and he had a point.

'All right Ant, I get the message. I promise I'll be more aware in future. Don't say anything about that guy in front of Uncle Poodie, he's suddenly turned into a protective old fashioned relative. I've already had a lecture about dating guys my own age, which I didn't need, by the way.

Let's get home, I'm famished, what's for dinner?'

19

Saturday morning and Gemma was telling Betty about their Special which this week was Carrot, pistachio and maple slices. They put some in the window, some under the counter and some cut into cubes for the customers to sample.

Clova walked around to look at the displays and gave her seal of approval. Not Three Bad was first in and sampled a cube, pronouncing it as very tasty but he would stick to his cupcakes, asking for a box of four.

Rosa came in followed by a lady who took her time looking around. Rosa was interested in the Homity pies, wanting 2 for her and her mum for their tea that night, she sampled the new cake while she waited and chatted to Gemma.

The lady who had been looking at the cakes asked if they did Eccles cakes, Gemma said no and to try Tollys. The customer who was deaf, was getting frustrated as she didn't understand what Gemma had said. Rosa tapped her on the arm and told her, using sign language. They had a five-minute chat, the lady bought one of the pies Rosa recommended and went away smiling, to try Tollys for her Eccles cakes.

   'Well,' Gemma said, for once nearly speechless, 'I can't believe you know sign language, how come you've never mentioned it?'

   Rosa shrugged, 'never came up. I learned B.S.L years ago. I had a deaf friend and wanted to be able to communicate better.'

'That's nice. I've always wanted to learn it too but never got round to it.'

'One of our after-school clubs was learning B.S.L. I thought about it but decided to do netball and computer skills instead.' Clova told them.

'All we had in our day was drama or the chess club.' Betty said, 'so I used to go to the town hall and do Keep Fit. It was very basic, not like the classes they have now, even my beginners class has equipment and great music and I've got my dance class which is very modern. I tried yoga, but it made me break wind.'

'If I got down on one of those mats, I'd never get up again and I don't need to do yoga to fart, I fart for England.' Rosa said, looking as if she was settling in for a long stay and a gossip.

'Right, anything else Rosa? I'm sure you want to get back to your mum. 'Gemma said, worried customers were going to come in and hear the conversation, flatulence, she felt was not the subject in a nice Bakery.

'Anyone would think you're trying to get rid of me, I am a customer you know.'

'Of course I'm not, Rosa, but can't stand around chatting, too much to do.'
Rosa looked pointedly around at the empty shop, empty apart from herself and the 3 women behind the counter.

'Betty, things to do in the kitchen please, then we'll have a drink. Clova, could you make up some cake boxes, come on, chop chop.' Clova raised an eyebrow at the unexpected command and snickered inwardly.

Gemma picked up her list and pretended to study it, scratching her head with her pen.

Rosa unconcerned, collected her pies, putting them in her bag, telling Gemma she was going to see if Bee was home as she fancied a proper chat over a coffee.

'Sorry about that,' Gem said to Clova 'but that was not a subject I wanted to talk about on a busy Saturday when people might walk in, and Rosa looked like she was settling in for a lengthy conversation.' Christine came in and Gemma greeted her with a smile, showing her the new cakes.

'They've got a green tinge to them,' Christine commented.

'That's the pistachio.'

'Geoff's heard of carrot cake, but I think the colour will suit. He'll think they are mouldy. Right, I'll take 2,' Christine decided, sampling a cube as she got her purse out.

Betty came out with the mugs just as Christine was leaving and Betty's gentlemen were coming in. They went straight to Betty and asked for Lardy cakes, their faces fell when she heard them first time.

'Lardy cakes, I haven't had them for years, no, my lovers, we don't do them. Try our Saturday Special instead.'

The men agreed and moved over to pick something from the savoury counter to go with them. Betty went to get the tray of cakes from the window, as she was about to reach in, there was an almighty crash and screech of brakes, and the front half of a car came through the window. It happened so quickly no-one had time to react. The window display and shelf had been pushed into Betty who was lying on the floor covered in glass and bleeding profusely, Gemma, standing behind Betty had also been knocked to the floor, Clova and the two men were unhurt. The driver of the car had banged his head on the steering wheel and was saying over and over, 'it was an accident, it was an accident. My foot slipped.'

Clova screamed at the driver: 'Carl! How could you. You've gone too far this time. You've killed Betty.'

'No, he hasn't, she's breathing. Calm down, we'll deal with one thing at a time.' David climbed over the broken counter announcing he knew first aid, whilst Clova dashed into the kitchen to get the First Aid kit. John was on his mobile calling for police and an ambulance. Matt, who'd been doing overtime with another builder, ran in to help, and Rosa who'd been halfway up the road chatting to an acquaintance, rushed back, calling Sindy on her mobile as she ran. Between them they helped Gemma up, she was in shock and bleeding from the hundreds of pieces of broken glass. David stemmed the worst of Betty's injuries with bandages but said they mustn't move her until the ambulance arrived. She was groaning and complaining that her wrist hurt and her ribs.

'Probably broken,' Matt said quietly to Clova, who was shaken but unhurt. 'They won't be able to do anything for her ribs, they don't strap ribs these days. Why don't you make a sweet tea for yourself and Gemma, it's good for shock, but don't give Betty anything in case they have to operate.'

Matt went into the kitchen and brought a stool out for Gemma to sit on, just as the emergency services arrived and took over. Matt told Gemma he and Gavin, the other builder would come back and help clean up. He said he would go to the yard later to get some wood to board the window up and make the shop secure.

'Thank heavens you were nearby Matt, thank you so much.'

An ambulanceman arrived to check Gemma over, two of his colleagues were seeing to Betty, and the police and another paramedic were attending to Carl. It was a busy Saturday but amazingly, no pedestrians had been walking past the instant the car had gone through the shop window. People had now gathered outside and were standing in a semi-circle around the scene of the accident, filming with their mobile phones and trying to peer into the bakery. Clova had started to cry. Matt put his arm around her shoulders and squeezed her into a hug, trying to stop her shaking.

'He did it on purpose, he hates us, poor Betty, look at her.' Clova sobbed.

The paramedics had put Betty on a stretcher with a collar around her neck as a precaution and were about to take her to the ambulance, Sindy pushed her way into the shop, telling the police she was the owner, she ran over to Gemma, who was still being treated by a paramedic.

'Sind. Don't worry, I'm ok but they want to check me over in hospital, I might have some bits of glass in me. It's mainly superficial, nothing broken, I just sting in about fifty places where the glass cut me Poor Betty, did you see her? She looked smaller somehow, frail and old. We don't really think of her as a pensioner when she's bossing us about and bustling to and fro.'

Matt followed the paramedics who were taking Betty to the ambulance and stayed with them until they had put her in the vehicle. Sindy bent down and hugged her partner then stood up and surveyed the scene. It looked like a bomb had gone off, rubble and glass everywhere. Gemma asked Sindy to stay and supervise, as she shakily made her way over to the ambulance. Rosa offered to drive Sindy to the hospital when she was ready.

Carl was put in a separate ambulance, then the police took over, moving spectators away and putting police tape around the scene, spoke to everyone who had been in Sins at the time and said they would take statements back at the station. Clova, David and John went in one of the police cars, Clova telling Sindy she would go on to the hospital after she'd given her statement to check on Betty.

20

The next day Poodie and Bee drove to their friends' house to see if they needed anything. Gemma and Sindy were sitting in the atrium, drinking coffee and looking exhausted. Gemma had tiny cuts all over her face, neck and hands, dark circles under her eyes indicating that she hadn't slept all night.

'We'll take the dogs out for you later,' Poodie said, as he and Bee made themselves a drink and came to sit with them. The incident had been on the local news and Sindy said that their phones hadn't stopped ringing.

'Have you heard how Betty is?' Bee asked.

'She was in A & E for 5 hours, 2 broken ribs, a broken wrist and multiple bruises and lacerations, they wanted her to stay in overnight to make sure she had no internal damage, they thought she might have bruised her kidneys, but she wouldn't. Clova stayed with her until David and John, the two men who had been in the shop when it happened, drove over and insisted on taking Betty home with them, as she lives alone, they wanted to look after her for a couple of days, it turns out they live quite near us, that big house on three levels that we always wanted to see inside. It could have been so much worse.'

'Yes, they could live in an old, terraced house on that bad estate,' Bee said, to try to make them laugh.

'Bee!' Gemma said, but it had made them smile, she continued, ' I can't really believe Carl did it on purpose, unless he's had a breakdown. We've never done anything to him. I can only think of a couple of reasons why he holds such a grudge.

Some time ago he had some ideas about wanting to make the street pedestrianised and was going to submit a plan to the council but none of the other traders would back him. I was told that he thought we had been talking behind his back and it was our fault no-one else was interested. Remember, Sind?'

'Oh yes. We hadn't been there long, and this guy came in and had a rant. We hadn't even talked about it to the other traders, we weren't that interested. You actually went to see him and tried to have a rational talk with him, but he didn't want to listen.'

Harley was sitting between Sindy's legs as if he realised she needed comforting. For all his faults, he was a very loving, instinctive boy with an emotional intelligence that surprised them sometimes. Sindy was stroking his ears absently.

Gemma put her head back, rolling her neck, trying to ease some of her aches.

'Ouch. You could almost hear my neck crack then.'

Chilli had jumped up on to Gemma's lap, deciding she needed to be a part of the consoling, after a quick cuddle, Gemma eased her down and picked up her coffee, sipping it slowly. Chilli transferred her attention to Bee, leaping into her arms.

'After that, Carl seemed to feel that anything negative that occurred to him must have originated from us.'

'Plus, he saw Sins as competition to Tollys. It's very odd though, if it was an accident, how come the car veered into our window in particular. Thank God the council were so slow in granting us permission to have the table and chairs outside. If they had, someone would have been killed for sure.

Well, it's in the hands of the police now.' Sindy held her drink in both hands, sipping it leisurely. Harley still pressed between her knees, his warmth a solid comfort.

'What about the shop?'

'The workmen have been brilliant, working for hours, it's cleaned up and made safe. The Insurance company have already been and assessed the situation. The glaziers will be there on Monday, and I suppose we'll be able to re-open in a few days.'

Sindy said, 'I'm making an executive decision, we'll close for a fortnight, I don't want you rushing back, you're in shock, and you can't stand behind the counter serving, looking like an extra from a horror film. We can go in at the end of this week to see if anything needs doing. I'll go down and put a sign on the door with our provisional re-opening date.

Meanwhile I'll text Jack and Clova and put them in the picture. Betty won't be back for at least 6 weeks, if she can face coming back at all.'

'Oh, don't say that, the place won't be the same without her.' Gemma looked stricken.

'Take it a day at a time,' Bee advised 'we'll muck in, and Kay rang to say to just let them know if you need any help.'

'Look on the bright side, firstly, it's starting to rain, and we've got out of the dog walk today, secondly, we can finally see inside David and Johns' place if we go and visit Betty tomorrow.' Sindy told her partner, looking over to Poodie and Bee giving them a half smile and a wink.

The following day, Gemma felt more able to cope with things, as they had decided not to rush into re-opening Sins, they took it easy, walking the dogs in the woods nearby and visiting Betty, who was doing remarkably well although in a lot of pain from her ribs. She told them she would be back, she was a tough old bird, her words, and even if her wrist was still in plaster, she could be there as moral support and serve one handed. David and John wanted her to stay with them until her ribs healed and were spoiling her rotten.

Clova called in to see Gemma later in the week and declared that Betty wanted to stay with David and John for as long as possible, she was having a whale of a time.

'She looks awful, but she said she looks worse than she feels, apart from being in pain from her broken ribs. Her wrist doesn't hurt now it's in plaster, but she's covered in cuts and she's black and blue. David and John love having someone to look after and of course, she's bossing them about and they're loving it,' Clova said.

Clova had Blue with her, and she and Gemma were going to walk into the village to see how the shop was looking. Gemma didn't look much better than Betty as she was also covered in a myriad of cuts and bruises. Gemma said she felt fine and had a chuckle over how many of their customers and neighbours of a certain age, phrased the question 'but how are you, in yourself?'

'Don't they say that in London then?' Clova asked.

'They probably do but the more I hear it, the stranger it seems.' Gemma chuckled.

They took their time, Blue walking sedately next to Clova. As they passed Tollys, Toni spotted them and came out, on the attack immediately.

'Carl has lost his job because of you and that email you sent about him having a grudge against you. He hasn't been charged by the police, nothing has been proved about the accident but the owners have decided to 'let him go.'

'For heavens, sake Toni, grow up. You don't know the full extent of things that have been going on and Gemma didn't accuse him of vandalism in her email, just said she felt he had a grudge against them – always glaring in at us and making sarky comments. We didn't make him drive into the shop, he's lucky no-one was killed or seriously injured, for all we know he got the sack for something he did, or didn't do as a manager.'

Gemma said calmly, 'I know for a fact Carl was selling tobacco and booze under the counter to selected customers. I know because one of our mates is a smoker and he was told to see Carl in the corner shop. That's a sackable offence.'

Exactly. You don't get the push because of one concerned email.'

Clova said, protectively pushing in front of Gemma,

'Why don't you mind your own business and leave us alone.'

Toni pushed her face about an inch away from Clova's and started to hiss 'he's got better things to do than cause trouble, the car damaging the shop was an accident,' then heard Blue, who was making a low rumbling sound, his lip twitching in a snarl.

'and keep that dog away from me,' she flung, over her shoulder, flouncing back into the store.

'Well, she's showing her true colours,' Clova said, 'I wonder if she and Gabe have split up? Why on earth would she be sticking up for Carl?'

Gemma shrugged.

'Shall we go into the Bakery or just look through the window?'

They decided to look through the window, joking that it looked as good if not better than before, being shiny and brand new. The shop had been cleared and the shelves replaced.

'It looks good to go,' Gemma said, 'I'll ring Jack and say we'll open in a week. They walked back to Gemma's, on the way her phone beeped with a message announcing a Pack Meet at the pub. Her friends deciding that she needed to get out, relax and forget about her problems.

'I'll feed Blue at my house and bring him to the pub tonight, then he can go home with Uncle Poodie.' Clova said, looking a bit sad at the thought.

They met in the beer garden, Bee leading the way, talking to Sindy about what she wanted to drink, wavering between a cocktail or a diet cola.

'Bit late for that, luv,' Sindy said, quick as a flash, getting in her favourite quip. Bee glared at her and stuck her nose in the air. The dogs were excited, greeting each other with licks and little whimpers and jumping up as if they hadn't seen their pack for months, even Blue pawed Bee and Poodie, and deigned to have his head scratched and his nose kissed. Although still aloof with strangers, he was becoming more affectionate by the day. Bee announced she loved kissing dogs on their furry noses as they were so cute.

'The noses that have usually been up another dogs arse,' Mark felt he had to say.

'I kiss the top of their nose, that part hasn't been near any arsehole, except maybe you,' Bee snapped and then immediately apologised, shocked at herself.

Mark waved the apology away; he had found it funny. They pushed two long tables together as usual. The beer garden was empty apart from one man in the corner enjoying a cigarette with his pint. Gemma, Kay and Poodie went in to get the drinks. Gemma asked if Bee was all right as it was unlike her to snap at Mark, she usually enjoyed a bit of banter.

'We had a chat about Blue in the van coming over. I suggested we give him to Clova but Bee is finding it hard to let go, even though she suggested it in the first place. I'll have another chat with her tonight when we get back from the pub. It's not as if she'd never see him.'

'Clova will be working full time, perhaps her family won't want a big dog in their house. Would Clova have time to walk him?'

'It was just an idea,' Poodie said, 'I haven't spoken to Clova about it, but their bond is so strong, and she's taken him out for quite a few walks since we were at the beach. Blue adored her from the first. I thought she might jump at the chance, and we'd still have him when needed. We love all the dogs, but Mac is a mummy's boy and Copper never leaves my side, Blue is happy enough, but I felt he wanted his own human and he had her picked out. We'll see. Now what is everyone drinking? I'm on the zero-alcohol lager as the designated driver. Bee wants me to surprise her with a cocktail of my choice…'

'Sex on the beach?'

'We would but the sand gets everywhere.'

Gemma rolled her eyes. They decided on the drinks eventually and took them back to the table.

'What, no crisps up your sleeves?' Bee asked, hopefully.

'Nope, sorry luv, I might treat you to some cheesy chips later,' Poodie said with a wink.

'Oh yes,' Rosa put in, 'they do great chips in here, we'll order some to share.'

Kay and Rosa went back to the bar to get them, and Bee raised her glass to Mark in a silent apology.

Clova looked up with anticipation each time the door to the bar opened then glanced away disappointed.

'Looking for Matt?' Gemma asked.

'No,' Clova said, picking up her shandy and taking a big gulp, 'just wondered if any of my mates were here. Matt treats me like a kid anyway.'

'He's too old for you,' Poodie said immediately, 'and a bit of a player by all accounts.'

Bee raised her eyebrows, Sindy and Gemma exchanged glances and Mark lifted his glass in Poodie's direction and sat back to enjoy the show.

Clova's eyes flashed, she placed her drink down carefully, putting her hands on the table she leaned across to face her uncle,

'I really can't believe you just said that ...'

'neither can I,' Bee muttered under her breath to Kay and Rosa.

'You of all people. Is Bee 7 or 9 years older than you?'

'That's different,' Poodie said, shifting in his chair uneasily while giving his girlfriend a sideways glance, 'I'd already sewn my wild oats Whereas you've hardly dated. What's wrong with the boys from college?'

'They're immature and I didn't fancy any of them. What does it matter if I've hardly dated, it's better than playing the field. From what I heard; you had a different woman every week after you split up with Dawn and you call Matt a player.'

'Takes one to know one,' Mark put in, for the fun of stirring it.

'Shut up, Mark,' came from various directions.

'I had a lot of female attention when I broke up with Dawn, I didn't have a different woman every week but I dated quite a few. The attention went to my head for a while,' Poodie said manfully defending himself.

'It wasn't your head it went to,'

'Mark!'

'You're worse than mum and dad, they haven't said a word to me about my social life, or even asked if I'm seeing anyone. They trust me. You've never given me relationship advice before so please don't start now and you don't even know Matt. You're basing your views on hearsay and gossip.'

'That's small towns for you.' Mark put in.

'Why are you sticking up for him? You said he sees you as a kid.' Poodie said, glaring at Mark and speaking to his niece.

'Your Uncle doesn't want you to get hurt, that's all,' Bee said, defending Poodie, they'd had a lot of heated discussions about his past and her age and she was finally feeling more confident in their relationship.

'We came out for a peaceful evening and to cheer Gemma up, so let's stay off certain subjects.'

Clova sighed, 'I know. I'm sorry. I think I'm over-sensitive about Matt and I'm sick of being told he's too old for me. Besides, it's irrelevant, he's not interested. Let's change the subject...'

The door to the bar opened and 2 men came through, one being the waiter carrying 2 dishes of cheesy chips for their table, the other following him, a blond-haired lad wearing a t shirt with a surfboard on, he came over to where Clova was sitting and started making conversation.

'Haven't I seen you somewhere before?'

'Do you come here often?' Mark suggested.

The lad raised an eyebrow but carried on, 'no, really.' He edged in a bit closer, distracted for a moment, he muttered, to nobody in particular, 'what's that noise?'

Then said to Clova, 'do you go surfing?'

'No, I go kayaking.'

'I bet that's where I've seen you, down at the cove, hey do you want to..' he paused, as the noise he was hearing got louder, 'what *is* that noise?'

Blue pushed his head out from under the table, sitting up to his full height which was considerable and continued his low grumbling growl.

'The lad backed away rapidly, nearly falling over in his haste, 'didn't know you had a dog, see you around.'

They all laughed.

'I don't think Blue liked him,' Gemma said, 'he's more protective than your uncle, be prepared for a lot of celibacy in your future if you keep bringing Blue with you.'

'I don't know what that means but I get the gist,' Clova groaned, as they all erupted again, 'at least it's taken our minds off our problems for a bit.'

Clova passed Blue's lead to Poodie saying she was popping to the loo and would see if anyone was playing pool.

'That's a flimsy excuse if ever I heard one,' Bee laughed, once she had gone, helping herself to a couple of chips.

'She's always had so many interests, was on the go all the time, off out doing this, that and the other. I've never seen her that keen on a bloke before, she's always had male and female friends, now suddenly men are looking at her in a different light. I suppose I didn't notice she had grown up.' Poodie said.

'She's a pretty girl, I'm sure a lot of the younger customers are coming into Sins just to see her.' Gemma commented.

Bee slapped Poodie lightly on the arm, 'stop glowering, you're acting like a Victorian father, she's allowed to have admirers. Look at you? It obviously runs in the family.'

'That's what he's worried about.' Mark said, laughing.

They looked round as they heard the door from the bar opening.

Clova came out followed by an older man who walked very close to her, touching her arm.

Bee narrowed her eyes, trying to see clearer, 'that's not Matt is it? It's an older bloke.'

As they all turned to look, Clova whirled and landed a punch in the man's solar plexus and they heard him try to take a wheezing breath in, obviously not expecting the blow, or tensing his stomach muscles. He doubled over as Clova said something before she stormed back to their table. She waved Mark and Poodie down. Both had stood up preparing to come over.

'What the hell was that?' Her uncle asked.

'Someone I saw at the gym; he's been coming on strong for a couple of weeks now. He's propositioned me twice and tried to touch me up. 'Leave it.' She added, seeing her uncle about to go over. 'I've dealt with it, he'll think again before assuming a young girl is easy prey. Who knew Boxercise would come in handy.' Clova smirked, rubbing her knuckles which were red and a bit sore.

'Honestly, Uncle Poodie, leave it. I think he'll take no for an answer in the future.'

Rosa was looking impressed, 'how many sports do you do?'

Clova took a sip of her shandy, watching the man skuttle back into the bar keeping his eyes averted.

'I did karate from the age of ten until I was fifteen, tried the usual exercise classes like Zumba, aerobics, jazz. Boxercise was great, it combined the exercises they give boxers to do, like high intensity training, skipping and using punchbags etc. I loved it but the place where it was held, closed down and the instructor moved on. Now I just do netball, kayaking, climbing, spin classes, a bit of gym and bouldering.'

Rosa pulled a face and picked up some chips, 'oh, is that all. Glad I asked.'

'I went to Boxercise once,' Bee said surprising them all.

'Did you?' Sindy said in a slightly disbelieving tone.

'I liked it, except the bit they did at the end of the session, supposedly for fun. I was heavier than I am now, and they did a relay race where you had to run giving each other piggy backs. I was embarrassed, imagining them thinking they hoped they wouldn't be partnered with me, so I said I didn't feel well and left.

It was a shame because I really enjoyed it up until that point.'

'You missed a chance, you could have squashed, I mean crushed all your opposition.' Mark teased.

Bee pulled a face at him, 'I'll set Clova on you if you don't behave.'

'Anyone you know playing pool?' Gemma asked Clova.

'No, it's quite quiet in there tonight, at least we can relax out here and enjoy the rest of the evening.'

Gemma nodded at her knowingly. Without thinking that Matt was in there and wondering what he was doing, she meant.

21

Sins was ready to re-open; The counters and the window were full of delicious looking cakes and savouries. Gemma. Clova and Betty waited behind the counter, all three in black and white with red scarves tied around their heads. Betty had a plaster on her wrist but declared she was fit enough to work. The Saturday Special was on the top of the front counter and in the window, Gemma had spoken to Betty about not overdoing it and tried to get her to sit down but she was having none of it and went out the back to make the drinks, saying that Clova would have to bring them out.

Not Three Bad was their first customer and he was so pleased to see them that he forgot to say his catchphrase. He bought double his usual number of cakes, possibly worried that lightning might strike twice, Clova suggested, when he had left the shop.

They had a steady stream of customers for the next hour, all saying how pleased they were to see them back and making a fuss of Betty.

'Here's Christine,' Gemma said, greeting her as she walked in. She was carrying flowers and a box of chocolates which she handed to Gemma, saying she had missed them and was glad no-one was badly hurt. She bought 2 of the Saturday Specials and went off with a smile.

'Blueberry, you're back!' Matt appeared, also carrying flowers and chocolates which he gave to Gemma.

'No, I'm not,' Clova said crossly, 'the black's fading and going a bit purple, that's all.' She picked up both lots of flowers and chocolates and took them into the kitchen.

'Like the new uniform,' Matt called after her.

Clova came back and put her hands on her hips, 'It's not a uniform, it's coincidence, apart from the scarves, and that's just for today.'

'Thanks for everything you did, Matt, you worked so hard. The shop looks great.' Gemma told him.

'My pleasure, and you paid me for it, after all.'

'I think you went above and beyond what we paid you, we really appreciated all your help.'

Matt shrugged it off, pleased but slightly embarrassed. He ordered a roll and a coffee which Clova prepared and gave it to him with a smile.

'Careful, you smiled then. I might get the impression you like me.' Matt said with a wink.

'Of course I like you. I like all our customers,' Clova replied, disappearing into the kitchen before he could see her blush, peeping round the door until she felt it was safe to come back out.

'Rug?' Gemma said.

Clova looked at her blankly, while Betty said they couldn't have rugs in the shop, it would be a trip hazard.

'Matt's nickname.'

Clova groaned and Gemma, struck by Betty's comment said, 'Trip Hazard. It sounds like a name; you could call him Trip.'

Clova shook her head. 'Your lateral thinking has gone way past me, and Matt would just think I'm an idiot.'

'Why are you so coy around him now? You were so confident before.'

'I don't know, since we went to the gym I feel like a schoolgirl with a crush. He's so good looking, I get butterflies as soon as I see him. Why is he still flirting with me, he can't seem to help himself.' Clova hadn't told Gemma about Matt saying he was too old for her. Gemma held her tongue dying to say that she virtually was a schoolgirl, having only left this year. Clova read her mind and said she hadn't been at school; she'd been at college.

'Okay,' Gemma said, holding her hands up, 'I'll drop the subject.' A few more customers came in including the new manager of Tollys who wanted to introduce himself and said he hoped that they would have a good relationship as the traders all seemed a friendly lot and if they needed anything not to hesitate to ask. He had brought a big box of biscuits which he said, might go down a treat with their tea break.

'Like taking coals to Newcastle,' Betty commented after he'd gone.

'What does that mean?' Gemma asked.

'It means I'm getting old and the youth of today doesn't understand me. I expected Clova to say that, not you. Oh look, David and John are here, Clova love, take the biscuits out the back and stick the kettle on. Then I'll make the drinks.'

David was holding a big bouquet of flowers and a card which he presented to Gemma, then leant across to kiss Betty on the cheek.

'I hope you're not over- doing it,' he said fondly. Then to Gemma, we can't even try to tease her, because she says we're mocking her affliction.'

'Plus, she's had an upgrade on her hearing aids, spoiling all our fun.' John added.

'Thank you for the flowers and for all you did for us, we should be buying you flowers,' Gemma told him, grateful but wondering where they were going to put them all as the back room was starting to resemble a florists.

'Nonsense. Anyone would have done the same and we've made new friends out of adversity.' David said, asking for 3 boxes of an assortment of cakes and savouries and inviting Betty back for tea. Sindy came in with Harley and Chilli to see how it was doing, before she met Bee for their walk.

Clova groaned, 'We've had no dramas up until now,' narrowing her eyes at Harley, who pounced on something that had been dropped on the floor, swallowing before it could be identified.

'Clova, I thought you were a changed woman regarding dogs?'

'No comment.'

'Come on, Sparkle,' they heard from outside.

'Bee's here. What is that in your hair? Is that why she's calling you Sparkle? I can give you some colouring tips if you want.'

Sindy rolled her eyes and glared at Gemma. Naturally, it was her fault, and she was sure she'd heard a snicker coming from her direction.

Dragging Harley away, Chilli walking sedately next to him, she took them out of the shop as Bee poked her head in and waved.

Gabriel came in as Sindy left, bringing a bottle of wine. 'To wish you luck,' he said.

Gemma gave it to Clova to put in the kitchen, thanking Gabriel and saying how nice people were. Gabriel was looking relaxed and more like his old self, he was taking a couple of weeks off from his evening job and mentioned that he and Toni had split up.

'Sorry to hear that, if you are,' Gemma said, trying to be diplomatic.

'I'm okay, I began to feel there were more cons than pros in our relationship, once I'd taken off my rose-tinted glasses, as my mum used to say. By the way, Clova, take a look at Kents Cavern website there are a few good events coming up in the caves and they mention some guided nature walks around the area. I know you like walking. Bye all, I'll let you know when I start baking again, if you're still interested, Gemma.'

The stream of customers became a trickle as their working day drew to a close. They'd had more gifts from kind people and Gemma told Betty and Clova to help themselves.

'I'll drop you home, Betty, you can't carry much with one arm in plaster.' Gemma offered, as she locked up. Thanking her staff for their hard work on their first day back.

22

Bee and Poodie drove to their favourite area to explore more of the paths and fields near The Pheasant Walk. There were so many different routes leading to other fields and woodland they were like a couple of excited kids.

'All the time we've lived in this area, and we've never explored here before, all the times we've said, 'I wonder where that goes and now we're finally checking them out.' Bee said.

She was wearing her new trainers, blue shorts and a pretty orange blouse with interlaced ribbons in place of buttons. Poodie was wearing jeans and a black tee shirt. He was striding ahead, giving Bee the chance to appreciate the fit of his jeans and the way his top accentuated his muscles, she belatedly realised that he had asked her a question and had to ask him to repeat it.

'Let's call this walk The Secret Garden.'

Naturally, the new walk began with a stile that had to be, in Bee's case, scrambled over with difficulty, which then led them up a steep narrow path, tall ferns grew on both sides and on the right, there was an orchard. Even narrower grassy paths criss-crossed the main track and Poodie led them along one of these.

Still climbing they reached a wall with a very narrow opening. Bee said she thought it was called a kissing gate.

'Don't think so, love, this is a dry-stone wall with a narrow gap so that livestock can't get through.'

'But that's what a Kissing Gate is.'

'They're not normally stone. We could try though.'

They attempted to squeeze through sideways but there was barely room for one person to inch their way through, let alone two. They decided to stop and have a smooch anyway.

'Your jeans are tight,' Bee observed, running her hands over his bottom in appreciation. Sometimes she liked to walk beside him with one hand in the rear pocket of his jeans but there was no chance of that today, he'd managed to squeeze his phone into one pocket but that was about it.

'Your top's loose.'

Bee glanced down at her top, 'no, it's not.'

Poodie deftly undid the ribbon, leaving most of the blouse open, 'it is now,' he smirked.

Bee smacked his hand away and did up the tie. 'Firstly, someone might walk past and catch us, secondly I'm not doing anything in a patch of ferns with three dogs looking on.'

'Spoilsport, you should be more daring,' Poodie said, his eyes twinkling. 'Our garden is very private. Not over-looked. It's nice making love outside. What do you think?'

Bee gave him a quizzical look. 'You said, our garden. You mean your garden.'

'Did I say that? You're there so much lately, you must have

brainwashed me. Are you sure you're not a cuckoo?'

'Very funny. Seriously, I have been staying there a lot. Is it too much?'

Poodie nuzzled her hair, 'of course not, I love having you there, in fact I was thinking...'

He paused, glancing at the sky and whispered, 'look, there's a kestrel. You can tell it's a kestrel because it's motionless in the sky. Beautiful, isn't it?'

They watched the raptor for a few minutes then catching her hand, Poodie pulled her into the next field, and they climbed higher and higher, trying various little paths, some made by animals. They stopped to give the dogs a drink before attempting to re-trace their steps. After twenty minutes Poodie tried to access the Sat Nav on his phone but couldn't get a signal.

'You can never get a signal here, it must drive the locals mad,' Poodie said, adding jokingly, 'Ask the next person you see, how to get back to the lane.' They hadn't seen a soul all afternoon. 'We should have stopped to muck about when I suggested it; I can guarantee walkers would have appeared just as it might have got interesting.'

'We're lost,' Bee said, stating the obvious, and ignoring the smut talk, 'you can download an app. that shows all the trails in the area, that might help, if we had a signal, which we don't, damn it and we've got no supplies, I gave the dogs all our water.'

'We're in Torquay, not in the Sahara desert, I think we'll live. We're like that tribe of Pygmies that live in the long grass … what are they called?'

Bee hit him.

'and every now and then one of them jumps up, sticks his head above the grass and calls out…'

'Don't say it! It's the oldest joke in the world.'

'I remember, the Wherethefuckarwi tribe.' Poodie chuckled, then catching sight of Bee's worried expression, 'don't be daft, this is an adventure, we're not lost, we just don't know exactly where we are, but we'll eventually get back to the road, we just need to start walking downhill.'

' Isn't that the meaning of the word lost? Also, didn't I suggest walking down the left path, not climbing and wending our way into the back of beyond. You must have been a mountain climber in a past life, you pick the steepest, hardest route and expect it to be a pleasant walk.

You'd think the dogs would lead us back.' Bee moaned.

'Ah but they don't know we're ready to head back. They just think they're having an extra-long outing. It *is* a pleasant walk and at least you're wearing decent footwear; this walk is breaking them in nicely.' Ouch, Bee thought, her feet hurt, and she had some blisters forming. Breaking them in nicely indeed, she couldn't wait to get home, take them off and put them in a dark cupboard behind her 6 pairs of trusty plastic clogs.

The path they were on, abruptly ended at a gate into another field, this one had cows in. Copper squeezed through the bottom slat of the wooden gate, headed for the nearest cowpat and rolled, in absolute bliss.

'Copper, come here!' Poodie looked at his usually obedient dog in horror, calling her again and again.

'Copper, biscuit,' Bee hissed, one eye on the cows still thankfully at the top end of the field, 'get here, now.'

Copper finished her roll leisurely and trotted back, wriggled under the gate and jumped up at Bee for her promised biscuit. Mac and Blue sniffed her approvingly.

Poodie glared at all of them.

'Don't be glaring at me,' Bee told him, seeing that he just couldn't wait to pin the blame on her, 'Copper is your dog. Your perfect, obedient, well-trained dog. You picked this route, I wanted to go down that left trail, I'm not going to be the one giving her a bath and … and you can both walk home.' She turned her back on him and looked at the vast expanse of bracken, ferns, trees and little paths, breathing deeply through her nose.

Poodie could almost see the steam.

'Appropriate noise, my little Taurean, puffing like a little bull, and may I point out that we came in *my* van, of which I have the keys.'

'Semantics,' Bee muttered but her mouth twitched as she tried to hide a smile, turning to him she said 'it seems to have escaped your memory that I have your keys as you couldn't squeeze them into your tight arse jeans along with your phone. Now can we try the way I suggested, half an hour ago?'

Bee started walking to be quickly overtaken by Poodie. She had observed that on walks where the path allowed for only one person at a time, there was a pack order, whether she was with her boyfriend or Sindy, she always brought up the rear, even her own little dog pushed past her to be in front. Eventually Poodie rounded a corner and called out that they were back at the original stile.

'Told you, I knew where I was going.' He said, triumphantly. Bee shook her head, giving another deep sigh but for once, gave up the argument, she was too relieved. Poodie stopped and gazed at her.

'What?'

'I've just realised something I love about you, you never sulk, you snap out of a mood really quickly, even if we have an argument you don't hold on to your anger once the row is over. It's very refreshing, don't think I've ever had that in a relationship before.'

'I like to be unique, and it was hardly a row.' Bee said lightly, although she was very touched, adding
'My family always used to say don't go to sleep on an argument.' Poodie held her gaze for another minute, then nuzzled her hair, breathing her scent in.

'I like these little explorations, this is a good walk, away from the crowds, we'll definitely come here again.' Poodie said, as they put the dogs on their leads, 'and the dogs had a great time. I love seeing them enjoying themselves. When we get in, I'll bath Copper if you'll cook the tea. After which, we'll stroll around the garden...'

'Stroll round the garden? We've just done a marathon walk.' Bee interrupted; eyebrows raised.

...'and I'll show you my appreciation.' Poodie winked.

'I hope that's not all you're going to show me,' Bee quipped, 'mind you, I need to go to my own house sometime this week, clothes to pick up, chores to do.'

Poodie gave her a brooding look, 'We should be thinking about taking our relationship to the next level. I was going to have a chat with you about it.'

Bee's eyebrows went up, 'Have a chat? Oh, very romantic. We're so good at the moment I don't want to spoil things. Let's see how things go.'

'You should at least bring some more stuff to leave at mine, you're there more than in your own house.' Poodie told her, not for the first time, when she didn't answer, adding

'I'll drop you home in the morning on my way to work.'

They finally reached the van, gave Copper a pre-bath, towel down and headed back to Poodie's cottage, van windows open and trying to breathe through their mouths. Arriving at Poodie s they saw Clova waiting by his gate.

'Ant dropped me off, you've just missed him,' she told her uncle. 'I wanted to ask if I could take Blue out?'

Bee sighed inwardly, her anticipation of a fun evening disappearing rapidly, looking at Poodie, she could tell by his face that he was disappointed too and wondered if it would be rude if she suggested that Poodie run Clova straight back home.

'Not this evening, Coop,' he said, 'he's just had a long walk.'

Bee wanted to know why Poodie was calling her Coop.

'It's her surname, Cooper-Dent. How about taking him out Sunday?'

Clova looked a little downcast but agreed. Giving Blue a pat after he greeted her happily on his way to his water bowl.

'Next time, ring first, it would have saved you a trip.'

'I tried but it went straight to answerphone.'

'Oh yes, we couldn't get a signal where we were. Would you like to stay for tea?' Bee offered, her innate politeness taking over and noticing she looked a bit down.

Clova cheered up, chatting away, she followed them into the cottage, asking what the smell was and offering to help Bee with the dinner.

Poodie muttered out of the corner of his mouth, 'should have taken advantage of me when you had the chance, hon.'

Bee ignored him, turning to reply to Clova, 'it's your uncle, he's filthy, I keep telling him to shower more.'

23

'Time goes so much faster when you get older,' Betty moaned, 'unless you have an injury or you're ill then it seems to take twice as long to recover.'

'We can manage,' Gemma told her, 'if you want to go home.' Betty looked horrified, 'and what would I do at home? Sit there feeling sorry for myself. I'm a lot better, I just had a bad night. I was too hot, and it made my arm sore under the plaster. I'll make a drink then Clova can help me bring them out.'

Gemma and Clova exchanged glances. Betty was not one to complain so she must have been feeling a bit under the weather. Once they had their drinks, Gemma made Betty sit on the stool behind the counter, which she agreed to, reluctantly.

'What's our special this week?' She asked, sitting on the stool and trying not to scratch at her wrist.

'Hummingbird cake.' Gemma told her with a smile. Betty was horrified, 'my hearing's been so much better since I got my new hearing aids, but they must be failing already, what a waste of money...'

Gemma interrupted her, telling her that she had heard correctly the first time. Jack had surpassed himself and had been enjoying the challenge of the Saturday Specials, taking a picture of his creations and posting them on social media. He and Sins were gaining a good reputation and Gemma was a bit worried that someone would try to poach Jack from them.

'He wouldn't go,' Clova said, 'he doesn't want more work at his age, you told me he was happy doing the amount he was doing. I think we're safe from rivals getting their dirty paws on him.'

Betty was still thinking about the Special.

'Is it like 4 and twenty blackbirds? Are you trying to do a nursery rhyme theme?'

'No Betty,' Gemma laughed, nearly choking on her coffee.

'Is it a savoury cake then? Chicken pretending to be an exotic bird?'

Gemma snorted with laughter, 'that's just its' name. It's a cake containing passionfruit, banana, pineapple and pecan. That's pecan Betty, not pelican or any other feathered creature.'

'Making my mouth water,' Clova said, licking her lips, 'it looks gorgeous. I hope there's some left at closing time.'
The shop started to get busy then. Gemma and Clova rushing to serve customers before Betty could get to them in the vain hope that they could get her to take it easy.

A small group of tourists came in on their way back from visiting the caves. The first couple homing in on the Saturday special and asking for two slices.

'I can't believe you're selling that.' The woman exclaimed excitedly, 'it was created in my country. It's Jamaican.'

'So I believe,' Gemma said, putting two slices carefully into a box. 'I hope it's as good as you would get at home.'

After the tourists had gone, Betty said that it was like English people going to Spain and only wanting fish and chips.

'Not quite, Betty but I get your point, we're going to sell out quite quickly I think. Oh good, Christine's coming, just in time.'

Christine looked in the window, did a double take and hurried in.

'Brilliant,' she said, practically rubbing her hands with glee, 'I absolutely cannot wait to tell Geoff. His brother and wife are popping in this afternoon and Bob is nearly as bad as Geoff, so I'll take four slices.'

Clova went into the back room and took the second Hummingbird cake out of the fridge, bringing it back into the shop she noticed Matt walk past with Toni.

'He didn't even glance in,' Clova fumed once the shop was clear of customers, 'what's he even doing with her? If that's his taste, good luck to him, she'll lead him a merry dance and make his life hell. If he starts dating her, that would kill my crush stone dead. He better not come in here and flirt and call me Blackberry or Blueberry.'

'Are berries going to be the flavours of the next Special?' Betty put in.

Clova ignored her, intent on her subject. 'Bastard. They're not suited at all. Can't see her doing anything physical with him.'

Gemma raised an eyebrow.

'I mean sporty. Ugh. Rotten pig.'

'Who's a pig?'

'Men. All of them.'

Gemma laughed, 'Don't jump to conclusions. They may have been walking up the road at the same time, after all, they both work in this street. It's probably a coincidence.'

'Hm,' Clova said, slightly mollified, 'I hate these feelings Gem, it's not me, how do I make it stop?'

'You can't, love,' Betty put in, eventually getting the hang of the conversation. 'Go and put the kettle on and I'll make us a nice drink in a minute. Keep busy and try not to think too much. Oh, the boys are coming.' She got off her stool quickly, explaining that they would only fuss if they saw her sitting down, thinking she was overdoing it. David and John came in, exclaimed with delight over the Hummingbird cake, bought the whole one that Clova had just placed under the counter and told Betty they were having a small garden party and would pick her up from work, providing, they said, that she would sit in the garden under a parasol and not keep trying to help.

'Fat chance of that,' Clova muttered, coming back out after washing their mugs ready for their next brew. She went over to the white board that she had purchased where she had listed all their Saturday Specials and gave the Hummingbird cake five stars.

'That will be brilliant to look back on,' Gemma enthused, and we'll know which cakes to make again. Your handwriting's lovely Clova, it's an under-rated skill, calligraphy.'

'Hardly calligraphy, Gem, I'm just neat.'

Gemma gave a slight shake of her head and wondered how they'd managed before Clova, and starting to dread the day she decided what career she wanted to pursue.

Mark and Kay came in on their way back from Tollys just as the phone rang. Mark leapt to answer it before Gemma could move.

His eyebrows started to creep higher and higher as he listened.

'What do you want exactly?'

The caller repeated himself.

'I think you've got the wrong number.'

Gemma widened her eyes at him gesturing for him to give her the phone, as he shook his head.

'This is a bakery … no I think you want the chemists up the road … hang on, I'll ask, Mark put the phone on mute and asked Gemma if she had the phone number for the local chemists, Clova googled it as Mark was talking and pointed her phone at him. He took the phone off mute and told the elderly gentleman the number. Putting the phone down, he bent over double laughing and gasping.

'Best yet!' he said finally, 'better than a dirty phone call. It was a wrong number, he thought he was speaking to the pharmacist. That's made my day.'

'Spit it out, Mark what did he say?'

'He wanted some cream to rub on his genitals as they were very sore and chafing. I can't believe he rang here. Betty, you would have given him some clotted cream and told him to go for it.'

'I'm not that daft.' Betty said but she had a twinkle in her eye.

'Do you want anything? Or have you just come in to show us all the baked goods you've just bought from Tollys.'

'That's a low blow, Gem, just when I've helped you out with yet another strange request. We came in to say hi, as we were passing.' Mark said, pretending to look hurt.

'As we're here, let's have 2 slices of that Hummingbird cake. I'm sure we had something similar when we were in Barbados.' Kay said, pushing her glasses up to sit on the bridge of her nose.

'Remember, Mark? We can sit in the garden, pretend we're on holiday and enjoy them with a nice glass of vino.'

'I might play some Caribbean music on my 12 string, if you play your cards right. You can put on that short skirt with the frills that you love, and dance.' Mark said with a wink.

Kay looked at Gemma and rolled her eyes, 'that **you** love. What have I started?'

Gemma handed her the cake box with a smile as she said goodbye.

'Only two slices left,' Clova said, groaning, they'll be gone by the time we close.

Gemma snatched them out of the window, put them in separate boxes and told Clova they were for the two of them. Betty would get a piece at the garden party.

'Now she can console herself with a piece of cake, like the rest of us do, when someone we fancy lets us down.' Gemma said to Betty as Clova took them out the back.

24.

Bee had the day off and she was dying to show Sindy The Secret Garden walk before she forgot it, they were always on the lookout for new walks for the dogs away from the tourists due to Harley's obsession with food and his love of pinching off picnickers and Chilli's nervousness around children and habit of growling at joggers. Walks could be stressful watching out for potential trouble, even Mac was badly behaved and chased other dogs if he didn't like the look of them, so it was nice to find somewhere quiet and let the dogs have some freedom without worrying about what they might get up to next.

Bee picked them up in her new second hand Honda Jazz. The day had started with fog and misty fine rain but had started to brighten up and it promised to be a nice afternoon for a stroll in the countryside. Poodie had taken Copper to work, as was his habit and they managed to squeeze the other four dogs into the back of Bee's new car, strapped in to keep them safe, glancing over her shoulder into the back seat, Sindy said she thought they looked like the stars of a Disney film, each dog a different size and colour but with identical half open mouths, smiling in anticipation of their walk.

'Nice car,' Sindy said, seeing it for the first time.

'I bought it on impulse. It was that day you and Gem had invited me to go to Newton Abbot then blew me out at the last minute, which meant I had a morning free, so I popped into that car dealership just to look. You cost me eight grand.'

'We didn't blow you out, we had a domestic emergency, and you needed a new car, your old one was falling to pieces. Nobody made you go out and spend that much. By the way, from a distance your number plate looks like it reads, 'Oh Shit' which is appropriate as the car is an unusual shade of dog poo brown.'

'Charming and for your information, the cars' colour is more sparkling bronze than brown, at least when the sun shines on it.' Sindy raised one eyebrow but declined to argue.

'How are you finding it?'

'I love it but it's the newest car I've ever owned, it's got so many knobs, switches and buttons. I don't know what half of them do and you need a master's degree to understand the manual. It nags all the time, tells me if I'm in the wrong gear ...'

'Which is most of the time,' Sindy interrupted.

'beeps if I don't shut the door fast enough, beeps if I don't put my seatbelt on, makes high pitched squeals if I open my door before removing the keys, makes a funny noise if I don't turn the lights off immediately. Honestly, it's like a very high maintenance boyfriend. Never mind the car, I've got loads to tell you,' Bee said excitedly.

'You're so weird, anyway, save it till we're on the walk,' Sindy said, as she always did, presumably in case they ran out of things to say, which hadn't happened yet, but you never knew. Instead, they discussed work and the weather until they reached a parking spot along the lane near to their destination. The dogs deafened them as soon as the car stopped, barking and howling with excitement until they got out of the car.

Pulling their owners frantically up a gravel path until it was safe for them to be let off their leads.

'Thank Heavens Blue doesn't pull; I'd never hold him.' Bee said gratefully.

'Are you going to re-home him with Clova?' Sindy asked, bending down to unhook their leads.

'I'm coming round to the idea, He's the type of dog that people refer to as 'a one-man dog'. I think he'd prefer to be the only dog in the house with his own special human, of course we don't know if Clova could have him or even if she would want to.'

Sindy scratched her head irritably, little midges already circling her. They never seemed to bother Bee, or if they did, she didn't notice.

'It's hard to believe Clova is the same girl who hated our dogs, she's had a complete turnaround. I hope these flies aren't going to be following me for the whole of this walk.'

'Wear a cap. I think Clova is only fond of Blue, she's not keen on the rest of the pack but she'll come round. Before I had dogs I said I would never be the type of person that spoke to their dogs like they understood every word and hearing people say 'come to Mummy' used to wind me up. I said I'd never do that. My first week as a dog owner I heard myself saying to Jess, who wouldn't come when called, 'hurry up, mummy's got to go shopping'. I made myself cringe but of course, I've done it ever since. It's as if you get possessed by a new dog owner persona.'

Sindy laughed and agreed. She would say to Chilli, 'where's Auntie Bee' and Chilli would run over to Bee and leap into her arms. They were all as daft as each other when it came to their animals. Bee, who had an overactive imagination and read a lot of Science Fiction, speculated that perhaps there was a secret element in a dogs saliva so that when they licked you, something got into your blood stream and created a symbiotic relationship. Sindy gave her a sideways glance and screwed up her mouth, finally deciding that the comment 'you nutter' was sufficient to convey her feelings about the subject.

They had reached the lower stile and Bee was pointing out the Secret Garden to Sindy just as another dog walker with a large dalmatian came along from the opposite direction. The woman, overhearing, said, 'it's not a garden, it's an orchard.'

Bee was about to say, I know, as the woman continued, 'I wouldn't go in there at this time of year, it's been raining, now it's warming up and the adders will come out. There are loads of them in the bracken. If your dog got bitten, you'd need to get it to the vet within 30 minutes, otherwise it would die.'

Bee and Sindy looked as horrified as they felt. Sindy asked if there was another route they could take, and the woman pointed up the path, telling them to go to the top, turn right, keep going until they crossed a little road, then they would find themselves at the lakes. It was a circular walk that would take about 15 minutes. They thanked her, taking her advice. Once she was out of sight, Bee said, 'loads of adders, oh my God, Poodie and I nearly had sex in the ferns last time we were here.'

'You tart.' Was the response.

'No, I'm not, as we didn't.'

'You just said 'nearly'. T.M.I and get a room … you tart.'

Bee ignored her, thinking about what the dog walker had said. '30 minutes to get to the vet. We'd never do it. It would take 20 just to get back to the car. What an awful thought.'

Sindy nodded.

'We won't be able to do the Secret Garden walk until the autumn and I think we should re-name it 'Garden of Eden walk', as it was full of temptation, has an orchard and at least one serpent.'

'Very good,' Bee said, having to give her credit for her quick thinking. Sindy was marching ahead, the path still climbing, fields on either side. The pack had arranged themselves in their natural order, Bee puffing a bit, bringing up the rear.

'Let me know if it flattens out,' she called to Sindy, who had reached the top and gone round a corner.

'Nope, still climbing. Now do we take the left or the right path?'

They picked a route and carried on climbing. The dogs were loving it, stopping and sniffing and trying to get into the fields, which were fenced off fairly securely. The path was still recognisably a path, although it had some big tree roots in places, which had to be clambered over.

After 40 minutes, Bee said, 'either that woman was a very fast walker, or we've gone wrong. We haven't come across a road. We're lost.'

They came to another split in the path and picked the one that seemed to be going slightly downhill. They were surrounded by trees and fields but in the distance they could see a roof and speculated that it might be somewhere in the village.

'I'm sure we're going in the right direction; I think I know where this will come out. Behind the church, where there is that really high stile that you can't get over.' Sindy said, looking at her short friend.

'Oh great. Well, we can't go back, we'd get even more lost. I'll have to get over the stile. Why are they obsessed with stiles here? What's wrong with a good old-fashioned gate that you can open and just walk through. It's a good walk though, if we ever get back to civilisation, what shall we call it?'

The walk had taken them an hour so far. Sindy suggested sarcastically that they call it 'The 15-minute Walk.'

Bee laughed and agreed then said she could hear voices, so they were on the right track.

Relaxing a little, pretty sure they knew roughly where they were, Sindy asked her what she was going to tell her. Bee tripped on a tree root, grabbing Sindy's arm to save herself, then said

'Oh yes, you'll never believe it, Poodie asked me to move in with him.'

'What, sell your place?'

'Well, yes, no point having two houses and I'm at his more than at mine lately, but I haven't said yes yet. It's a huge step and I'm a bit worried about the age gap and the fact that I'm punching above my weight. He's always getting women coming on to him. Seriously. People sometimes ask him if I'm his sister, they obviously can't imagine that he'd be in a relationship with me.' She added as Sindy rolled her eyes.

'He says he hardly notices. He can be at the bar waiting for the drinks and will get chatted up by some attractive younger woman, one day the temptation might be too great.'

Sindy tutted, 'I thought you'd got all that insecurity out of your system last year. He loves you, it's obvious by the way he looks at you. If he wanted to still date other women, he wouldn't have asked you to move in with him.'

I know and I do trust him, I just worry about the future. The age gap isn't going to get any smaller and I might not age well. What if I look old and wrinkly in a year or so?'

'Well you do turn forty next year so it's quite possible.' Sindy said, rolling her eyes.

'Don't worry. Poodie works outside, he'll soon start to look weather beaten. Before you know it, people will think you're the same age.'

Sindy lied.

Bee relaxed, clambering over another couple of tree roots and holding on to a branch for support. She looked at her friend, raising her eyebrows, 'Do you think? It's nice that Mum likes him, so I think she'd approve but she might be wary about me selling the house.

We've been seeing each other for about the same length of time as he and Dawn were together, and you've seen her, you know what she looks like. He got bored.'

'She's shallow, I'm not surprised he got bored, was he even in love with her? Besides, you're eccentric, he won't get bored.'

Bee managed to insert a sarcastic 'cheers' as Sindy carried on.

'To be honest, the thought of boredom shouldn't even enter a persons' head regarding relationships. Everyone goes through periods of routine and it's a comfortable feeling to understand your partner so well that you sometimes finish their sentences and know without a doubt, how they are going to react in any given situation.

Most people don't want excitement and spontaneity every day. It would get tiring.

Your relationship survived him working away for those six months, when he was in the Isles of Scilly and please don't say. 'I don't know what he sees in me', I had enough of that last year. Just go for it. Rosa will be so jealous, not of Poodie but she really covets his cottage.'

Bee chuckled, 'I know, it's small but perfectly formed.'

'again, T.M.I.'

'Do you mind? The cottage of course. Poodie's got big feet which tells you everything you need to know.'

'Tart.' Sindy said again.

The trees were thick and overhanging the path on both sides, letting no sunlight in. They were walking down a steep slope and had to watch their footing on loose stones, branches and tree roots but eventually they came to the stile, Sindy laughing at her friend who took about four tries before she managed to get over it. Sindy heroically not recording the event on her phone, even though she was sorely tempted.

'Yay, we know where we are,' Bee declared.

They reached the car and gave the dogs a drink, then settled them down on the back seat.

Sindy got in the front seat and put on her seatbelt, glancing over her shoulder at the dogs. 'They'll sleep the rest of the day after that walk. So, what are you going to do about Poodie's offer?'

'I'll let you know when I've thought it through. Now let's get home. Shall I come back and help you finish off that wine I know you've got in the fridge? You can water mine down with soda.'

'Oh, can I now, how kind of you.'

25

Clova and Betty arrived at Sins just after Gemma got there. She was saying goodbye to her partner and the two dogs, handing Sindy poo bags and dog biscuits.

'Bye Sparkle,' Betty called out.

Gemma could see Sindy hunch her shoulders and hurry off without looking back and chuckled to herself.

'Is she still changing her name?' Betty asked, as they went into the back room to get ready.

'No Betty, she's going to keep the name Sindy.'

'Oh good, because it would have got very confusing, never been around so few people with so many names between them. Clova's young man calls her a different name every time he come in. Your friend Bee calls her partner all sorts and he's got a strange enough name to begin with.' Betty paused for breath as Clova muttered Matt wasn't her young man as she watched Betty put an apron on over her head then trying to tie a scarf around her hair with one hand, moaning to Clova that she'd given up wearing bras as she couldn't get them on very easily. Clova tied her scarf for her then did her own. She told Betty she would come round any time and help with anything at all.

'Thanks, my lover, might take you up on that but I've got my friend Iris, who pops in most days, she helped me have a bath. I was worried I might slip.'

Gemma put the kettle on and went into the shop to open up, leaving the other two to make the drinks. They brought them out, still chatting. Betty was seeing a lot of her new friends, David and John and went to their home several times a week to be waited on hand and foot.

'They are playing classical music for me now and I haven't the heart to tell them it's a bit too high brow for me, I'd rather have a bit of Adele. They're taking it as a challenge to find a composer that I'll love, quite liked those planet ones by, um...'

'Holst.'

'Clova, wow.'

'I'm not a complete Philistine, Gem. We've got very eclectic tastes regarding music in our house. Dad listens to some of the lighter classical composers. I like Holst.'

Gemma finished putting all the cakes out and slicing up some of the Saturday Special for people to sample. This week it was Lemon and Rosemary cupcakes.

'Bee tells me you're taking the hound of the Baskervilles out tomorrow.'

Clova narrowed her eyes, 'Okay, now you're doing it on purpose to test me. I'm guessing that's a character in a film probably something to do with wild beasts eating people in the wilderness?'

Gemma tried to force her curly chestnut hair back under her scarf where it had been trying to escape for the last five minutes.

'There are books out there, Clova, that preceded the film adaptations but that'll teach me to try to be clever. I haven't seen or read it. I know it's a Sherlock Holmes book, but I only know the title. I always imagined giant wolf like beasts that attacked and killed anyone who was on the moors after dark. Think it was set on Dartmoor but could've been Bodmin Moor.'

'Wuthering Heights?' Betty put in.

'Different book, different author, but also set on a moor. Yorkshire moors I think.'

'Bloomin eck Gem, how many books do you know that are set on moors? Anyway, Blue is not a hound of the Baskervilles, he's a good dog, he wouldn't even pinch food,' here Clova gave Gemma a sly look, 'and he's not even one year old yet.'

'Bloomin eck? Girls your age don't say that. Where did you get that from, your gran? All right, all right, saved by the bell,' Gemma said, after a raised eyebrow from Clova as the shop door opened with a little ding, and she greeted the first customer of the day. Clova went out and hooked the door open to save Betty trying to do it one handed.

Betty served Not Three Bad, who asked for his regular dainty cupcakes but took one of the specials to try as well.

Gemma nudged Clova, pointing out one of the lads working on the shop refit, pretending to look at the cakes in the window.

'Bet he's plucking up courage to ask you out.'

'Oh no,' Clova had a pained expression on her face, 'what shall I say?'

'Yes?'

'No. I don't fancy him, look, he's coming in, you serve him.' Clova pushed herself behind Gemma and pretended to tidy things on the back shelf.

'What can I get for you,' Gemma asked, smiling at the lad, who looked about 10 but was probably the same age as her assistant.

'pizza slice please want to go for a drink?' He said in one breath, directing the comment to the back of Clova's head.

Clova turned round, 'sorry, no thanks but thank you for asking.'

'what about going to see a film?'

'Um, no thanks.' Clova handed him his slice and took his money, trying to keep a smile on her face.

'a meal?'

'no thanks.'

After he'd gone Betty said, 'he may look like a young teenager, but you've got to admit, he's got man sized balls. I bet he'll come back with a new suggestion.'

Gemma gave Betty a surprised look.

'I mean for a date.'

'Betty! You've finally shocked me, you said balls,' their boss said, her eyebrows nearly touching her headscarf.

'I have had a life, Gemma. I know more about men than you do.

Sometimes you sound quite old fashioned.'

'You said balls.' Gemma said.

Clova laughed at them both and told them that he'd been in her class at school, he was 19. She felt mean and didn't want to hurt his feelings, but she didn't fancy him.

More customers began coming in, ending the chat and they were kept busy, selling a lot of drinks as well as pastries.

Gemma was still trying to tuck her hair into her scarf, moaning about it, in-between customers, saying it grew faster than anyone else's and that she needed at least ten more hairgrips to keep it in place.

'I've got a phobia about a customer finding one of my hairs on their cake.' She muttered, thinking privately that as her hair was curly and wiry it might look like a pube. Groaning again, just at the thought.

Clova gave her a wry smile and told her she was paranoid.

Christine arrived and asked for 2 of the lemon and rosemary cupcakes and 2 vegan banana cakes, hoping that one or both would annoy her husband, as he thought the only fruit in cakes should be sultanas and had started asking why Sins didn't sell normal cakes like doughnuts or iced buns and what was the world coming to? She had made it worse the week before by buying some colourful feathers and placing them around the Hummingbird cake, making her sister-in-law roar with laughter, Geoff and Bob frowning had made the situation even more funny.

Gemma told her that they did sell 'normal cakes' if she would like to please her husband.

'I know you do, my lover but can't have him knowing that, can we? Don't want to spoil all my entertainment. I've told him this is a Specialist bakery, not your usual run of the mill.'

They laughed. Betty fiddled with her hearing aids, saying that while she enjoyed hearing most of what their customers were saying, it wasn't as much fun.'

'Don't worry Betty, I'm sure your batteries will lose power eventually.'

'What?'

'Yes, very funny.' Clova had nearly repeated herself but stopped just in time.

'You youngsters do mumble though and talk too quickly. We're nearly out of milk should we get some more for the last couple of hours?'

Gemma took some money from the till and asked Clova to go to the corner shop, making a note to order more for the following Saturday. Clova strolled up the road enjoying the sunshine, outside Tollys she could see Toni, wearing a very short white skirt and an almost transparent yellow blouse, she was twirling her blonde hair as she chatted to a man, in a very flirtatious manner, as Clova reached the couple she saw with a shock, that it was her Uncle Poodie. He hadn't seen her, so she stayed back slightly, pretending to look in the newsagent's window. Toni was asking if Poodie was going to The Eight

Bells that evening, adding that she was and giggling in what she must have thought, was a cute girlie fashion.

'I've split up with Gabriel,' she informed him, 'he was such a drag, always working. I bet you enjoy a good night out.'

Poodie smiled but didn't reply.

Toni giggled again, putting a curl of her fair hair into her mouth, then asked him if he was single.

Poodie told her that he had a girlfriend.

'not that woman I've seen you with before, I thought she was an older relative.' Toni giggled again then spotted Clova unabashedly eavesdropping.

'Yes?' Toni's voice turned glacial.

'Hello Uncle Poodie, how's Bee?'

'Hi Coop, shouldn't you be at work? Bee is fine, I'm just picking up some groceries before I head home, I lost a bet, so I've got to cook us a full English breakfast and then... um, well never mind, you don't need to know the details.' He said a polite excuse me to Toni, and went into Tollys, Clova following at his heels, Toni glaring at their backs. Clova grabbed a basket, threw 2 litres of milk into it and asked him what he was playing at?

'Just being polite, it's nothing new, some women aren't backward in coming forward and good for them. I'm not interested but I don't have to be rude about it.'

'She's desperate to get her claws into any man. I've seen her in action.'

'Charming.' Poodie said, looking taken aback at the vehemence in his niece's tone.

'She's toxic, that's all and I like Bee.'

Poodie ran his fingers through his dark hair, wondering if it was time to pop into the barbers up the road. Then put a companiable arm around Clova, who still had a face like thunder.

'Clo, I'm not into girlie girls like Toni, or any other women for that matter. I love Bee and we trust each other, now come and help me find the bacon and eggs and whatever else goes into a full English, and stop worrying.'

They paid at the till and Poodie walked Clova back to Sins, telling her he would drop Blue off the next day.

'Who'd have thought that woman would have such a negative impact in the short time she's been in Torquay,' Clova moaned, after recounting what she had heard, 'The good news is, she and Matt aren't dating, I heard her say she was single. I hope she stays well away from my uncle, she was practically offering it to him on a plate.'

'ooh, is someone giving free tasters up the road?' Betty said, not wanting to miss out.

'You could put it like that,' Clova said darkly, 'your batteries going already?'

'No, my lover,' Betty said, looking puzzled. 'Here comes your young man.'

Clova looked around eagerly, her face falling when she saw the lad from earlier.

'sausage roll and a coffee please.'

Clova made his drink and bagged up the sausage roll.

'I like your hair.'

'I'm changing it soon. Bye.'

'Do you want to come to the beach party with me next week?'

Clova sighed and said, 'look Ben, I'm sorry, I don't like you that way, I'd prefer to just be friends.'

Ben rolled his eyes, 'relegated to the friends' zone, okay, I get the message.' He left, looking a little dejected.

'Just as well,' Gemma said, 'you'd eat him for breakfast.'

'me?' Clova squeaked

'yes you, you need a stronger man who'll keep up with you.'

'I thought you said he had balls.'

'That was Betty.'

'A few more people came in, followed by two lads working on the shop re-fit. They were chatting about Matt. Clova served a man in front of them with half her attention on their conversation.

'He asked that pretty paramedic out after that car went through the window here. Talk about a quick worker, got her number and took her out the other night.'

'Jammy git. Yeah, Gav said she was a looker.'

Clova had finished serving her customer and had turned her back. Her eyes brimming with tears. Gemma had heard and quickly served the men, telling Clova to go into the kitchen. Once the customers had gone, she asked Betty to hold the fort and went to see how Clova was. Clova was sitting on the stool, sniffing and trying to stop her tears.

'I'm being stupid I know, it's not as if we are dating, I just didn't expect him to ask someone else out. When I said I thought he saw me as a kid, I didn't really mean it, he looks at me as if he fancies me and he's always flirting, you know he is.' she sniffled, the sobs turning into hiccuppy cries, the tears running down her cheeks. Oh God Gemma, I really liked him.'

Gemma put her arms around her, giving her a hug. 'I know you did. Try to think positive, as far as you know, it was one date, maybe it didn't go well. Bide your time, keep playing it cool, he obviously does like you, it might lead to something one day or you might meet someone else. Get out there, meet people. You're young, free and single.'

Clova tried to stop crying and put on a brave face. 'Oh no, the Saturday cliches. I can't believe I'm crying; I've never cried over a man before and you sound like Uncle Poodie. I wasn't looking for a relationship, I was quite happy with my life until I started seeing Matt everywhere I turned.

My first boyfriend lasted six months and we drifted apart. The second, became really controlling. I only dated him for about 2 months, and he started telling me who I could see and criticised my clothes, so I finished with him and just felt relieved. I didn't cry over either of them.

I barely know Matt but when I see him this wave comes over me, butterflies in my stomach, I can't stop looking at him and wishing we were together. Perhaps it's not logical but in my gut I feel we were meant to be with one another.' She gave another little sob then dabbed her eyes with a tissue.

'Sorry Gem. I'll pull myself together.' Clova took a deep breath and stood up.

'Don't be daft, I understand.' Gemma gave her another consoling hug.

'Don't say 'I was young once.' Or 'I've been there.'

'Would I.' Those were going to be her next words, instead she said,

'Cheek! How old do you think I am? Ancient to you, I suppose. Hi Betty, sorry, we're coming out now.' This said, as Betty poked her head round the door and Gemma added, 'now let's get on, it's like a soap opera in here today. I think I hear more customers coming in.'
They went back out into the shop, Gemma suggesting a few jobs to Clova, to keep her occupied. After an hour in which they had a steady stream of customers, Gemma looked at Betty, whose face was screwed up as if she was in pain.

'Betty, I think you're trying to do too much too soon. You don't look so good. How are your ribs? Do you want to go home?'
Betty was looking tired and drawn, obviously still in some discomfort and agreed to call it a day. Clova took her into the kitchen and helped her with her jacket and bag and told her to ring if she needed anything. Gemma popped one of Sindy's spiced fruit cakes into her bag as she

was leaving, and Betty said she thought she would be a lot better by next Saturday.

'It's lucky I am very active, at least I can still walk. In fact, walking is easier than trying to get on the bus one handed which is just as well, as I'm eating twice as much as I used to. The boys are trying to fatten me up as well, I think. Bless them. See you next week.'

26

Blue was dropped off at Clova's house, to the delight of both of them. Poodie telling her to ring when she was ready for him to come back and take him home.

She grabbed her keys, phone and bag and she and Blue headed out. It was a warm day, so Clova walked in the direction of one of the quieter dog friendly beaches off the beaten track, as it lost the sun by mid-afternoon, it was mainly used by locals. Clova felt the stresses and strains of everyday life start to fade away as she strolled along, enjoying the sights and sounds of nature all around her. Walking was beneficial, and animals were therapeutic, combining the two was good for both body and soul, and Clova realised how much she loved being out with a dog. Blue was happy and excited. Clova was discovering that she could read his body language and tell his feelings by looking at him. His tail was up and slightly waving, his ears were pricked, and his mouth was half open in a canine grin.

They'd walked for a couple of miles, crossing the green which was bordered on their right by woodland that was very steep and almost too difficult to negotiate, unless you found the right route. To their left, the sea road twisted and turned, a few cars using it but not many. Across the road, over the pavement a high stone wall protected the walkway and road to some extent from the sea and severe flooding in stormy weather, although the sea always came over the wall at its peak, with huge waves that threw up pebbles from the beach to the extent that a clean-up crew had to arrive in lorries after each incoming tide to sweep the road, and on stormy days, the road was often closed when bad weather combined with the tide at its peak.

The wood to their right was frequented by owls at night and buzzards during the day. Two of whom were swooping and gliding above their heads. A few brave crows were dive bombing them to no avail.

Clova and Blue crossed over the road, walking down the storm ravaged, battered, partly broken slipway which hadn't withstood the power of the waves over the last few years and wasn't likely to be repaired by the council any time soon. Just about manageable, they could get down on to the rocky beach. The tide was out so they were able to walk the length of the part shingle, part sandy beach without having to go up the steps and re-join the path next to the sea road. The high tide would flood in to fill one end of the beach first, giving the impression that there was plenty of time and beach to enjoy before the tide came in. It was sneaky, Clova had always thought, as if the beach was saying 'yay, I'm safe, come and walk on me' until the waves seemed to rush in at speed, trapping you in the middle with no dry route back, if you weren't careful. Clova's father used to quote 'trapped between a rock and a hard place' every time they heard of people being caught out by the incoming tide. Plenty of rocks, Clova used to argue but no hard place, unless you counted the sea wall at your back.

It had left plenty of unwary visitors stranded and panicking, so Clova always checked the tide times before she came out.

Reaching the far end of the beach, she stopped at the kiosk which was up the second slipway near the brightly coloured row of beach huts and bought a drink for herself, water for Blue and treated him to a doggy ice-cream, then they sat on a large flattish rock to enjoy their refreshments, listening to the waves lapping on the shore, the water moving the sand and shingle creating a pleasant shushing noise. Clova folded her top under her head and lay on the sun warmed rock, even though the sun had long gone from the beach. She could hear the staff in the kiosk starting to close up shop, sometimes they stayed open late, but they'd obviously decided to call it a day.

Clova lay there, not thinking about anything in particular, especially not Matt, while Blue sat next to her observing everything around him. Eventually Clova stood up, left the beach and chose the woodland path across the road that eventually took you up to the caves. The cavern often had special events and guided walks and she could hear something happening further along the high, very steep winding path which was also a nature trail. They followed all its' twists and turns, up steps and more steps, finally encountering a few people who had been to the cavern bar and were now sounding merry, they passed by with a friendly greeting and Clova turned right, walking on a straighter path that would take her back down nearer the town. She'd barely gone more than a few steps when she encountered more stragglers. She groaned inwardly, it was Matt and his friend Tom whom she'd met on the disastrous Dartmoor walk, with Toni and Carl behind them.

'Hi,' Matt greeted her, seeming to give her a brooding look from out of his dark eyes that she could have interpreted as desire if she was feeling fanciful, but was more like wishful thinking she told herself sternly.

'Tom, remember Clova?' Tom nodded, smiling and saying hello. Matt continued: 'Fancy bumping into you, is this your dog? I thought he belonged to one of your friends. He's a handsome boy. Can I stroke him?' Matt held out his hand for Blue to sniff, then patted him on the head.

'We've just seen Lovers Leap performing in the caves, they were amazing, weren't they, Tom?'

'Don't talk to her,' Toni called out, trying to catch them up, 'she's a troublemaker and a shit stirrer,' Carl was pulling at her sleeve trying unsuccessfully to take them in the opposite direction.

'You've gone down in my estimation, Matt,' Clova said coldly, 'I didn't think you'd be hanging around with them. She's already made a play for my uncle, looks like she's leading Carl around by his … nose, as if he's not in enough trouble.'

'I'm not with them, they just followed us after the gig.' Matt told her, 'I was there, remember, after Carl went through the window.'

'It was an accident.' Carl mumbled.

'That's for the police to decide,' Clova said hotly, 'what about

Gemma's scratched car, and the broken letterbox and the abusive phone calls, not you either I suppose.'

'You've no proof, stop trying to pin everything on Carl,' Toni finally pushed her way to the front, you're just trying to cause trouble and show off in front of Matt cos you fancy him. She had her eye on Gabriel too.' Toni added, for Matts' benefit.

'I think you've had one too many. If you came here with Carl, then I would suggest he takes you home.' Matt said coolly.

'How dare you, mind your own business, you didn't hear how Little Miss Perfect talked to me the other day.' Toni snapped, red in the face with temper.

'What, when you were trying to chat up my uncle and dissing his girlfriend? Grow up, you stupid little girl, this is like playground shit.' Clova snapped back.

Toni lunged forward; her arms outstretched about to give Clova a push which would have seen her tumble off the narrow path down the steep cliff, then caught sight of the impressive might of Blue who had forced his way in front of Clova with his lips raised in a warning snarl. Toni veered at the last second and accidentally cannoned into Matt who fell backwards with a startled grunt. Carl, with a look of horror on his face, finally managed to pull Toni away and they staggered off in the opposite direction.

Clova peered into the rapidly fading light and saw Matt had fallen halfway down the sharp incline, near a deep rocky hole. She took charge telling Tom to go back to the caves and get help, and some rope. Sternly telling Blue to stay, she edged her way gingerly down the cliff, telling Matt not to move.

'You're really near that hole, it might lead into the caves, they honeycomb this entire area, and they are still discovering new ones, you don't want to fall down there, we don't know how far down it goes. Can you wriggle to your left?'

'I've sprained my ankle,' Matt groaned, 'I can't put any weight on it.'

'Are you hurt anywhere else?'

'My right wrist but it's not broken. My ankle is worse. I can't get any purchase, there are no footholds for me to stabilise myself. Look at us, two good climbers and we can't get back up a slope.'

'Speak for yourself,' Clova teased, 'and it's a bit more than a slope. Just don't move right whatever you do. Stretch out your left arm, there's a big tree root, try to grab hold of it and pull yourself across away from that hole.'

Clova had edged down on her bottom, hanging on to branches with each move, getting stung by nettles and scratched by brambles which were catching in her clothes and in her hair, muttering 'ouch' under her breath every few yards, each time causing Matt to say 'careful, Blueberry, are you all right?'

Matt was right, they were good at climbing under the right conditions, down rockfaces with safety equipment or in the gym on the climbing wall, wearing the correct shoes but this was a very overgrown steep area, covered with brambles and almost impossible to force your way through them in some places.

Eventually Clova found a relatively secure spot about six feet above Matt's head and managed to squeeze herself into the fork of two branches, with only one hairy moment when she nearly slipped, sending stones rattling down the steep incline. Telling Matt, who was fussing, that she was fine now and safely wedged in.

'I might have to call you Cliff, if you were worthy of a nickname, which you're not.' Clova mused, unsettled by her strong feelings which hadn't faded a bit.

'What?'

'Talk to me about something, take your mind off our dilemma.' Matt screwed up his face trying to think of something to say, his ankle was very painful, throbbing, sending shooting pains up his leg every time he moved slightly, and his right wrist was weak and felt swollen. He wasn't used to feeling helpless and he didn't like it.

'Are you going to keep coming to the gym?'

'Probably, I quite enjoyed it and they're a nice group, all very supportive. Did you like it?'

'Yes. I'm like you, into anything sporty. Football in the winter, hiking, occasionally swimming but I don't like cold water, it's got to be really hot before I'll go in the sea.'

'Wimp,' Clova laughed.

'I can't reach my phone. It might be an idea to put your phone torch on if you can, so they can spot us.'

'I'll put it on shortly. Can you believe that Carl and Toni just walked away? They knew you had fallen and didn't even stay to try to help. Unbelievable.'

'I didn't fall, I was pushed.' Matt said, trying to joke.

Clova frowned thinking about the cause of their dilemma and wishing she had said more to her, but she knew people like Toni didn't listen to reason. They'd all tried to be pleasant to her for Gabriel's sake but she didn't seem to have a single redeeming feature. Maybe she had put on an act to hook Gabriel then shown her true colours when she didn't get her own way. Clova felt herself getting wound up thinking about her so took a deep breath in and tried to think of a safe topic of conversation while they waited for help to arrive. Before she could think of anything, Matt said, 'Is your dog all right? What breed is he?'

'Mixed breed. I take him for walks but he's Uncle Poodie and Bee's dog. They found him by the side of the road when he was a puppy and kept him, it's funny though, he thinks I'm his and we are perfect for each other. When I first saw him he wouldn't leave me alone, kept staring at me. It was a bit weird really, I'd never had an animal take to me like that, I didn't know what to make of him, but it was love at first sight on his part.
Really sweet in retrospect although I didn't appreciate him at the time.' Clova thought her comment had a secondary meaning relating

to Matt, but it went over his head. Insensitive idiot, she thought darkly, really wanting to say something soppy like, 'you don't appreciate what we could have, if you'd only give us a chance and get over your hang up.'

Instead she said, 'I take him out when I can, and we've talked about me adopting him, but I haven't asked my parents yet.

Ugh, what was that?' Clova squeaked as several shadowy shapes flashed close to her face.

'Bats, you see loads of them at dusk. I could watch them for hours but hopefully, not tonight,' craning his neck to try to follow their movements, glancing up at her to check that she hadn't moved and telling her not to worry, they wouldn't get tangled up in her hair as so many people seemed to think.

'I wasn't worried,' Clova lied. 'So what was the band like? Who else have you seen in the caves?'

'The band was great, seen them before, then a couple of years ago a girl I was going out with, was into Shakespeare and we came here and saw Romeo and Juliet. That was a real experience. We had to follow the actors through the caves and a few times they jumped out at us from behind rocks. It was a very energetic and dynamic performance but I'm not really into Shakespeare – don't understand half the flowery language but I enjoyed the sword fighting, argh.' Matt groaned, as he moved his leg slightly.

Clova looked down at him, worried but he was secure enough.

'Tom will be back soon with help, just stay still. You must have been about 21 then, guys that age aren't usually into Shakespeare.'

'I was doing it to please my girlfriend but I'm glad I did, not many people can say they've followed actors through prehistoric caves and seen the entire play on the move.'

'Yeah, sounds unique. I'll have to check out their website, see what else they're doing this year.' Clova said, managing not to make any sarky comments about Matts' girlfriends, even though she was dying to ask how many girls he had dated and if he was still seeing the sexy paramedic.'

'Bet you bloody are.' She muttered.

'What? Are you okay?'

'I'm good. Settled in a stable position. More to the point, are you?' Matt had taken her advice and had pulled himself further out of danger, holding on to the tree root, and told her he was in no danger of slipping. Clova managed to get her phone out and put the torch on, shining it around herself, down to Matt, then up to where Blue was waiting, his eyes glowing red in the torchlight, looking like a hellhound.

'Hound of the Baskervilles, indeed.' Clova murmured to herself then heard people rushing down the path.

'We're here,' she called out, waving her phone, 'mind out for the dog, don't scare him, he's in protective mode. Be a good boy, Blue.' She added.

Four men, including Tom, three of whom were experienced climbers, arrived with rope and soon rescued Clova and Matt. Clova got back on the path, shakily embracing Blue, who was ecstatic, nuzzling her and licking her. Matt was next and once back on the path, put his arms around the necks of two of the men and managed to hop his way back to the caves where he'd parked his car. Sitting Matt down at one of the picnic tables outside the cavern, they bandaged his wrist and strapped his ankle, telling him to go to hospital to get it checked out, when he refused, saying he could tell it was not broken, they told him to go home and put ice on both and see how he felt in the morning. Thanking everyone, Matt gave his friend his keys, telling Tom he'd have to drive and offered Clova a lift home.

'You were pretty amazing, you know that?' Matt said, 'taking charge like that, it could have been a lot worse, I might be lying at the bottom of a hole leading to God knows where, waiting for the cave rescue team if it hadn't been for you.'

'If I hadn't been there, you wouldn't have been pushed down the cliff in the first place, not that I did anything to set Toni off, she was gunning for me as soon as she caught sight of me.'

'Don't start feeling guilty, you were great.' Matt said, his eyes flashing.

'It was nothing, anyone would have done the same.' Clova said, looking embarrassed.

'No, they wouldn't, Clova. For a young girl you were incredible.' Matt looked at her with admiration.

'Not so young,' Clova mumbled.

Matt nodded slowly, 'no, not so young. Some people twice your age wouldn't have kept such a cool head. Come on, you can help me hobble to the car.'

Hooking an arm around Tom, he limped and hopped to the car as Clova supported his other side, then she rang her uncle to tell him she'd be home in 15 minutes.'

Tom dropped her and Blue off and Matt thanked her again. In the car she had asked him if he was going to report Toni to the police, but he said she had been drunk and he didn't think she had meant to do it. No, she'd meant to push me, Clova had thought but didn't say it, as far as she was concerned, Toni had burnt her last bridge and she sincerely hoped, she'd stay out of her way from now on.

No sooner had Clova got in the door and given Blue a drink when Poodie arrived, he pulled on Blue's lead and the dog refused to budge.

'You were a really long time. I was starting to get a bit worried. Did you have a good walk?' Poodie asked the pair of them, Blue obviously not wanting to leave Clova.

'It was eventful, tell you about it next time I see you, but Blue was as good as gold.'

'You look like you've been dragged through a hedge backwards, where did you go?'

'Mainly local and through the woods. The paths are really overgrown, and I got stung by nettles, anyway I'll tell you all about it later.' Widening her eyes and nodding towards the front room where her parents were.

Her uncle got the message. He turned to the dog, picking up his lead. 'Come on Blue, we've got to go home now. Going to have some dinner?'

Blue planted his feet, clearly not intending to move. Poodie dropped the lead and walked into the front room to have a chat with his half-sister Mary and her husband Stuart, Ant was out. Clova took charge of the conversation.

'Blue doesn't want to go home with Uncle Poodie, can I keep him?' She asked her parents. 'He likes all of us and he's very protective of me.'

'Are you sure he's a dog?' Stuart asked his brother-in-law, 'he looks at least half wolf.'

'Of course, he's a dog, Dad,' Clova said before Poodie could get a word in, ' how could a bitch get impregnated by a wolf in England?'

'Might be wild wolves on Dartmoor, escaped from that zoo. Paudric, where did you get him again?' Stuart always called Poodie by his given name.

'Dad. He's a dog. Just a big dog, some kind of mixed breed. In fact, technically he's still a puppy.'

'Jesus God, he's probably not even finished growing. How much does he eat?' Mary was looking worried, the Irish part of her emerged when she was concerned about something, 'and if you're working full time how can you look after him properly, love?'

'I'll get up early and walk him before work or college. We've got a big garden: you could let him out in the afternoon if he needs to go. Please?'

Poodie said, 'I know it's a big commitment, so I propose that I help towards feeding and vets bills and can take him out whenever you are too busy. Give it a trial for a few weeks but Mary, Blue attached himself to Clova at first sight and has decided she is his owner. You can see how he is with her. Did she tell you what happened on the beach, when Blue rescued her?'

'No. I don't believe she mentioned anything about a rescue.' Mary narrowed her eyes at her daughter, 'I told her never to go out of her depth, but she doesn't listen, you have to respect the sea.
 Clova, you told me that dog had swum out and joined you and you both swam to shore. You said it was cute. What's this about being rescued?'

'Uncle Poodie's exaggerating,' Clova also narrowed her eyes and glared at her uncle, 'Blue thought I was in trouble so swam out to help but I was fine.'

'You stay out of the sea unless you've got that dog with you.' Stuart told his daughter, unwittingly giving his approval of the fostering. Clova threw her arms around his neck and kissed his cheek, 'thanks dad. He won't be any bother, I promise.'

'What? What have I just agreed to?'

Mary rolled her eyes and asked her brother if he wanted to stay to tea. Poodie declined, saying Bee had started dinner and he'd told her he wouldn't be long.

 I've got some dog food in the van to tide you over for tonight, have a proper chat and a think about it and let me know. If you agree, I'll bring his basket and the rest of his stuff over tomorrow.'

'Win, win,' Clova said to her parents, 'he won't cost us anything and he'll be a burglar deterrent. What will Bee say though?'

'We've already talked about the possibility; she'll be fine and it's not as if she'll never see him. Right, that's settled for now, let me know when you decide, I'll just go and get the food in.'

Poodie went out to the van and returned with the food to find Blue had settled himself on the sheepskin rug and was pretending to be asleep.

Stuart gestured to the dog as if to say, 'he's made himself at home' and Mary said 'we've decided. He can stay for a trial run, as Clova said, if you are helping with the costs and the walking there are no obstacles in our way. I'd better stay up until our Ant gets home though, else he'll get a hell of a shock.'

27

'How was your Sunday off?' Gemma asked, as they got ready for opening.

'Hectic? Eventful? I can't believe a person can go for weeks without anything of significance happening, then have so much occur in one day.' Clova replied, tying her hair back and tucking it in to her purple scarf adorned with butterflies.

'I don't know whether to change my hair colour or not, what do you think?'

Gemma looked at her list, told Clova they needed some breakfast baps heated up in the microwave for 10 o'clock and advised her not to colour her hair for a while to give it a break and improve its condition, adding hastily that it looked fine but over colouring it could dry it out too much. She touched her own curly chestnut mop, commented that she really ought to book in for a haircut soon as she had started to resemble a scarecrow, then carried on fulfilling the daily orders.

'Fancy Toni being so nasty,' Gemma said, getting the gist of the story in between customers, 'it could have ended in a tragedy. She should be made to face up to the consequences of what might have happened.'

'What did happen, was bad enough. Matt had a really badly sprained ankle.'

'Did you get the chance to talk? Did you ask him if he's still seeing that nurse?' Gemma said, thinking it was unfortunate that Matt might have a new girlfriend perfectly qualified to take care of him.

'Gemma! Thanks for reminding me. No, I didn't. The adrenalin was coursing through me, and I was concerned about getting Matt back up to the top and about Blue waiting for me on the path. She's a paramedic anyway, but he hadn't taken her to see Lovers Leap. It was just him and Tom.'

'Is Lovers Leap a part of the caves?'

'Gemma. They're a band.' Clover said, with a laugh.

Gemma gave a slight shake of her head, annoyed with herself. She liked to keep up with the latest bands, but she hadn't heard of them.

'I'm fostering Blue,' Clova announced, three hours later, having waited for a lull in customers to finish talking about her Sunday.

'No, really? What happened to the girl who hated dogs?'

'I've never hated dogs. Blue is different, he's like my guardian angel in animal form and he's so clever.'

'That's almost word for word what Bee said about Mac when she first got him. Will you have time to walk Blue before work? Talking of Bee, did she mind you adopting Blue?'

Gemma and Clova both skipped from subject to subject, as if they had two trains of thought on the go at once, but each seemed to follow the others conversation without a problem and could backtrack to answer a comment made hours ago.

'Uncle Poodie said she didn't, and she can still see him and take him out when I'm not free. I got up early this morning, and we were out for an hour, walking across the fields behind the house, I never knew there were so many rabbits in those fields; first time I've been up at that time of day. Then tonight I can give him another long walk. I might have to give up a couple of my classes, but I don't mind, I'm still getting my exercise, maybe I'll start jogging, Blue might enjoy that. Oh, and you don't resemble a scarecrow.'

'Glad to hear it but I still need a cut. Want to come to the Eight Bells Thursday after work? The gang are all going. The pub is having a curry evening.' Gemma managed to say before another steady flow of customers kept them busy for the rest of the day.

As they were winding down, clearing up and getting ready to close, two police officers walked in and asked to speak to Gemma. She looked worried and asked Clova to lock the shop door and turn the sign to closed.

'Nothing to worry about, miss. Some information has come to light regarding your complaints. In the course of our investigations we've discovered a person who has been the cause of some of your phone calls and has admitted to scratching your car. Does the name Oliver Franklin mean anything to you?'

Gemma frowned, racking her brain. 'I don't think so, I don't know anyone called Oliver.'

Clova said, 'what about that lad who worked here before me?'

Gemma scratched her head, trying to cast her mind back to a time when Clova hadn't been there.

'Oh yes, now you come to mention it, he was called Oliver. He was useless, didn't do a stroke of work, only did the one Saturday and I told him it wouldn't work out.'

'He said you didn't pay him, miss.'

'He didn't do any work!' Gemma was incensed, 'spent the whole time on his phone.'

'We haven't charged him due to his age at the time of the occurrences but he has received a caution and a talking to in front of his parents. If you want to press a private charge against him and inform your insurance company, that is your right. With regards to the accident and several other incidences they are still under investigation. Have a good day, Miss.'

Gemma unlocked the door and let the officers out. Shutting it again she turned to Clova, shaking her head, her mouth still agape.

'I need a drink after that,' she said eventually. 'Coming?'

'The Eight Bells was tucked away down a side street and not easy to find unless you stumbled upon it by accident. It was an old-fashioned pub, what some people used to refer to as 'spit and sawdust'. It looked rough and ready from the outside and even if some tourists had sat navved it, they were often put off by its exterior, and didn't bother going in, which was how the residents liked it. Therefore, it was mainly used by locals, and you could always get a seat even in the middle of the tourist season.

Once inside, it was more spacious than its scruffy exterior suggested. A small stage, with neon lights around it, unoccupied unless it was a live music night, was at the back, a pool table in front of it. The long bar ran along one side with a door leading to the kitchen. Opposite the bar, an archway led to another room, with plenty of tables and chairs throughout, although the carpet was a bit sticky, and some of the upholstery was in need of repair, the tables were clean, the staff efficient and the food excellent. The beer garden at the rear of the property, was large and also decorated with neon lights. The door leading from the bar led on to a patio and two large grassy areas with pretty solar lights evenly spaced along the edges, one lawn was set in a dip giving the customers the illusion of privacy. An outside tap had big water bowls beneath it, with a sign telling people to help themselves for their dogs.

There was an eclectic mix of garden furniture. Along the path bordering the lawns, five white plastic tables and chairs had been evenly spaced along its length. On the grass there were more solid circular tables with umbrellas, some benches and a few heavy oblong wooden tables that groups of people liked to commandeer and arrange to their liking.

 It was a warm evening in mid-summer, Bee, Poodie, Kay and Mark were the first to arrive and arranged two of the tables to their liking. Mark had some dog biscuits in his pocket and was trying to teach Mac and Copper tricks, to no avail. They would give a paw and knew that 'high five' also meant holding up a paw, but that was it. Mac understood 'sit' but didn't see why he should do it on command. His long body and short legs weren't conducive to sitting, he went from standing to lying down in one movement. Copper sat immediately and looked at Mark expectantly for her reward, while Mark was waiting for Mac to follow suit.

After a fruitless wait, Mark sighed and gave up then turned his attention to Bee, telling her she looked nice, and he liked her dress, commenting on the unusual colour.

Bee frowned giving Mark a suspicious look but all he said was, he would get the first round in, as Mark got up to go to the bar, the rest of their friends arrived and Sindy went to help Mark bring the drinks out, leaving Gemma to be pulled into the garden by Harley and Chilli, Rosa trying to help, closely followed by Clova and Blue. All the dogs went wild with excitement, whimpering and kissing each other and the humans. Blue pushed himself between Poodie and Bee to receive his share of strokes and kisses before looking around to make sure he could see Clova.

'He always has his eyes on me, he hates it if he can't see me,' she said, smiling fondly at Blue.

'German Shepherds are like that; they can't bear their owners to be out of their line of sight. I expect he's got some Alsatian in him.' Bee told her, taking her drink from Mark and thanking him as he and Sindy came out with trays.

Bee was slightly obsessed with mixed breeds and which breeds made up their genetic make-up. She'd had Macs' DNA sent off to be analysed and advised Clova to do the same with Blue.

'When she was out with Mac, strangers often asked what breed he was and she drove Sindy up the wall, listing all the breeds found by the DNA check, that Sindy had to listen to, time and time again.

'I bet Clova would like some Albanian in her,' Sindy said in a loud whisper.

Gemma hit her on the arm, shushing her furiously and going red. 'Bee's talking about Blue, and she said Alsatian.' She hissed to her partner.

'I know luv. I'm not an idiot, at least it proves I listen when you tell me stuff.' Sindy said, unrepentantly.

'It proves Bee's managed to drag you into the gutter with her.'

'Eh?' Bee asked, hearing her name, while Sindy and Gem looked at her innocently, raising their eyebrows and shaking their heads slightly.

They settled the dogs down under the table, promising them chews later, when the food was served. Because naturally, the dogs understood every word and had grasped the concept of 'later', as Mark observed, hearing the comment.

'Oliver.' Gemma said, for the tenth time, 'wait till I tell Betty. That snotty little shit and to think I blamed everything on Carl.'

'I wouldn't let Carl off the hook just yet, he probably contributed to fifty per cent of our trouble. Try to forget about it for tonight.' Sindy told her partner, wanting her to relax and enjoy the evening.

'Don't you think Bee has picked the right outfit for tonight?' Mark asked the group, when there was a lull in the conversation.

'It's a nice dress for a summer's evening,' Kay agreed, giving her partner a puzzled look.

'Unusual material with the swirls of browns and orange. Congratulations Bee, a perfect dress to eat curry in. No-one would notice, even if you spilt the whole lot down yourself.'

'I knew you were up to something Mark, when have you ever paid me a compliment, I suppose we're betting again?'

'Naturellment. A fiver, is it?'

'That reminds me,' Poodie interjected, turning to his girlfriend, 'don't you owe me a fiver from the last time we were here?'

'No, I gave you that,' Bee said breezily.

Poodie put his arm around her and nuzzled her hair, 'are you sure?' He said, elongating the last word.

'Yep. This shampoo is expensive. It's five pound a sniff.'

Poodie chortled and Kay, who had finished her glass of wine quite quickly laughed and said, 'I love our get togethers, I do.'

'She's gone Welsh already, did you have a drink before you came out?' Sindy asked her.

'No but I haven't eaten all day. I was saving myself for tonight. I love a curry, I do.' Kay answered, pushing her glasses back, as they had slipped down her nose, and poured herself another glass of wine from the bottle on the table.

Gemma and Clova related the previous Sundays' shenanigans to their friends, who hadn't yet had all the details. Bee, who had, went in to order more drinks, before it got busy.

Rosa couldn't believe Toni could be so vindictive. 'She looked like butter wouldn't melt. Gabe's such a nice guy, what on earth did he see in her?'

'She's a pretty girl, I don't think he saw much beyond that in the first few months, and you find out what a person's really like, when you live with them.' Gemma said, taking a sip of her dirty martini.

'You can relate to that, Uncle Poodie, Designer Dawn didn't have much to her either.' Clova put in, adding, 'men!'

Poodie raised his eyebrows at his niece, and grimaced, not keen on having his past relationship brought up in company.

'Charming. Coop, you're much too young to be so cynical, you haven't even had your heart broken yet. Besides, I didn't live with Dawn, just stayed with her for a few weeks in-between moves.'

'I'm joking,' Clova said, a bit too quickly, realising she shouldn't have said it, 'listening to the way my brother and his mates talk about girls, has put me off.'

'They're young and full of hormones,' Sindy laughed.

'Full of something,' Mark said, earning a scowl and an embarrassed giggle from Kay.

The remark went over Clova's head.

'So am I but I don't talk about the opposite sex like he does.'

'I think you might be in the minority there, I've heard gaggles of girls your age talking about blokes. It would turn your hair white just to hear them.' Mark commented.

'Well. We're not all the same,' Clova said, taking a sip of her shandy and petting Blue under the table, whilst thinking maybe she should go for white or silver as her next hair colour.

'I understand people of your age, I'm on the same wavelength.' Mark said, putting a hand to the back of his head to make sure his ponytail was still in place.

Bee, coming out with the first tray of drinks, heard. 'You can't remember that far back Mark, so don't pretend you relate to the youth of today.'

Poodie gave Mark a warning glance as he opened his mouth about to comment that Bee was older than him and what would she know. Bee returned to the bar to collect the rest of the drinks, content in the knowledge that she had got the last word, for once.

'Mate, you're spoiling my fun.' Mark said with a laugh.

'I know it's fun, I do it all the time, but you can let her have the last word once in a while, besides I've been winding her up all afternoon, she's only got one nerve left and one of us might get on it.'

'Very clever. Isn't that a bumper sticker?' Sindy asked.

'All right,' Mark sighed, 'as long as she doesn't spill any food, I'll keep my mouth shut.'

Sindy said, as Bee brought the rest of the drinks out, 'you've got two hopes of that. No hope and Bob Hope.'

'Who's Bob Hope?' Clova asked.

'An American comedian from the early twentieth century. Sometimes they show old films with him in, Betty likes him.' Gemma told her.

'I wonder why Toni was out with Carl anyway. He's not her type, although she was sticking up for him that day, outside Tollys. Sugar Daddy, do you think? There must be something in it for her.' Gemma said to Clova.

'She probably hasn't got any friends and latched on to Carl. I expect he was flattered; probably thinks she fancies him. Carl lives near the caves. I expect they went for Happy Hour in the bar and didn't leave.' The food arrived then, halting the speculation. The dogs got their chews, and everyone settled down to enjoy their curries.

Bee lifted the last large forkful to her lips and announced triumphantly, 'nothing down me, see?'

Poodie couldn't resist nudging her elbow before she could get the food into her mouth, and she leapt backwards nearly falling off the seat in an attempt to miss it dropping on her dress.

'Poodie,' she hissed, in mock anger, 'not funny. You'll suffer for that later and I'm not giving Mark any money, it actually missed my dress.' Poodie and Mark were laughing, and Harley cleaned up, under the table.

'Honestly, you two, I think you're more on the wavelength of teenagers than I am.' Clova said, about to add more when Matt came out of the bar and limped over to her.

'Blueberry, I hoped to see you tonight to thank you for the other day.' Matt ran his fingers through his black hair. Looking a little uncomfortable to be the centre of attention as everyone had stopped talking and were watching the two of them.

Clova stood up, taking hold of Blues' lead, telling them she was just taking him on to the grass for a wee.

'Blue or Matt?' Mark quipped.

The others laughed and Matt limped along beside her, resting his hand on her arm as they moved to another table out of hearing range.

'Rosa, you know BSL, can you lip read as well?' Gemma asked her.

'Sadly, no but I'm sure she'll tell you everything tomorrow.'

'They look good together. I think they make a handsome couple. I hope they get it together.' Gemma said.

'Then at least she'd stop mooning about like a lovesick teen at work.' Sindy said, speaking with no knowledge of the facts at all.

'She is a lovesick teen.' Poodie said, trying not to glare across the garden at the pair of them.

'She's a mature nineteen-year-old woman, she's very professional and she doesn't moon about at work.' Gemma told them, sticking up for her friend.

'Doesn't that mean baring your bum? Flashing people out of a car window?'

'Mark!'

'Blue seems to like him,' Bee observed, watching the way Blue nudged Matts leg with his nose. 'He's a good judge of character. Now leave them in peace.

Anyone want to see the dessert menu?'

28

The following day Gemma opened the door to the bakery and saw an envelope on the floor addressed to Clova, she put it on the back shelf and got on with her first jobs of the morning, served a couple of her regulars, greeted Sindy and Bee who were returning from a very early morning walk and had called in, wanting something for breakfast.

'I'm never usually hungry this early,' Sindy moaned, 'I must have stretched my stomach with that curry.'

'and my naan,' Bee put in, 'where's Clova? Dish the goss.'

'I said she could start half an hour later if she wanted, because of Blue. She's not used to having a dog, just needs to get a routine going.' Bee groaned, 'oh well, you'll have to text me later.'

She and Sindy asked for a couple of cheese salad rolls which Gemma had already made up and Bee asked for a cherry scone that she intended to have for brunch.

'Harley's got his nose in your bag,' Gemma pointed out.

'Harley! One dog biscuit left. He's cleaned me out, he's such a tea leaf.'

'Bee. Why didn't you zip it up, you know what he's like.'

'You zip it,' her friend said, not meaning the bag, 'Bye Gem'.

They walked out of the shop, Sindy still telling her off.

Gemma popped into the back and quickly put the kettle on, before her next customer and Clova came in.

'Hiya, make us a drink, will you? The kettle has boiled. Oh, a note came for you today it's on the back shelf.'

Clova picked up the envelope and went into the kitchen to make the coffee and put a hairnet on, as she had forgotten her scarf. She returned a few minutes later with the drinks, served a customer, then handed Gemma the note to read.

Gemma read it, shaking her head. 'Not a love letter then, I thought it might be from that lad that fancies you. Would you believe it, a note from Carl, apologising. Money as well, for the fish through the letterbox incident which he said he thought it might have been a practical joke by a mate of his, after he'd given him the idea in the pub. Claims he felt partly to blame and hoped that the cash would cover the cost of the new letterbox. He obviously couldn't bear to address the letter to me, if he even knows my name'.

Clova shook her head. 'I think he's covering himself in case I try to bring charges against Toni.'

'He still insists the car going through our window was an accident, he says his foot slipped but he's saying sorry for causing a little mischief that may have got out of hand. I notice he's being careful not to put any hard facts in writing. He's not admitting to anything I could go to the police with, but at the very least, we now know he was connected to the person who broke the letterbox and I reckon he probably got some people to make dirty phone calls, it wasn't all Oliver.

Can you believe he and Toni are moving to Wales? As friends, she was probably looking over his shoulder when he wrote that, didn't want you to jump to conclusions. I bet she thinks he must have some money and he's going to set her up in business. Well, good riddance to them both. I hope he was the sole cause of all our problems here and I can stop looking over my shoulder now and relax.'

Betty came in and they showed her the letter, she was delighted, and echoed Gemma's words. She was on the mend, she told them, her ribs were the worst but healing slowly and she wanted to come in to work at the weekend.

'I'll take 3 Maple and Pecan Danish pastries please: I'm going round to the boys.'

'The boys must be at least 70.' Gemma laughed, emphasising the word 'boys'.

'No-one feels their age these days, 70 is the new 50, so they say,' although who 'they' were, no-one knew.

'I'll be in tomorrow; shall I make you a drink before I go?' Gemma refused payment for the cakes, said they'd just made a drink and told Betty to come in a bit later on Saturday if she wanted.

'Morning Christine, don't usually see you on a Friday,' Gemma greeted her next customer.

Christine leaned across the counter, 'Geoff wants to go to another bakery tomorrow,' she hissed, saying the word 'bakery' as if she was telling them her husband was converting to another faith.

'Why don't you bring him in here so he can choose a cake for himself?'

Christine looked horrified at the thought that her husband would find out the truth, 'No, absolutely not. It's my guilty pleasure ...well, not guilty. I'll have to think of a way around it. Wherever we get the cakes from tomorrow they won't taste as good as yours, I'll sabotage them, leave the bag open so they taste stale, or sprinkle salt on them, then Geoff should relent and let me pick the cakes on my own. I just popped in to let you know. I will be back, it just won't be tomorrow but please keep doing your Saturday Specials, everyone likes them.' She scurried out of the shop, looking harassed.

Gemma parroted Christine, 'I'll be back.' She said, trying to do an Austrian accent.

'Some people's lives are so strange. Now come on Clova, what happened last night with Matt. I'm itching to know.'

In-between customers, Clova told her that she and Matt had got on really well, chatted all evening with no awkward pauses.

She thought back to their conversation, she had casually mentioned that she had heard he was dating and asked where his girlfriend was. Matt had looked puzzled, he replied 'Do you mean Helen? The paramedic? Hmm. We had one date; our small talk consisted of her telling me all about her fantasy of getting married. It was her childhood dream and she made a scrapbook at the age of 10 that she filled with pictures from Bride magazines.

She had already picked her dress, the venue, the honeymoon, all that was lacking was the groom.'

Clova had laughed, inwardly cheering.

Matt said she had asked him what his surname was, said that if they got married, he would have to change his name to hers as she didn't like his, then asked him how many children he wanted in the future. Clova was laughing so much by this time that she could barely ask him was his surname was.

They stayed until closing and one of Matt's friends dropped them home, as Matt still couldn't drive.

'We've exchanged numbers and he's texted me this morning.' Clova was glowing.

'I'm really pleased for you. I like Matt. Looks like you finally got your man, I told you playing it cool was the way to go.'

Clova smiled but she knew that playing hard to get hadn't got Matt's attention, he'd told her that he'd found her confidence and courage a real turn on. He loved her relationship with Blue and he certainly didn't see her as a kid anymore. She smiled to herself, remembering the feel of his lips on hers in the car park while they were waiting for his mate to bring the car round. He was a good kisser, not that she had much to compare it to, but he made her feel warm inside. A gentle, tender prolonged kiss, containing a hint of the passion he was holding inside. She wanted to ask if they were dating now but didn't want to seem pushy. Though after the wedding fantasies of the paramedic, asking if they were dating was hardly coming on too strong.

Instead she asked him why he'd been so standoffish when they were on Dartmoor.

Matt had paused for so long she didn't think he was going to answer, but in the end he had said he realised how much he liked her, when he couldn't seem to stop turning round and looking at her.

'I didn't like it,' Matt admitted, 'I really did think you were too young for me. That's one of the reasons I asked Helen out, trying to get you out of my system.

I thought that if we got together we would get in too deep, and I didn't think I wanted a long-term relationship. Sorry, I was a bit of a dick that day.'

'A bit?' Clova had squeaked, 'you were horrible. I wondered why you asked me along in the first place.'

'I know,' Matt said ruefully, 'my friends gave me hell after you'd gone. They know that's not like me at all. Are you going to let me make it up to you?'

Clova had tapped her foot and pretended to consider it before saying she would give him another chance.

'It's early days, Gem, once the glow of his gratitude has worn off then we'll see. I'm trying to hold back a bit when I really just want to throw myself into his arms. Oh God, that sounds so cheesy. Pass the sick bucket. I'm not talking about him to any of my friends, only you. When my friends had a new boyfriend that's all they talked about. I

always said I had too much going on in my life to obsess over a man.
I didn't think I was the romantic type, but I even pinched the beermat his drink had been on in the pub. Pathetic. My mates would be crying with laughter if they knew. I think I've got it bad.'

'It's not pathetic, it's sweet. He didn't ask you out, out of gratitude. He's not the type. It sounds as if he really likes you and has done for a while.

What is his surname?' Gemma asked, curiosity getting the better of her.

'Kryezi.'

'Oh, nothing wrong with that. I was expecting something rude sounding, like Piddlebottom.'

Clova laughed, 'I shouldn't think Piddlebottom is a very common name in Albania.'

'Was he romantic? What were you talking about?'

'This and that,' Clova said evasively, 'but he did say he loved my laugh.'

'Your laugh?'

'He had trouble describing how it sounded to him, he said it was unusual, a cute liquid giggle was as near as he could get. I've never thought about the way I laugh, have you?'

Gemma shook her head, thinking it was a slightly odd thing to focus on.

Matt's got a thing about voices, he can't stand Toni's for example, too squeaky, apparently. Also the way some people laugh grates on his

nerves but seemingly my laugh has an almost pure bell like tone to it.'
She laughed, unconsciously demonstrating it.

Gemma put her head to one side, considering it. Then told her that she did have a very pleasant laugh and although she thought it was a slightly strange thing to say, it made a change from unimaginative comments like 'your eyes are like deep pools, I could let myself drown in them.'

'Oh yeah, he said that too.

I'm joking.' This, at the look on Gemma's face.

'Once his ankle is better we are going to do a long walk with Blue, Torquay to Paignton probably.'

'Rather you than me,' Gemma said, cringing at the thought.

'Well better get on, extra orders to make up for Saturday and I must ring Jack and remind him that we'll need extra bakes with the Slimming Club on tonight. They'll be flocking in, in the morning with a whole week to go before their next weigh-in.'

29

Poodie and Bee had driven to a National Trust woodland, a walk they really enjoyed but hardly ever did.

It was a large area, with a very long winding trail stretching ahead of them, a river on the left and a little stream on the right, trees extending as far as the eye could see, beyond the water on each side. The white gravel path meandered ahead of them, for Bee the best thing about it was that it was flat, which was a treat in hilly Devon. There was a new coffee kiosk near where they had parked that Bee had noticed, which sold home baked flapjacks and other interesting looking items. Bee loved having coffee out, especially after a walk and if they were out long enough, she felt she might have earned a cake as well, not that Poodie cared what she ate.

Mac and Copper ran ahead of them, Copper crossing the stream, running into the trees, coming back periodically to check where they were. Mac trotted in front, sniffing and scent marking each side of the path, looking for his favourite grass to eat and generally having a good time. It had been a dry couple of weeks and their feet kicked up white dust from the path with each step, half a mile further on, the path changed to earth, hard, dried, impacted red soil which could turn to mud after one heavy downpour, with no rain forecast, they could enjoy the flat, easy to walk on, natural path. Red dust kicking up to join the white on their shoes.

'I'm not missing Blue as much as I thought I would.' Bee mused after they'd been walking for a while. 'Knowing he's in the same town with an owner he loves helps, and I expect we'll still see a lot of him with Clova being family.

She and Matt make a nice couple don't you think?

I hope they start dating properly, we could use a carpenter/handyman in the family.' Bee said, after another long comfortable silence, the two of them just enjoying the birdsong and gentle sound of the river flowing over pebbles and rocks to their left.

Poodie actually stopped and turned to look at his girlfriend.

'What?' She laughed.

'That's very conniving, that's what. Although I could use some help with the cottage renovations,' Poodie pondered.

'It's early days, they're both young, might only last a couple of months,' he added.

'Exactly. Get in there, while we can.'

'Bee!'

'I'm joking. Some people meet their life partner when they are very young and stay together. Time will tell. Meanwhile we should invite them both over to the cottage for a barbecue, then we can get our claws into Matt.'

You said 'we', does this mean you're going to move in with me?'

Poodie took her hand as they resumed walking, watching Copper paddle in the stream, she was lifting up her paws as she ran and appeared to be getting an aesthetic pleasure from hearing the plink plink sound her feet were making in the water, her mouth open in a canine grin. They glanced back to see where Mac was, and he was just as happy to be out of the water, enjoying all the smells and animal trails and insects to try to catch. He was running to catch them up after stopping to eat grass, looking like a little cartoon creature. Sindy called him Pepe Le Pew, after a skunk from an old animated TV show.

'Do you really think it would work? How will you feel when I'm 40 and you're still in your thirties.'

'I hardly think a year will make much difference,' remembering Bee was turning 40 the following year, although she had convinced herself that she was still in her mid-thirties, had picked the age she wanted to stick at and hoped that was an end to it.

'I'm old for my age and you're young for yours, we've discussed it over and over, time to not mention it again. Besides, I read that there is no such thing as time. Time is a construct, human beings have created it for their own reasons.'

'That's a bit profound, so does that mean we can pick the age we want to be? In which case we could both be 35.'

'Nope. You'll always be seven years older than me.'
Bee hit him.

'Seriously, what did your family say about my age?'

'Nothing. Now don't mention it again.'

'Okay, okay, see? I'm boring you already.'

Poodie drew her closer and kissed her, 'you'll never bore me.'

Bee broke off the kiss after a minute to say 'wow, that's the nicest thing anyone has ever said to me.'

'Really? You seriously haven't lived, have you.'

Bee pulled a face at him and smacked his arm again, 'do you think the cottage is big enough for two people and two dogs? What about when you need your own space? You're used to living there on your own.'

'I work outdoors, I've got plenty of time for solitude and reflection if that's what you're imagining I do or I need. When you wind me up I can go and sit under the willow tree.' Poodie looked at her with a twinkle in his eye.

'and when you wind me up you can also go and sit under the willow tree. You'd better put a bench under there, you'll be spending a lot of time contemplating the error of your ways.'

Poodie chuckled before saying, 'yes, the cottage is tiny but until recently, Blue was also living there, you've been at the cottage practically every day for the last month, what do you think? We weren't getting under each other's feet.'

'No we weren't but if I move in I've got a whole house filled with furniture and stuff. I don't want to get rid of everything.'

'Oh I get it; you're hatching a devious plot regarding getting Matt to do a total makeover. Conservatory, extend the kitchen, stick another floor on the top, oh and then we could have a roof garden. I'm sure he'd be thrilled and naturally, the council would grant us planning permission for all our freebies that Matt will do because he's practically family.'

Bee rolled her eyes, 'when you start with the sarcasm, you take it to the next level, you twonk.'

Poodie laughed, 'Coming from the queen of the sarcastic comment, I'm flattered.

Come on Bee, we've thrashed out all your possible objections, you only live once, what's holding you back, frightened you might fall in love with me, like I'm in love with you?'

'You idiot. I've been in love with you since the day I saw you walking Copper in the park.

I said, 'Good morning', you stuck your nose in the air, I thought, 'stuck up pig' and went back at the same time for weeks, hoping to see you again.'

'Aw, really? Love at first sight?'

'Well, a mixture of love and contempt but I couldn't get you out of my mind. Do you remember when me and Sindy saw you at Ashleigh Manor? We'd progressed to nodding and a quick 'good morning'. Sindy asked you what your name was, because she was sick of me guessing.'

'I saw you at least once a week after that,' Poodie said, 'often falling face first into a muddy puddle or dropping food down yourself in the café. Once I saw you catch sight of me and sweep all the food on your plate into your handbag, presumably in case I saw you eating. You were behaving very oddly, oh, and Mac kept chasing Copper and barking at her. I'd think, there's that nutter again.'

'Don't exaggerate and don't call Mac a nutter.' Bee teased. 'But you always seemed to appear when I had spilt something down myself, or got covered in mud from the dogs. You still do, you must have a sixth sense. I do remember putting a toasted teacake in my bag, in case you saw me eating cake. You must have eyes in the back of your head.' Poodie chuckled as Bee continued, 'I thought, doesn't that man work, until I saw you gardening one day.
You still barely spoke.'

'I'd had a year without Dawn and was happily single.'

'Oh yes, please do remind me of your young, free and single days.' Bee had a glint in her eyes which meant the opposite of what she was saying.

Poodie pulled her towards him again, nuzzling her hair, 'they ended because I couldn't get you out of my mind either, now for the love of God, are you going to move in with me or not?'

Bee laughed, kissed him and said, 'Oh go on then.'

They stood on the mud path kissing, until a dog walker with six dogs walked past and Mac went nuts, barking and warning all the big dogs away from his pack. Bee put Mac on the lead, apologised to the dog walker for Mac terrorising her Rottweilers, called Copper, glancing up at Poodie with a silent question.

Poodie grabbed Bee's hand and turned to walk back, 'come on, let's pick up a cream tea on the way home and call in to see your mum and give her the good news.'

THE END.

Printed in Great Britain
by Amazon

10053592R00180